THEIR
ANGEL'S
CRY

BOOKS BY SHANNON HOLLINGER

SHANNON HOLLINGER

THEIR ANGEL'S CRY

bookouture

Published by Bookouture in 2023

An imprint of Storyfire Ltd.
Carmelite House
50 Victoria Embankment
London EC4Y 0DZ

www.bookouture.com

ISBN: 978-1-80314-888-5
eBook ISBN: 978-1-80314-887-8

To all the dogs I've loved before, especially the real Tempest and Sullivan. A more formidable duo there never was.

PROLOGUE

A lone hiker scrabbles up the trail. Every step carries them higher, farther from other people, from help, should they need it. Their labored gasps and the sound of the scree shifting beneath their boots is the only sound, and even that is snatched up and carried away by the wind, as if it's trying to erase any evidence of their existence.

And it just might.

This far from civilization, even a small mistake can be fatal.

It's the risk you take entering the woods, especially at this elevation, where the weather can change in an instant. In a region already so remote, most of the territory remains uncharted and unexplored. At a time of year where a snowstorm can descend unexpectedly, obliterating your ability to orient. One false move and you've lost your way. Possibly forever.

As if to drive this home, frigid air blows against them, trying to bend them into submission. The cold bites at the hiker's exposed skin, digging its teeth in deep, leaving them chapped and raw.

The hiker glances at the eerie stillness around them, scalp

tingling, skin tightening over their bones. Suddenly, they realize that this is a really dumb idea. Hiking a mountain all alone.

If something happened, what would they do? No one knows they're here—their friends and family wouldn't even know where to look. They'd be one of those people who simply vanished.

Distracted, they trip and stumble, rolling an ankle painfully. Catching themselves perilously close to the edge of a cliff, where the trees and earth on one side of the trail vanish, opening into a breathtaking vista.

The view is spellbinding, mountains rippling in the distance as far as the eye can see. A thick cloak of fog hangs low in the valley, turning the boldness of the evergreens beyond into a faded wash of watercolor, but it doesn't conceal the steep, vertical drop below. Or how the pristine landscape appears untouched by signs of man. The isolation is so complete, it's easy to imagine that they're the last human on earth.

But, rounding a switchback, it turns out they're not alone out here after all.

Another hiker stands in the middle of the trail, back turned, body rigid. And beyond them, three people lie on the ground, sightless eyes revealing their fate.

The mountains can be a dangerous place.

1

MAGGIE

The body dangles from the gnarled branch of an elm, turning slightly as the wind catches it, the sign pinned to its chest fluttering in the breeze. The words slit my belly open like a knife, leaving me empty, gutted, disemboweled. This is personal. Someone wanted me to see this.

They're probably watching right now.

I fight the urge to react, teeth clenched painfully together, hands curled into fists as I think who could have done it, but it could have been anyone. Truth is, people in the tiny Northwoods burg of Coyote Cove have never been too welcoming. Something about a female police chief hasn't sat well with them, but after what happened this past fall—well, let's just say I'm not expecting to win any popularity contests anytime soon.

And that's fine. They don't have to like me, or the way I run this town. But if they think they can run me off? They're mistaken. It's better they learn that now than waste any more of my time.

I debate whether to ignore it, brush by and continue on to my office like it isn't even there, but something about the indignity of it has crept under my skin. I feel twitchy, overheated despite the way my breath fogs in the chill morning air. Only moments ago I'd been freezing, winter in Maine seeping into my bones, making my joints ache. Now all I feel is anger. Correction. Rage.

"Sometimes I hate people."

I glance toward Sue, standing beside me, not surprised that I didn't hear her approach over the sound of blood boiling in my ears.

"Only sometimes?" I ask.

"Eh. There's Christmas. My birthday. If they give me a gift I try to make a twenty-four-hour exception, but they still suck. Want me to help you get it down?"

She stamps her feet against the cold, drawing my attention to the *Winnie-the-Pooh* pajama pants tucked into the tops of her snow boots. Perhaps not the most professional attire for the receptionist of a police department, but she won't hear any complaints from me. Without her, I'd be running a one woman show.

"No, you go ahead inside and get warmed up. I'll take care of it."

Sue pauses a moment, the silence between us thick, filled with our unspoken loss. Our grief. And guilt. Though that last one is mine alone to bear.

She gives my shoulder a gentle squeeze, the contact so unexpected, so needed, that I don't know whether to freeze up or melt. Before I have to choose, she drops her hand, shuffling off inside to crank up the heat and start a pot of her high-test coffee.

A frigid gust of wind bowls into me, kicking up a swarm of dead leaves, sending them rattling down the sidewalk. The dummy, wearing a khaki shirt and pants much like my own, twists and sways at the end of its noose. I wonder where they got the uniform as I reach up to still its movements with one hand, unsheathing the knife I keep strapped to my hip with the other.

The sign is only inches from my eyes now, the words written in red, the now-dry paint allowed to drip down the paper in a way I assume was meant to mimic blood trails. But it's the words that I find disgusting. I consider donning gloves, processing this as a crime scene, charging whoever was behind this grisly prank.

Instead, I slice through the rope and let the straw-stuffed body tumble to the ground. Gathering it up, I carry it to the trash can around back, staring straight ahead, refusing to acknowledge the people who have stopped along the street to watch. The mailman. The school principal. One of the cashiers from the trading post.

Any of these people could have done this. Any of them could be planning worse. They could be planning together. And yet, it's still my job to protect them. To respond to calls, wherever that might take me. Alone. You don't have to be a gambler to realize how bad those odds are.

The edge of the paper with its despicable message saws against my hand with each step. Shifting my grip, I crumple it into a ball inside my fist, and keep a hold of it as I stuff the dummy inside the bin, shoving it down inside my pocket as I replace the lid.

My former lieutenant deserved better than what he got. I know the people here hold me responsible, and I get that. I do, too. My part in what happened makes me sick. But this makes me sicker.

At the end of the day, I'm an outsider, and I always will be. But Dale? Dale Murphy was one of them. This town is full of his friends, his family, and for them to mock him so blatantly like this while he rots cold and alone in his grave? It almost makes me glad that he's no longer around. I'd hate for him to see this.

Sue's right. People suck.

I march back around to the front of the building, telling

myself that the moisture in my eyes is from the cold, thinking of the paper in my pocket. Maybe I will give it a look, see if I can pull some prints. Crack some heads, levy some fines, do something...

Catching sight of Sue standing outside the door, I draw to a sudden halt. She looks paler than she had just minutes ago, her eyes red-rimmed, glistening under the weak morning sun. She rocks back on her heels unsteadily, teeth chattering, arms wrapped tight around herself, and it's then that I notice that she isn't wearing her jacket.

"What's wrong?" I take a reluctant step forward, then another. "Did they do something inside, too?"

Sue shakes her head, her glasses falling low on her nose. She takes a deep breath, gasps the air in too quickly, and chokes. Closing the distance between us, I wrap an arm around her shoulders and rub briskly.

"Let's get you inside and warmed up."

She shakes her head again, clears her throat, searching for her voice. "A call came in."

It must be serious, for her to be reacting like this. Instantly, my legs feel weak. *Steve*, I think. *Or one of the dogs. Something bad.* I release Sue, bracing myself against the side of the building to keep standing. My throat's gone too tight to swallow. I can barely draw air.

"What's happened?" It comes out as a whisper, but I know she's heard me. I want to scream at her, shake her, anything to get her to tell me what's going on, to stop the barrage of scenarios assaulting my brain, each more horrible than the last. I say her name, begging her to end my agony, to make it quick. "Sue?"

"There's been an accident up on Rattlesnake Mountain."

My throat relaxes, letting oxygen find its way to my lungs.

"A fatality."

A single word is all it takes for me to become one of those

people who suck. The relief I feel is at the expense of another. And I want it that way, would choose for someone else to grieve the loss of one of theirs over me experiencing the loss of one of my own.

"Hiker?" I ask, my voice wavering.

Sue nods. "A family."

I curse.

"Dead. All of them."

2

BRAD

Life was supposed to be more than this. *He* was supposed to be more than this. As a teenager he'd been sure he was meant for great things—climbing Mount Everest, exploring uncharted territories in the Amazon, braving new frontiers in extreme sports, really seizing destiny by the balls to show it who was boss.

Maybe a part of him had known he'd been setting his sights a tad too high for some poor redneck kid from West Virginia, but still. What he lacked in funds, education, and lineage he'd made up for with large quantities of hope. He figured it had been enough to help lesser men conquer their place in the world, why not him?

If he'd known how it would all end up, stuck in some far-flung corner of Maine in a town just as small and backwoods as the one he'd started from, he never would have tried. At least back home he'd had some friends. Some family. A girl or two to call his own. Or at least to call.

Here he had three days a week working retail for a cranky old man who let him escape on the weekends to lead crabby tourists on guided tours for a fraction of the take. Bandaging blisters, breaking his back under the pack full of bottled water he was forced to carry for the "hikers," who were too soft or weak or lazy to carry enough of their own. Tiptoeing among the easily bruised egos of the weekend warriors, in hopes of getting a gratuity in exchange for babysitting them and their bratty spawn, and keeping them alive on what was usually a moderate hike at best.

He couldn't understand why they didn't appreciate the beauty of the mountain. Why they felt the need to ruin the tranquility of the hike with their shouted conversations. And every time he was forced to watch them toss their trash and privilege around like confetti, he felt another little part of him die.

He can't wait to escape this place. Already has one foot aimed toward the nearest highway. So when the phone rings on Thursday morning, it's with a distinct lack of enthusiasm that he answers the call. "Northern Maine Sports, this is Brad speaking."

He doodles on a pad of paper, a stick figure aiming a gun at its own head, Xs for eyes, a grisly cloud of blood spatter and brain chunks mushrooming opposite the shot, or at least it might be grisly if he had anything other than blue ink to draw with. He tips the pen cup over, searching for another color while he waits to be asked if they sell socks, or gloves, or the ever eyebrow-raising athletic cup, because, as he'd told the last kid, "If you need one of those for hiking, you're doing it wrong."

"This is the place that leads the guided tours, right?"

"Yeah. Every weekend." He breathes the words out on a bored sigh, pulls the reservation book across the counter and flips it open. "What day did you want to book?"

"This is Chief Riley with the Coyote Cove Police Department."

Brad straightens in his chair even though he knows she can't see him. He sniffs his fingers, checks to see if they still smell like the joint he smoked on his way in this morning.

"I have a favor to ask, was wondering if you guys might be able to send someone over to help me out?"

"Uh, yeah. Sure. Totally. What can I do for you?"

"Got a call I need to respond to up on Rattlesnake Mountain. The Glacier Falls trail. You familiar with it?"

"Yeah, I know it like..." His mouth has gone dry, but he swallows hard anyways. "I know it."

"Can you take me up?"

"Now?"

"If possible."

He knows he'll catch hell from Horace for closing up shop early, but he'll deal with that when the time comes. If the time comes. "Let me grab my gear. Meet you in twenty?"

"Ten would be better."

"Okay. Sure. I'm on my way."

He sets the phone back on its cradle, stares at it like it's a friend who betrayed him. Pats his pockets, checking that he has everything that he needs—keys, wallet, phone—and nothing—drugs, paraphernalia, other items he shouldn't be caught with—that he doesn't. Stands unsteadily, feet dragging as he grabs his pack from a hook behind the counter, wishing more than anything that he could rewind time five minutes and be happy with his low-key, under the radar existence. Wishing, more than anything, that the call had been from a tourist enquiring about a pair of socks.

3

MAGGIE

I'm hoping the caller was mistaken. It wouldn't be the first time. The last report I received of a fatality, I responded to find a man passed out, yes, but very obviously alive from the thunderous pitch of his snores. With any luck, that'll be the case here, too. I'd much rather drag myself up the side of this mountain to discover there's nothing to investigate than to confirm that an entire family is dead.

I struggle to pant quietly, not wanting my guide—a twenty-something who looks like he just stepped off the pages of a print ad for Abercrombie—to know exactly how out of shape I am. Sweat slicks my skin despite the freezing temperature. My muscles burn, my legs feel like soggy noodles, and my head throbs from the change in altitude. Why the hell would anyone do this for fun?

We round a bend, one side of the trail dropping away, and I get my answer. The view is amazing. Soft greens and grays and shades of white blanketing the rolling profile of the mountain range as it extends in every direction. The beauty is almost over-whelming.

It also drives home how far we are from the rest of humanity

—I take a step closer and make the mistake of looking down—and how much higher. I scramble back from the ledge and continue forward. I know the tiny valley town of Coyote Cove is nestled somewhere below us, but I can't, for the life of me, see it. I can't see a single sign of civilization, for that matter.

This would be a really bad place to need help. As each step across unstable ground brings me closer to the clouds and further from the safety of shelter and medical attention, it's easy to see how an entire family might have perished out here.

I think of the dummy hanging outside my office this morning, the dark looks and unfriendly stares that follow me on a normal day as I walk down the street, and I wonder if I made a mistake asking this kid to be my guide. Maybe I'd have been better off on my own. But it's clear I'm out of my element here, and it makes me nervous like few things do.

The temperature dips as a cloud drifts over the sun. The skeletal hands of bare branches claw at us from the sudden shadows. A ripple of unease shivers along my spine, spreading into my limbs with goosebumps like it's some kind of omen.

But I'm too old to start being superstitious. I focus on the things I can control, the cadence of my steps, the rhythm of my breathing. The job I'm here to do. And though it has everything to do with the hard knot that's formed deep in the pit of my stomach, I try not to think about what waits ahead if the caller was correct.

She hadn't said much. Hadn't been able to, according to Sue. She'd simply stuttered out what she'd discovered and promised to wait until I arrived on the scene.

Though that part's taking a little longer than I expected. I hadn't realized that mountain miles would be so much different than flat miles. But it could be worse. I pause as I catch a glimpse of a whitecapped peak through a gap in the trees. Snow. That could definitely complicate things and slow us down.

We've been lucky so far—usually by this time of year there's at least a foot of snow on the ground. Nothing's stuck yet except at the higher elevations, but the *Farmers' Almanac* has predicted that this winter will be a doozy. And this would be a very bad place to be when conditions change. I swallow down a surge of apprehension.

The straps of my pack—a promotional freebie, the name of the company where I purchase the department's fingerprint powder emblazoned in navy across the cheap yellow nylon—bite deep into my shoulders. I bend my arms behind my back and lift the bag from the bottom, trying to get a moment of relief, wondering if the few supplies I shoved in on my way out of the office quadrupled in weight because gravity pulls harder on a mountain. I suspect that I'm creating my own laws of physics, but I'm not willing to acknowledge the alternative.

My guide, Brad, pauses at the curve of a switchback ahead. He grabs a water bottle from his pack, takes a sip while he waits for me to catch up. "Want one?" he asks, holding out a spare.

"Thanks." I jog a couple steps to close the distance between us. "Ouch. That looks like it hurts," I say, gesturing to his outstretched hand as I take the drink. Cracking the seal, I chug half of it in a single swallow.

He frowns as he looks at the gash on his palm. "Not so much anymore. But when it first happened..." He meets my gaze as he nods his head, eyes opened wide. "Oh yeah."

"It probably could have used a few stitches."

Brad shrugs. "I was guiding a hike when it happened. Knew from the time I ripped my calf open on a branch during an overnighter that the doctors usually won't sew you up after too many hours have passed. By the time I got the tourists off the mountain and back to town, I figured there'd be no point."

"Is your job always so dangerous?"

Another shrug. "Parts of it are worth it. I mean, look around. It's gorgeous, isn't it? And there's something about challenging yourself, both physically and mentally. It's almost spiritual, you know? I'll take the fresh air and serenity of a mountain over an office any day." Taking in my expression, he adds, with a note of disappointment in his tone, "You're not much of a hiker then?"

"I'm from Florida." My voice sounds strained, hoarse. "I think there's, like, three hills in the entire state."

"Flatlander, huh? But that doesn't matter, you can work your way through that. If we were up here just for fun, I bet you'd love it."

I seriously doubt that. "You from around here?" I ask, more interested in buying extra time to hold still than the answer.

"Nope."

He stashes his bottle back in his pack and shoulders it, ready to forge ahead already. I groan internally, then struggle to force a smile as he looks over his shoulder, making sure I'm following.

"West Virginia. Less bears, more coal, otherwise it's pretty much the same."

"What brought you up this way?"

I watch his broad shoulders shrug. "Seemed like a good idea at the time. How about you?"

"Same."

Sometimes a lie is more convenient than the truth. And I don't exactly feel like rehashing my past with this kid, the tragedy that caused me to crash and burn at the height of my career. Besides, no one in Coyote Cove needs to know that I ended up their police chief because I didn't have any other options.

As if he can sense the tenderness of the subject, he lets it drop. We hike in silence, the only sounds the slap of our boots against the rocky trail, loose scree skittering behind us, and my labored breathing.

"What are we doing up here, anyways?"

I startle at the sound of his voice, rub a hand along my collarbone to dispel some of the tension tightening my chest. He asked the question like we were mid-conversation, despite the lag in talking, which lets me know it's something he's been thinking about. It's been bothering him. Truth is, it's been bothering me, too.

"A hiker called in to report something I need to investigate."

Should I elaborate? Prepare poor Brad for what might await us? Or should I allow him his blissful ignorance for as long as it has a chance to last?

"On the Glacier Falls trail? Not many people hike that way this time of year."

"Oh, yeah?"

"Yeah. You get better views taking the Snake's Tail trail. Or the Sunset Loop. The falls are pretty much frozen by now. All you can see is a hump of ice at the top. Not really interesting."

"Hmm." I wonder what brought the family of hikers out this way then. If it was some unfortunate twist of fate—a bad idea, a wrong turn, a faulty guidebook—that led to their possible demise.

"No reason to come up this way at all right now, really. Not unless..."

"Unless?"

"Never mind."

"No, what were you going to say?"

"It's nothing."

I come to a stop, feet planted firmly on either side of a rock in the trail, refusing to move forward. The shakiness has gone from my limbs, the weakness has left my body. Realizing I'm no longer following behind him, Brad turns, checks to see where I am.

I study his face, searching his expression. It might be my imagination, a trick of the light perhaps, but it looks like his skin has blanched beneath the tanned surface. "Why don't you tell me, let me decide."

His eyes go a little wide. His mouth tightens into a thin line. I take a step closer, smelling fear.

"Really, it's nothing. It's just. You hear rumors."

"About?"

He toes a line in the dirt with his boot. Must be a pretty interesting glyph since he can't seem to tear his eyes away from it.

Just when I think he's going to refuse to elaborate, he says, "About what goes on up here. In the off season. You know."

"I don't, actually."

"Just—illegal stuff. Drugs. Smuggling." He shrugs, lifts his gaze to mine reluctantly.

"Up here? Actually *on* the mountain?"

"Like I said, just rumors." He shakes off whatever was troubling him and closes the distance between us. Breaks out into a lopsided grin, revealing a dimple in his cheek. "You've got something..."

He lifts a thumb, runs it along my jawline. I shiver at his touch. Find myself torn between the urge to bite and sever the digit from his hand—because how dare he erase and ignore the invisible barrier between us—or feel flattered because I'm probably fifteen years his senior, a woman fast approaching middle age, and an attractive younger man just chose to voluntarily touch my sweaty, dirty skin.

"Anyways." His eyes meet mine, shyly. "It's not much farther."

I look toward where he gestures, at the sky, at my feet, at the thin line of gray dirt snaking between some brush in the opposite direction, anywhere but at him and his fluttery lashes. I track the narrow trail as far as I can see it, wondering where it leads.

Brad starts walking the other direction. I put a palm on his forearm to stop him. He flinches. Hisses. Guess I'm not the only one uncomfortable with unexpected physical contact. I drop my hand and try not to read anything into the way he gingerly fingers his jacket where I touched him.

"Hello? Is someone there?"

I jump, the panicked emotion in the tone triggering an uneasy release of adrenaline that makes my skin bristle. A cloud of dust precedes the owner, small rocks tumbling down the incline ahead of them. I move past Brad, putting myself between him and the person approaching too fast for a safe descent. My hand moves to the butt of the gun holstered at my side.

"Oh, thank God."

A mid-fortyish woman appears and flings herself at me. Her body hits mine with such force that I'm knocked off balance, my backward momentum stopped only by a painful meeting between my spine and a tree. She collapses in my arms, sagging against me. Bark bites painfully into my flesh as she sobs, near hysterics.

"Get me the hell off of this mountain. Everyone's dead here."

4

STEVE

A strange sensation draws my skin tight across my bones. I rub a hand across the back of my neck, trying to erase the feeling, but it's no use. Whatever it is that's crept under my flesh remains. I look from the dogs—watching me like hawks from the kitchen floor, ready to pounce on anything I drop—to the phone.

I want to call Maggie. Want to check to make sure she's all right. I try to convince myself that the source of my sudden anxiety has nothing to do with her. Even if it does, though, if I'm somehow picking up on some vibe she's tossing out to the universe, I can't.

She's an adult. A cop. Just because I love her doesn't mean it's appropriate for me to act like some kind of overprotective parent every time I get an odd feeling. Besides, if what I'm feeling really were some kind of cosmic call of distress on Maggie's part, wouldn't the dogs be picking up on it too?

I eye the terriers, canine evolution at its finest. The phone. The wiry butts, one black and one white, now shaking with the wag of their stumpy tails, thinking my interest is an invitation to share my lunch. The phone, cold and hard in its plastic cradle.

The dogs. The landline. Maybe it wouldn't hurt if I made a quick call, just to ask what she feels like for dinner.

I know I'm wrong even as I convince myself that I'm right. I reach out hungrily, greedily, needing to hear her voice. Almost fall over backward when it rings before I even lay a finger on it.

"Hello?" My pulse needles like a tattoo gun at the base of my throat as I wait for the voice on the other end of the line. What if this is it? The call I've been dreading since I realized I wanted to spend my life with a woman who occasionally finds herself on the wrong end of a loaded weapon.

"Steven."

"Mother?" My lungs, finding they can once again inflate, suck the word into my chest so deep I almost choke.

"Were you expecting someone else?"

I swallow my reply, not wanting to get into it with her right now. There are easier battles to be fought. Like finding the cure for cancer.

"Who's this woman your sister told me about? The one you asked to marry you?"

I pinch the bridge of my nose, ruing the day I stopped being an only child. Then I get a brief flash of what my life would have been like had I been my mother's sole focus, and quickly recant.

"I've told you about Maggie before."

"You never said it was serious."

"I never said it wasn't."

"Whatever happened to that nice girl from Weston you were seeing? Jasmine?"

Nice girl? My mother hated her at the time, and she wasn't exactly shy about her feelings. It's been the same with all my past girlfriends. She acts like it's some kind of contest. It's not that they're not good enough for me so much as they're not good enough to compete against her for my affection.

"Julie. And I stopped seeing her over six years ago."

My mother sniffs to fill the silence. "I suppose this means you'll be staying in that place?"

"It's my home."

She sounds genuinely upset when she says, "Your home is here in Boston. With me. Your sister. Grampa Joe."

A sudden wave of homesickness sweeps over me. A lump forms in my throat. I kneel down, let the dogs nuzzle my face as I deal with the unexpected realization that even though my mother and I have never gotten along, I still miss her.

"So when do I get to meet what's her name?"

"Maggie."

"Uh-huh. When?"

"Soon."

"Could you be any vaguer? I mean, what? Do you expect me to wait to meet my future daughter-in-law until the wedding?"

Ideally? Yes. I want Maggie to be my wife. There's a greater chance of us actually making it to the altar if she doesn't get a chance to know the family she's marrying into first. I swallow the reply, instead saying, "There's plenty of time. We haven't even set a date yet."

"How about I come up this weekend?"

Icy dread shoots through my veins. "No."

"Why not?"

I might miss my mother, but that doesn't mean I actually want to see her. She's not an easy woman to get along with. She's pushy. Meddling. Aggressive. And for once I'm with someone who won't be cowed and back down. Putting Maggie and my mother in the same room together could be catastrophic.

"Maggie's working."

"That's ridiculous."

"Um."

"I insist. I'll email you my flight information once I've booked."

"Mother..."

"It's settled. Can't wait to see you and Mary."

"Mother!"

But the line is dead, the call ended. I scowl at the phone in my hand like it's a sworn enemy, wishing I'd never picked it up in the first place. The betrayal of this inanimate object burns deep.

I don't know how I'm going to tell Maggie. I don't know how either of us are going to survive the weekend. The only thing I do know is the probable source of the unease I was feeling, which is nothing compared to the dread that I feel now.

5

MAGGIE

I glance over the shoulder of the woman who's turned to jelly in my arms, at the pale face of the man who's appeared behind her. My muscles tighten involuntarily, my body instantly wary. So obviously not *everyone* is dead. It's an important distinction. One she should have mentioned. I shift my weight, resting my palm against the firearm on my hip.

The man runs the back of his wrist across his mouth in a way that makes me suspect I'll find vomit somewhere around my possible crime scene. But I don't have time to worry about that right now. I've got to manage the situation.

Brad's sidestepping like a skittish colt, moving back down the trail. His eyes flash, whites showing, and his lips curl back from his teeth.

"What's she talking about?" He inches farther away toward the trailhead.

I've got to stop him before he bolts. I need him, his help and expertise.

I give him a sheepish look over the head of the balling woman. "A fatality was reported this morning. I won't know what's going on until I see for myself."

Brad swears under his breath.

"Listen, Brad, I know you don't owe me anything, and I really appreciate you bringing me up here, but I still need your help."

He wipes a hand over his face, now damp with sweat. Casts a longing look over his shoulder at his escape route.

"If—what's your name?" I ask the man.

"Glen. Glen Coffrey."

"And yours?" I ask, slowly extricating myself from the woman's embrace.

"Cheryl."

"If Glen and Cheryl are right, I'm going to have to report this to the state crime lab for investigation. I'll need someone to meet them at the bottom. Lead them up here. Do you think you can do that for me?"

He doesn't look sure, but he says, "Yeah."

"Let me go with him," Cheryl begs, her hand gripping my arm tightly.

"I'm afraid I can't. I'm going to need to ask you some questions while the details are still fresh in your mind."

Her head shakes violently from side to side. "I can't stay up here another minute. Not with... I just can't."

I need her statement. But an uncooperative witness is a useless witness. Besides, I still don't know what I'm dealing with here. "Tell me what happened," I prompt, fighting to keep my voice steady, compassionate. Patient.

"I already told you."

I don't point out that it was Sue she spoke with, not me. "Can you tell me again, please?"

"I'm here on vacation. Went for a hike."

"What time did you start?"

"First thing this morning."

"Was the sun up?"

"Not quite yet."

I nod for her to continue.

"I was making good time, came around the bend, tripped on a loose rock. That's when I saw the body. The first one. The son." Her voice tapers into a shrill whine.

"Then what?"

"Then nothing. I dialed nine-one-one, got connected to you. You told me to wait for you here, I did, now I'm done."

"Did you notice anything else?"

"No."

"See anyone else?"

"Uh-uh. Not until he got here." She gestures toward the man.

"So you two didn't hike up here together?"

"No," Cheryl says, in the same tone someone might say *ew*.

Glen stares down at his feet. "I, uh, actually got here before. Not before Cheryl," he rushes to say, eyes widening in panic. "But before she made the call. I must have been close behind her, I hit the trail right at sunrise. Didn't see anyone or anything until I rounded the bend and stumbled on..."

He swallows hard, pressing the back of his fingers against his mouth. I take a small step to the side, just in case.

"How long are you in town for?"

He draws a deep breath before answering. "Two weeks. I'm renting a cabin with some buddies. We're planning to do some fly-fishing. I got here last night, no one else is getting in until tomorrow, so I thought I'd take a hike." Under his breath he adds, "Really regretting *that* decision."

"Where's the cabin?"

"Loon Lane. Twenty-eight Loon Lane."

I know exactly where he's talking about. It's two doors down from where I live.

"And you?" I ask, turning toward Cheryl.

"Just the weekend. I'm leaving Sunday night."

But I can tell by the way her eyes dart hard to the side that she has no intention of staying for the rest of her trip.

"Where are you staying?"

"The motel in town."

"Margot's?"

"Yes."

"Do you guys have your IDs on you?"

Pulling my phone out, I take a picture of their licenses. As soon as I hand Cheryl's back to her, she shoves it into her pack without looking and shrugs her arms into the straps.

"So, can I go?"

I nod, making a mental note to call Margot when I finish with the staties. Assuming Cheryl stops by her room to retrieve her things, Margot will find a way to get her to stay. Her method might not be strictly legal, but I'd rather find the money in my operating budget for a car repair or two than be tasked with trying to track down a witness who doesn't want to be found.

Glen raises his hand like a timid student. "Can I...?"

"Go ahead."

Brad gives me a grim look before he joins them, one that lets me know that there's no way he'd trade places with me right now. I don't blame him. I'd prefer not to be here myself.

I watch them make tracks down the trail until they disappear from sight. The sound of their retreating steps fades into the distance, leaving me by myself. Except for a handful of corpses, that is. The thought makes my spit thin.

As much as I don't want to admit it, I wish I wasn't on my own right now. But I can't let my nerves get the best of me. Looking toward the path, I force myself forward, thighs burning as I hike briskly up the incline and around the bend of a switchback.

And there they are.

I take deep belly breaths as I pull my phone from my

pocket. Lick dry lips, trying to rehydrate them as I find my voice. Clear my throat.

I take a hesitant step closer as I dial, not wanting to disturb the scene, but needing to make sense of what I'm seeing. And what I'm not. Because the family before me—a mother, a father, their son—are indeed dead, strewn across the trail like winter leaves shed from the trees. But for the life of me I can't tell what killed them.

6

ERIKA

I'm obsessing when I receive the email. It's been almost a week since I went out with Devon in the print lab last Friday. We haven't spoken since.

I saw him Monday while passing the breakroom. I should have said hi to him then, but I didn't want to seem too desperate. Or needy. Especially not lonely. Even if I am all of those things.

But I didn't want it to be obvious, so I kept walking without even a second glance in his direction, figuring he'd make the first move, but he hasn't, and now we haven't talked since our date. Too much time has gone by. It's morphed beyond awkward into painfully uncomfortable.

Now I'm destined to spend this Friday on the couch watching Hallmark movies with my cats, and it's all my fault. I might have to find a new job. In a new town. Or maybe I should just retire completely and give in, become a full-time crazy cat lady.

This is why you should never date a coworker.

Only, then I wouldn't even have the one and a half dates I average a year. Even sadder? That half-date usually consists of me listening sympathetically to whoever's had too much to drink at the annual Christmas party.

I'm knee-deep in berating myself, partaking in the kind of self-loathing pity party that borders on self-flagellation. Admitting that my mom was right. And the jerk I dumped in college, who I'm not sure was ever really my boyfriend to begin with. And my fourth-grade teacher who really was a crazy cat lady, the kind who delights in being cruel to children.

So when I click on the lab-wide email requesting volunteers to assist with the collection and investigation of three unattended deaths in some tiny little town up north, I jump on it. Which probably isn't the best idea considering that I'm not someone who works in the field. Ever.

I'm too uptight. I like a controlled environment. My lab. Possibly long walks on the beach if I ever tried them, but honestly just the idea of the sand and the wind and the salt spray seems unpleasant. But so is obsessing over whether or not to end my career just to avoid an awkward encounter with a coworker who obviously isn't interested in asking me on date number two.

So now here I am, riding shotgun in a crime scene response van along winding mountain roads. Trying to hold on to the donut I shouldn't have self-medicated with this morning. Wondering if I can really trust my neighbor to take proper care of my cats.

I grab the dash to steady myself as we zip around a curve too fast. Cut my eyes at the driver, a crime scene technician named Bridgette who's young enough to be my daughter. She's pretty and perky, smart and ambitious, and genuinely nice, everything I've come to hate in another human.

Bridgette reaches toward the radio then hesitates, looks my way and smiles. I wish she'd keep her eyes on the road.

"Do you mind?" she asks.

"I'd rather you not."

"Oh. Okay." She drums her hands on the steering wheel, which is even worse than whatever racket she probably would have chosen to listen to. "Have you ever been to Coyote Cove before?" she asks.

And now I've trapped myself into making small talk. I should have just let her play the radio. "I have not." I stare out the window, wondering if I should say something back. Finally I decide on, "Have you?"

"Yeah, once. Not that long ago, actually. Just this past fall."

I shift in my seat, giving her my attention. "For a suspicious death investigation? Is this place dangerous?"

She shrugs, shifting her grip on the wheel so she's holding it at the bottom. Not a proper driving position. "A homicide, actually. I got the impression that case was kind of a one-off. But, I mean, we're heading up there now for a triple, so, maybe?"

"Should I be worried?"

"Nah, I wouldn't." She looks over at me again. Again with the smile. "The police chief seems very capable."

I huff air out my nose, roll my eyes at my reflection in the window, an image playing through my mind of a hunky cop straight off the cover of a romance novel. "Is that so?"

"Well, yeah. She's kind of like you."

"And what do you mean by that?" I turn, narrowing my gaze at her, wondering what kind of game she's up to.

This time there's no look, no smile. Brigette keeps watch on the road. But her cheeks? They're pink. Her hands grip the wheel tightly at ten and two. Her teeth dig into her lower lip.

She releases the bite. Her voice is soft, barely above a whisper, her cheeks flushing almost red as she says, "You know. A strong woman. Someone who doesn't conform in a male-dominated industry just because society expects it of them."

A what? I study her profile, but she doesn't seem to be joking. If anything, she seems genuinely embarrassed, like me when I say too much. "Um. Thanks?"

The smile returns, but her eyes still stay on the road. "I volunteered for this trip when I heard you were going. I'm really looking forward to working with you."

What I say is, "Yeah. Me too." What I think is, *Oh, crap.* The awkward situation with Devon in the print lab was bad enough, but this? It's ten times worse. It's one thing to embarrass and disappoint myself, I'm used to that.

But this young woman might actually look up to me. I'm not sure how, or why, or even that I've ever been in this position before. I probably won't be ever again. And I really don't want to let her down. The pressure's on, and of all the things that I'm not, good under pressure tops the list.

7

MAGGIE

The body closest to me is that of a young man, someone whose life was really only just beginning. His arm is stretched above his head, hand slightly curled as if he's reaching for my help. But it's too late for that. Now the only thing I can do for him is find out what happened.

As I study him, I try not to think about all the experiences he'll miss out on, the lessons he's learned during his short life that he'll never get to put into action. His eyes are open, his lips parted, his brows high in a way that suggests surprise.

But there's no visible sign of what killed him. No blood, no wounds, no body fluids to suggest sickness. No nothing. It's eerie. It's like he just dropped dead in his tracks.

My eyes slide past him to the woman beyond. I'm struck by how close she must be to my own age. She's petite, her features delicate, almost elfin. Even before death she must have been pale, but now her skin is pure alabaster, the translucence marred only by the network of blood vessels already starting to collapse beneath, spidering like veining in marble. She looks like a statue, forever frozen in time.

The gray in her neatly tucked flannel shirt is an exact match to her hiking trousers, the laces of her barely worn boots matching the blue. She's the kind of woman who would make me look twice if I passed her in the grocery store, the kind who seems like she would have tissues and Band-Aids and maybe even a miniature sewing kit in her purse, the kind who has it all together. But none of that preparedness is of any use now.

I feel myself growing strangely emotional. But I can't allow that. I can't identify with this victim. I can't wonder if we listened to the same bands growing up, if we liked the same shows. That's how the job destroys you. I need to remain detached.

I shift my attention to the third body. The man is a similar age to the woman, to myself. His vacant, staring gaze confirms death. His uninjured body denies me the cause. Which might be why I'm breathing so shallowly. What the hell happened to these people? Maybe I should put a little distance between us.

I study my surroundings as I retreat back to the bend, searching the trees, the dirt, the rocks littered along the edge of the path, but nothing appears out of the ordinary. Yet I can't stop looking, because something happened here. Something that left three people dead without a discernible trace.

I think of what Brad said earlier, about the rumors he'd heard of illegal activities up on the mountains. Is that what I'm dealing with? Did this poor family observe something they weren't meant to see, and get silenced because of it? But, surely, if that was the case, there'd be a sign of what killed them.

A gentle vibration from my pocket interrupts my thoughts. It's Sue calling with an update.

As she talks, I remind myself that the state police investigate all major crimes in Maine. This is not my case. There are other duties I need to attend to. A town to police, all on my own until I find a new lieutenant. That's my job, that's what should be my focus, not this.

I try to pay attention as Sue rattles off a list of applicants, but it's tough. My traitorous body begs for rest. My shoulders are knotted tight. My thighs burn. And my feet ache.

Dropping my gaze to the ground, taking in the track I've worn on the dusty trail from all my pacing, it's no wonder. There's a boulder to my right that's a comfortable height for sitting. A fallen log several yards beyond that would also do. And past that? Like a car wreck that you're not supposed to look at, my eyes are drawn to the pale hand half-curled into a fist on the dirt path.

I glance away quickly, clear my throat as I resume pacing and return my attention to Sue on the phone. "Sorry, can you repeat that?"

"Sure. I said that none of these guys are a good fit."

"Tell me something I don't know."

"You shouldn't be up on that mountain by yourself."

The truth is, I know that, too. I catch myself just as my focus returns to the bodies, force myself to turn my head away. March farther down the trail so it won't be so easy for my eyes to betray me.

"Yeah, well—" I move the phone away from my mouth for a second so Sue can't hear my sigh "—that's why we've got to settle. Now come on. Let's go through the list again. A few of the applicants have to be worth interviewing."

"*Mmm.*" Sue's low growl of disapproval does little to help.

"Do you deny that we need a new lieutenant?"

Her silence is pregnant with the emotion we're both feeling.

"We're not replacing Murphy," I say softly. The back of my throat tightens and burns. I give my eyes a wipe, then my runny nose, pat my cheek a few times to ground myself. "We're just hiring someone to do all the things that neither of us want to do. Now, seriously. Are you telling me that not one of the candidates has foot massages listed under special skills?"

My attempt at humor falls flat. Sue spikes my volley back over the net.

"No, but here's one who says he can gut a pig in under three minutes."

"Um, do you mean dress a pig?"

"No, I do not. There is no mention of utilizing said pig for consumption. Or hunting, for that matter. The resume says, and I quote, 'I can gut a pig dry in under three minutes.'"

"Yeah." I shift the phone to my other hand, rub my ear like I can erase what I just heard. "Let's move that one to the probably-no pile."

Sue snorts. "You must really want someone to trade places with you right now."

I fight the urge to glance behind me. "You have no idea."

"You want me to pick out the applicants who are least likely to be serial killers and arrange interviews?"

"That would be great."

"You got it. Anything else?"

"Yeah. Could you call Steve and let him know what's up? That I probably won't be home 'til late?"

I hear myself swallow. I hear the wind rattling leaves. What I don't hear is Sue's reply.

"Hello?" I check the phone, make sure the call hasn't dropped. It hasn't. "Sue? Are you there?"

"I'm here."

"Oh, good. The call must have faded out for a second."

"That's not what happened." I hear her fingers drumming angrily across the line.

"Okay?" The tapping gets louder. "Then what did?"

"Nothing. I just didn't reply. Doing your dirty work is not part of my job description."

"Actually—"

"Don't actually me, you know what I mean. Call your man and tell him yourself." When I don't reply, she asks, "Is there something going on between the two of you that I need to know about?"

"Not really."

"Not really," she mocks. "Girl. If you can't tell me, who *are* you going to talk to about it?"

It's a low blow and we both know it. We both also know that it's true. I don't exactly have a lot of friends. And I could use someone to confide in.

"It's nothing, really. We just, kind of, you know." I draw a deep breath, force myself to spit the words out as I exhale. "Got engaged."

"Engaged! But that's a good thing. Isn't it?"

I look at my nails, start picking at the lines of dirt wedged beneath them from the hike. "Sure."

"Then why don't you sound happy?"

"I'm just worried, I guess. That it's going to change things."

"Well, it is."

"But I'm not sure I want things to change."

"Maggie, dear. You lovable little rock. You take it from me. You need this. Him. Someone to soften your hard edges. And Steve? He's a good man. Don't blow this. I'm hanging up now. You do what you need to do."

And just like that, she cruelly leaves me alone with my thoughts. I stare down at my cell long after the call has ended. My stomach shifts and churns, turning on itself. I sink onto a fallen log, the wind suddenly out of my sails, leaving me exhausted.

Because what Sue said is only half-right. I am a rock. And Steve is a good man. But those hard edges? I'm not sure I could survive without them.

8

BRAD

Brad's eyes track the woman, Cheryl, as she hurries down the trail ahead of him and Glen, practically at a jog. Something's off about her behavior. Before, in front of Chief Riley, she was panicked, her actions frantic, almost spastic. Now, her movements are careful and controlled.

"Hey. You might want to slow down a bit," he calls after her. "There's a stretch of loose scree up ahead. Makes for sketchy footing."

As if to prove his point, Glen grunts as his boot skids, a handful of pebbles scattering down the trail as his ankle buckles. Brad grabs his shoulder, steadying him until he regains his balance.

Cheryl tosses an annoyed glance at him over her shoulder, her pace not easing up a bit. "Don't worry about me."

Brad scowls as he carefully threads a finger under the sleeve of his shirt and wipes the sweat away from a stinging abrasion. It's freezing out. They're descending. There'd be no cause to sweat if she'd just slow down. "Yeah, well. Kind of have to. The chief told me to look after you."

It's a convenient lie. One that should garner a little respect. It doesn't.

But it does make the woman stop. She spins to face him, cheeks flushed, but whether from anger or exertion, he doesn't know. The finger she raises in his direction, however, stabbing it through the air at him like a sword as she closes the distance between them clues him in. He touches the phone in the top pocket of his jacket.

"The chief." She rolls her eyes. "Do you really think I give a damn about anything she has to say? Made me stay up there with those—those—bodies like some kind of sick sadist."

"She didn't *make* you," he mumbles.

"I'm getting off this mountain of death and out of this Podunk town as fast as I possibly can and I'm never looking back."

"Okay, but—"

"And if anyone even tries to stop me." She doesn't finish the threat, instead turning on her heel and marching forward.

He casts an annoyed look at Glen as they both start walking again, following along behind her, but the other man refuses to meet his eye. Brad calls after Cheryl. "Yeah, but—"

"So don't worry about trying to keep up," she interrupts. "Probably better for you if you don't. You can tell her that by the time you got to the parking lot I was already gone."

"Fine by me." But he matches her pace, maintaining the short space between them. He glances behind him to where Glen is struggling to keep up. Or is he purposely dawdling? "But, hey. Cheryl?"

She raises her head toward the sky, shaking her head. Yells, "What?"

"Don't take offense or anything, but don't you think you're acting kind of suspicious?"

She turns slowly, head cocked at an odd angle as she fixes

her narrowed eyes on his face. "What the hell are you talking about?"

"I mean, seriously. No offense." He holds his hands up, palms forward as if preparing to ward off an attack. "But it just seems kind of strange. You're acting completely different than you did in front of Chief Riley."

"What's your point?"

"Well, um." He pulls at the front of his coat, adjusting it. "Just that, you know. You're the one who found the bodies."

"And?"

"And, uh. You keep talking about how you plan to go against police orders to leave town. It just, well, it seems a little bit fishy if you ask me."

"Oh. My. God." Cheryl digs her hands into her hair, close to the roots, and pulls. "Screw you. Screw you, screw this mountain, screw the bodies, and especially screw your precious police chief."

Spittle flies from her mouth as she shouts in his face. "And another thing. Back off. If you don't stay off my heels there'll be a fourth body getting carried off this mountain. You hear me?"

"Loud and clear."

Brad watches her back as she storms down the path, kicking up a cloud of dust behind her. He listens to her muttered curses, the crunch of her boots over rocks and roots, the trickle of pebbles stirred up by her angry strides. When all signs of her are gone, he discreetly lifts the phone out of his jacket pocket, holds it down along his leg as he turns to face Glen.

"That was strange," he comments.

"You're telling me." Glen stops as he reaches Brad, swipes at the sweat dripping into his eyes. "That lady's a weirdo, plain and simple. To tell the truth, I'd rather have been up there alone with the bodies than there with her. Them I didn't have to worry about."

"That's... interesting. You need to make sure to tell the chief that."

"You bet. I just didn't want to say anything in front of her," he says, gesturing toward the trail where Cheryl has already disappeared. "Because, well, you know." He makes a face as he draws a finger across his throat in a slashing motion.

"So you're saying you felt threatened by her?"

"Let's just say that if looks could kill, I know what happened to those people up there."

Brad stifles a snort, saying, "Yeah, that's definitely something the chief should know," before thumbing off the recording.

9

MAGGIE

I know I should call Steve, but I can't figure out what to tell him. That I'm alone on a mountain with three dead people and no idea what killed them? That, even though I have enough on my plate, and this crime falls under state police jurisdiction, it's a struggle not to dive in and investigate? That even though I'm spooked and more than slightly concerned that I'm exposing myself to something that could be fatal, I'd rather be here right now than there?

It's that last part that keeps me from making the call.

Because even though I'm hungry, thirsty, and so far beyond cold that saying I'm freezing my ass off would be the understatement of the year, I've got the overwhelming urge to stop ignoring the bodies behind me and do some damn detective work.

It wouldn't be so wrong. It's not like I don't know what I'm doing. I wouldn't make some rookie mistake that botched the scene or anything.

Once upon a time, in a past life, I was a homicide detective. A good one.

Somewhere between being a child who loved puzzles and a

teen who loved mysteries I stumbled into being an adult who loved solving crimes. I lived for it. Excelled at it. Defined myself by my skill for it.

Yet, when it was personal, when it mattered the most, I failed.

Because that detective I used to be? The one in that other life? She had a little brother.

Past tense. Had.

Maybe we weren't close. I was already a cop by the time he was born. But that didn't mean I didn't love him. That his loss didn't almost destroy me.

I would have done anything for Brandon. And I still would.

Some crimes can't be forgiven. Some scores need to be settled. And when the right time comes around, I'll exact my eye for an eye.

I know that nothing I plan to do will make much of a difference. My brother will still be gone. My parents still lost to me. But knowing that one day, the man who destroyed my life as I knew it will pay for what he did? That's the only thing that lets me sleep at night.

This is the wedge that festers like a painful splinter between me and Steve, because revenge is not a dish best served cold—it's a dish best kept to oneself, to be consumed in private. Like that pizza you know you shouldn't have on your diet, or the parents who eat their kid's Halloween candy. The "innocent" flirtation at work. That misplaced decimal on your credit card application. Some secrets other people just won't understand.

Sure, the things that make us feel good about ourselves are hard to give up, but so are the things that make us feel bad. Because giving up anything that you're used to—good or bad—is uncomfortable. And human civilization is nothing if not forged around comfort.

So here, now, as much as I know that I need to stay hands off, that this isn't my case so I shouldn't become attached and try to work it, I need it. I crave it. Like a favorite blanket, it would bring me comfort.

Just knowing there are people who somehow lost their lives —a family, no less—in my jurisdiction, on my watch, and that I'm trying to ignore them, is tearing me up inside. Opening old wounds. Flaying the raw meat of my heart. Gutting me like a pig. In under three minutes.

I turn around, allowing myself to face the bodies. Like an intravenous drug, the effect is immediate. My muscles relax. My breath comes easier. The static in my head fades to background noise.

I know I'm being stupid—I don't know what killed them. It could be contagious. I could be putting myself at risk. But like a diabetic with a donut, I want it anyways.

I pull my phone from my pocket and open the camera app. If I'm going to do this, I'm doing it right. Shooting my way into and out of the scene, preparing the case for prosecution on the off chance that there's someone to charge for this. And if there's not? It'll be my guilty little midnight snack secret.

Decision made, I feel better, lighter. Happier. There's a lot in my life that doesn't make sense, but this does.

I backtrack to where Cheryl heard me talking to Brad, preparing to take video of the approach to the scene. I roll my shoulders to release some of the tension holding them tight and raise my phone, when something rustles in the brush beside me, making me pause. It's a bird, maybe, or a chipmunk. Even though I haven't seen a single sign of wildlife since I've been up here. Whatever.

I shrug it off. Hit the button to start the recording. Say my name, the date, and the time. Startle at the sound of a high-pitched whine. It isn't feedback. But it is a sound I recognize. I am not alone on this mountain.

10
ERIKA

I crane my head down low to get a better glimpse out the windshield. Debate whether or not it's too late to turn around. That early retirement as a crazy cat lady thing seems like a pretty good idea right about now.

"It's beautiful, isn't it."

I glance at Brigette, decide it's too early to disappoint her and agree. "Yes. Very." Turn around in my seat as we pass a sign marking the turnoff for Coyote Cove. "Wasn't that our turn?"

"Nope."

"It said Coyote Cove."

"I know."

"Isn't that where we're going?"

"More or less."

It's like talking to the Sphinx. I like riddles, but I'm more of a *did the clogged artery cause the myocardial infarction or just contribute to it* kind of girl. I bite my tongue and count to ten, trying to be patient. Then I count to twenty. "So, then, where is our destination, exactly?"

"You're looking at it."

"What? Where?"

"There." She points out the windshield.

"The mountain?"

"Uh-huh."

I'm praying for patience. Salvation. The discernment to know whether jumping out of this moving vehicle will somehow wake me up out of what I'm hoping is just a very cruel dream, or put me in the hospital. Either seems acceptable as I gape at the giant rockface before us and pose myself a riddle. *Did the mountain cause the myocardial infarction, or the stroke?*

Brigette's perfectly arched brows crease at my lack of enthusiasm. She frowns. "You didn't know?"

"Uh. No."

"But I thought. Um." She nervously licks her lips.

"Thought what?"

"That you volunteered for this. The field assignment."

My stomach tightens into a hard little stone. Could I really have been so stupid? So desperate to get out of the office and away from an awkward situation that I failed to read the entire email before I hit reply? Yes, yes I could. And, apparently, I was.

"I have a confession." I glance in her direction but fail to make eye contact. "I may not have read the full description of what I agreed to do."

"Oh." It's a single word, but it's loaded. The sound of the tires on the road beneath us grows deafening, filling the silence between us. An insufferable amount of time passes before she says, "Well, I'm sure you'll be fine."

"Are you?"

"Do you like hiking?"

"No."

"Nature?"

"I'm an indoor cat."

"Fresh air?"

Now she's really stretching. Which does not bode well for my immediate future.

"Level with me," I say. I pull at a piece of chapped skin on my lip, putting off the inevitable, which is Brigette replying to the question I've yet to ask. "How painful is this going to be?"

I look over, checking her expression. I wish I hadn't.

She at least has the decency to look sympathetic as she asks, "Have you ever hiked a mountain before?"

"I don't even take the stairs if there's another option."

"Oh. Okay." I hear her swallow across the car. "Well, then. Pretty painful."

I let loose with a string of words that would make Satan himself blush. Catching her watching me, I say, "You must think I'm pretty pathetic, huh?"

She glances between me and the road several times before asking, "You going to make me turn around?"

"No."

"Fake an injury?"

"Well, not now."

"Okay." Her lips twitch. Her mouth bends into a grin. "Then no, I don't. In fact, I think you're being a badass."

I groan but can't help returning her smile with a smirk of my own. "Yep. I suspect that's the part of my anatomy that'll be to blame when I can't get out of bed tomorrow morning."

She whoops out a laugh and I join her. I sound a little manic, like a sorority girl at the all-you-can-drink night at the bar. But inside, I'm terrified. I'm not athletic. Or strong. I don't even have a good attitude. What I do have is a living will and the unsettling suspicion that it's going to need to be used very soon on my behalf. It'll be a miracle if I make it off that mountain alive.

11

BRAD

Brad's perched on the hood of his ancient sedan eating a protein bar when the first car pulls into the dirt lot. He hops up, brushes the crumbs off the front of his jacket, wipes his hands on the seat of his pants. His mouth goes cottony as he watches the small trailhead lot fill with police vehicles until some are forced to park along the road.

He feels nauseous, his tongue coated with a thick paste, overly sweet crumbles from his snack still lodged in his molars. Taking a swig of water, he tries to swallow his nerves along with it. There are an awful lot of cops milling around in their dusty blue state police uniforms, many more than he expected, although, had he thought about it, it shouldn't have been a surprise. They have to get those bodies down somehow.

But still. He's surrounded by law enforcement, and he's not exactly the world's most law-abiding citizen. His heart strikes a ska beat as he thinks about all the illegal things he's done. These people are not his allies. But they don't have to know that.

What was it that his mom always used to say? *Fake it 'til you make it?* Yeah, something like that. All he has to do is keep his cool, feign the confidence he doesn't feel, and get the job done.

Two hours, three, tops, depending on the pace, and he'll be free to run down the mountain and hole up in the crappy apartment he rents until the staties clear town. Now that his roommate's gone, and he has the place to himself, he doesn't even have to worry about wearing pants or sharing the TV. He just has to get this over with first.

A tall man with a bushy mustache separates from the pack, narrowing his sights on Brad. He strides through the chaos, ignoring the chatter as supplies are distributed, gurneys withdrawn from the back of transport vans, teams chosen.

The cop gives Brad a smile and a nod, extends a palm in his direction. "Officer Kevin Miller, State Police."

Brad clears his throat, once again wiping his palm on his pants, this time to dry it, then gives the statie's hand a firm shake. "Nice to meet you, sir. I'm Brad Peterson. I'll be your guide up the mountain."

"Drew the short straw, huh?" He gives Brad's shoulder a knock with his fist. "Well, we appreciate it, son. And Kev will do."

Brad realizes, with a strange sense of amazement, that the man thinks he's a fellow cop. He glances down at his khaki hiking pants, the brown jacket he's got buttoned to the collar over his Lil Wayne sweatshirt to fend off the cold. Figures there's no harm in rolling with it.

"All right. Kev." Brad glances around. No one seems to be paying any attention to them, too busy bustling around, preparing for the hike, so he seizes the opportunity. Leaning closer to the statie, he says, "So, what do you think about this case? It's a weird one, right?"

"Eh." Kev shrugs a shoulder like recovering three dead people off a mountain is all in a normal day's work.

"I, uh, saw them. When I was up there. Couldn't see

anything wrong with them. Would have looked like they were sleeping if they hadn't appeared a little..."

"Ripe?"

"Well, no. I wouldn't say that."

"Sometimes you've gotta love the cold. But I know what you're saying."

"So, what do you think?" Brad asks again.

"About?"

He wipes a hand over his mouth, checks to make sure no one's listening. "About what happened to them? I mean, guy like you, you probably have a good idea what you'll find up there already, right?"

Kev smirks beneath his mustache, stands a little straighter. "'Course I do. Ten to one we've got a murder–suicide on our hands."

"You think?"

The statie blows a hard *eff* sound. "You kidding? You ask me, this whole thing's a waste of time. I mean, they didn't even send a detective. Can't be much investigating to do. Hoping to get up there and bring them down in time for beer-thirty, if you catch my drift."

Brad leans back on his heels, out of the cloud of the other man's breath, and nods. "Sure thing, Kev. You just let me know what kind of pace to set and I'll have you all up to the crime scene in a mountain minute."

A mountain minute is much like a mountain mile. It occasionally takes five times as long as normal and seems like it will never end, which is probably exactly how this experience is going to feel to them all by the end, but a part of Brad is looking forward to it. It'll be like a social experiment. Like he's gone undercover.

"Don't you worry none 'bout my guys. They'll keep up. The ladies, on the other hand..."

Brad follows the orbit of Kev's eyeroll. Spotting the two

women lingering at the edge of the action, he watches them with open curiosity. "They aren't with you?" he asks.

"The younger one, she's one of our techs, seen her around a bit. Not that concerned 'bout her. The other one, though." He shifts until he's standing beside Brad, shoulder to shoulder. "She's one of the state's medical examiners. Doesn't look like they let her out of her cage much, does it?"

There's something about the wary way her eyes flash, the pale, almost transparent hue of her skin that suggests the cop is right.

"Think she'll be able to make it up?" Brad asks.

"She better. We can't touch a thing until she's done her job and given us the okay."

Any hopes Brad had that this would be quick or easy have gone. He wipes a hand over his mouth to hide his grimace. But the statie openly aims a nasty look in the woman's direction.

Noticing, the sick feeling in the pit of Brad's stomach spreads. He needs to find a way to get the cop to play nice. He needs a miracle. Because when tempers are short and tensions are high, the worst place you can be is on a mountain.

12

MAGGIE

I squint at the brush lining the trail. Eye the jagged-ended branches at the edges. Crane my ears for a sound, any at all, that would let me know that I'm not imagining what I heard, but there's nothing. No movement, no noise, nothing but a feeling in my gut.

That's all I need.

I could say that it's a detective thing, or even woman's intuition, but both would be a lie. The fact is, there's a network of over a hundred million neurons lining the insides of your stomach and intestines. Your gut is in constant contact with your brain. I've learned that, in my case, it's the smarter organ. So when it tells me something, I listen.

Squatting, I peer into the scrub. Call. Clap. Cluck. And am rewarded by a faint whimper.

I follow the sound to a dense thicket and start breaking it away piece by piece, thorns snagging my clothes and skin, the weak sounds of distress I now hear every time I pause snagging my heart. The undergrowth just ahead of me moves.

My pulse quickens. I redouble my efforts, gouge a hole in my hand, the skin tearing as I pull back, the flap of flesh purple for several moments before blood starts gushing through the rip, rolling in dark red trails that drip to the ground. I barely feel it. Because now I can see the chocolate brown eyes rolled mournfully in my direction.

The dog's a mixed breed, about the size of my own pups, somewhere between twenty and thirty pounds. It's lean, trembling from the cold or fear or both. I punch through the last barrier, get a thorn under my nail as I reach into the briars and free the dog's collar from the branch it was hung up on. It earns me a feeble tail thump. I sit back on my haunches, getting jabbed in all my soft parts as I encourage the dog to come forward.

It doesn't. Won't. Can't?

Maybe it's not cold. Maybe it's in shock. Or too weak. Or suffering from the deadly effects of whatever killed the human members of the family.

It makes a pained moan in the back of its throat, and I consider my options for only a fraction of a second before plunging myself into the thicket. As I get closer, the dog shifts to the side, revealing the reason why it wouldn't leave even after I freed it. I gasp, blinking several times because I can't believe what I'm seeing, but it's true. Real. And I have no idea what to do about it.

An icy nose touches against my wrist, prodding me into action. I reach forward with shaky hands. The baby stirs when I touch it, rosebud lips tinged blue, opening in a silent cry. I draw a deep breath of relief, whispering a prayer, stroking a tuft of blonde hair before I loosen the folds of the tightly swaddled blanket and run my hands over her body, checking for injuries.

All I find is a fully saturated diaper, which I remove before bundling her back up, my fingertips lingering on the two small snags in the fabric from where the dog dragged her to safety, and I can't resist giving the pup a pet before zipping the infant into my jacket for warmth. I gather the dog gently in my arms, then, hunching over, I use my back as a shield against the thorns and pull us all free.

The dog stares up at me as I stroke her distractedly, wondering what went on here. Trying to make sense of it all. Because someone's missing a baby, and I find myself hoping, as unlikely as it seems, that it's not the family lying dead behind me.

And my gut tells me, this poor little pup with the sad eyes, this tiny baby cradled against my chest? They have the answers to all my questions. They know what happened up here on this mountain. It's just too bad they can't tell me.

13

STEVE

When I hear the frantic edge to Maggie's voice, I think the worst. She's hurt. In trouble. Needs me and I'll never be able to make it in time. The bitter shard of helplessness wedges deeper between my ribs.

As I struggle to make out what she's saying between her ragged puffs of breath, it occurs to me that she's sick. Hallucinating, maybe, but certainly delirious. Then I register the part about a dog. I look at the pups sitting at my feet, watching me with concern, picking up on my growing worry. Possibly still delirious, but maybe she just fell asleep and had a nightmare.

"The dogs are fine, Maggie. I'm looking at them both right now."

"No, not *our* dogs. *A* dog. The family's, I think."

"What family?"

"The dead family's. On the mountain."

"Maggie, you aren't making any sense."

"There was a call. This morning. Three dead on Rattlesnake Mountain."

"And you're there now? Alone? With the bodies?"

I don't like the sound of this at all. Actually, I hate it.

"Yes. And a baby. Did you hear the part about the baby?"

I hear a gasp, a crunch.

"Maggie? Maggie!"

"Sorry, I dropped the phone. Got my hands full, kind of juggling here."

"They're alive then?"

"For now, but I'm not sure for how long. I've got to get them down, get them help."

I toss a hurried glance toward the water bowl in the corner, checking to make sure it's full as I grab my keys, then I'm out the door.

"Well, slow down," I tell her, imagining her trying to dismount the mountain in leaps and bounds. "Be careful. It's not going to help anyone if you get hurt."

"I'm not prepared for this. I don't know what I'm doing."

"Sure you do. Have you called Sue?" I ask, one foot in my SUV.

She curses. "No. Not yet. The state police are on their way to the scene, but I wasn't thinking. I haven't told anyone about—I just, I panicked, and I called you."

A tiny zing of elation throbs through me as I back out, shift into drive, and surge forward down the road at an unsafe speed. "I'll take care of it, have her get an ambulance out there." I calculate the time it will take them to make the drive from the nearest hospital, figure it's roughly half the time it'll take Maggie to get down the mountain. "And I'll give the vet a head's up."

I hear a catch in her breath.

"Seriously. I'll handle it."

"I left the bodies. Unguarded."

"I'm already on the way."

"I probably shouldn't have done that."

"What do you think is more important right now?" I ask. "The dead or the living?"

I already know but hold the line patiently while she struggles to come to terms with the answer. Her voice is high and tight as she says, "The line between the two is too close for comfort right now. This baby, it's, she's—she's small, Steve. Really tiny. And cold. Her lips are blue. If something happens to her…"

"Nothing's going to happen, not bad, anyways, now that you've found her." Tires squeal as I take a turn too sharply. "Stop worrying. You trust me, right?"

She swallows hard into the phone, says, "Of course."

"You just focus on getting down the mountain safely and let me do the rest."

I punch in the station number as I skid around another corner, leaving tire tread on the road behind me. Press the pedal down harder as I listen to the line ring, waiting for Sue to pick up. Stare at the peak looming in the distance, getting closer with each passing second.

I'll be there well before Maggie makes it down, but it doesn't matter. I'll start hiking up, meet her halfway. There's no denying things have been tense between us lately. I've been feeling guilty because I lied. She's been pulling away, probably because she knows it. This could be the bandage we need to patch things up. God knows I can't use the truth.

14
ERIKA

I'm a smart woman. Sure, sometimes I might show a lapse in good judgment, and I'm not immune to making stupid decisions, but I can't, for the life of me, figure out how I got myself smack dab into the middle of this mess. On the side of a mountain, no less.

I backhand sweat from my forehead, then knuckle it from my stinging eyes. Grab onto a tree along the trail for balance as I lift a leg and scoop a finger into my shoe, trying to dislodge a pebble. I'm soaking wet, freezing cold, and every part of me aches. I don't think I've ever been more uncomfortable in my life.

"Come on. You gotta keep up, little lady. It's not fair to hold us men up just because you swapped one too many spin classes for the ice cream shop."

I take the deepest breath I can manage and let it out noisily. I've had just about all I can take of Officer Kevin Miller and his misogynistic attitude. I flinch as he cups his hand around the back of my arm to help me along and snatch it free from his grasp. Fight the urge to snarl as he rolls his eyes.

It's bad enough that he's decided to make me his trail buddy for the hike. I've been subjected to his philistine personality, I refuse to be subjected to his sweaty paws, too. "I need a break," I say.

Behind me, a fresh round of groans breaks out. Screw them. I don't care. I'm the only one here actually necessary. I have a stitch in my side that feels like I'm being sewn in half, my legs have gone wobbly, and I can't draw enough breath to banish the lightheadedness creeping around the edges of my skull. Let them wait.

Then I'm the one groaning as Brad comes over to no doubt give me another one of his little pep talks meant to inspire me to keep up. Like it's a lack of motivation that's my problem.

"You doing all right?"

He seems like a nice kid. He'd have to be, to have shown me the patience he has, patience the others, including Bridgette, lost a while back. Instead of answering him, though, I just give him a glare. It's a look I learned from one of my cats, and if I'm doing it right, I have no doubt he knows what it means.

His smile sags, and I almost feel bad, but not quite. His lazy, confident grin reminds me too much of the frat boys in college, guys who wouldn't give me the time of day unless they needed my help to pass a class. In a different situation, he wouldn't even notice my existence.

"Let's try something different, okay? Kev, how about you take the lead for a while, and I'll walk with the doctor."

Um, no. "Is that safe?"

"Why wouldn't it be?"

"He could get us lost."

"I know this trail like my own backyard. Not going to happen." Brad gives me an encouraging look, one that promises that the next hour of my life will be easier this way. Taking my silence as acquiescence, he says, "Slow and steady, Kev. Like a walk around the mall."

The statie grumbles something under his breath that I can't

quite hear, but I don't need to. I've been exposed to enough of his ignorance for a lifetime. I shift my gaze to Brad. He's certainly nicer to look at. Not as annoying to listen to. Maybe this arrangement will be better after all.

"So, doc."

"It's doctor. Dr. Ricky."

He gives me a magazine ad grin and a wink. "I gotcha. So... Dr. Ricky. Is this your first mountain hike?"

Officer Miller, bastion of professionalism, snorts ahead of us. It figures he's eavesdropping.

"Is it that obvious?"

Miller jeers, "Completely," only half trying to disguise the comment as a cough.

Brad shrugs, too polite to say that it is. "What's kept you from giving it a try before?"

The sweating? The physical exertion? I don't want to tell him the truth, so I say the first alternative that pops into my head. "Bears."

"Bears?"

"Yes, bears. They live on these mountains, don't they?"

"Well, yeah, but the black bears we get up here are notoriously shy. They'll run off as soon as they catch sound or scent of us. You have more to fear from a moose than a bear."

"Is that true?" I ask.

"Every bear I've ever come up on has run from me."

"That's not an answer."

He gives me that easy grin of his. The one that would be adorable if he was a four-year-old and not a cocky twenty-four-year-old. Or somewhere around there. I try not to do the math between his age and mine because I suspect it would be a case of dividing by two.

But there's no denying that, strangely enough, our easy banter has energized me. Now that I'm not bogged down under the weight of Officer Miller's judgment, it's easier to maintain my pace. And a competitive part of me I never knew existed wants to make the others eat my dust.

I lean forward, into the winter breeze that's using our trail as the path of least resistance down the mountain. My face feels wind-burned and raw, but the branches of the evergreens beckon me onwards. I obey, continuing my forward march, finding my rhythm.

The burning in my legs lessens. My muscles feel strong and able. I'm forty-seven and experiencing an endorphin rush from exercise for the first time. So this is what all the fuss is about. I could get used to it.

I click into autopilot, thinking of the gear I'll need. A good pair of hiking boots. Some of those trekking sticks I've seen people using on TV. Maybe even one of those backpacks with the drinking straw marathoners use. I'm so wrapped up in my future plans that I don't notice the dark shadow lumbering toward us on the trail until it's too late.

15

MAGGIE

It's been a long time since I've held a baby. Not since my brother, Brandon, was born, actually. I wish I could say it was like riding a bike, but this time it's completely different.

It's harder. I'm harder. I've had to become that way. It's the only way I've survived.

Because this time I fully understand and am all too aware of the gut-wrenching, soul-shredding devastation of the untimely loss of a child. Whose life will I destroy if I should fail to bring her back to civilization safely? Who is left to mourn this baby?

The responsibility is almost too great for me to bear.

I cradle her in my arms as gently as I can, worrying that I'm being too rough. Jostling her too much. Doing a worse job of taking care of her than anyone else would.

I couldn't even help my own baby brother. I'm the last person who should be entrusted with a child's care.

Then I hear it. Voices. And they sound close.

I quicken my already hasty steps, eager to meet the people approaching on the trail. It has to be the state police dispatched to the scene. Relief overwhelms me as I round a bend and they come into view. Their arrival's not a moment too soon.

I'm rushing to meet them when a frightened shriek shreds the air between us, catching me by surprise. I freeze mid-step, the hair on the back of my damp neck bristling. The dog shifts her weight in the pack on my back, growling softly.

I slowly lower my foot to the ground, tightening my hold on the baby, shifting her over to my left hip and arm as my right drops to the butt of my gun, unsnapping the holster strap. I take a controlled breath in for a four-count, release it for a five-count as I spin to face the trail behind me, simultaneously drawing my pistol. My finger is alongside the trigger guard but ready to move swiftly if I need to shoot.

Nothing's there.

I attune my senses, seeking movement in the shadows, noises among the trees, animal scents. Continue with my steady four-count in, five-count out as I check with my body, my nerves, my gut. I'm coming up blank.

My heart still feels like it's rolling logs as I turn back around with a questioning look. "What is it? What's the matter?" I ask, my voice hoarse, vocal cords tight.

"What's the matter? You! You're the matter!"

The state police officer glares at me with wide eyes. He strokes the ends of his overgrown mustache in a self-soothing manner. His pulse strobes against the taut muscles in his neck.

"I thought you were a bear," he growls in a voice much deeper than the one he used only seconds ago.

His nostrils flare as, behind him, a short lady snickers. Beside her, Brad does a poor job of hiding his amusement behind a hand cupped over the lower half of his face. I give him a nod and reholster my sidearm, use the freed hand to reach over my shoulder and give the dog a reassuring stroke on the head.

"Who the hell are you, anyways? What are you doing up here?"

"Chief Riley." Bridgette smiles warmly as she sidesteps past the others. "It's good to see you again." She stops short as she notices the tiny head protruding from the bundle zipped in my jacket, her outstretched hand hovering in the air between us. Her face folds in confusion. "Is that a... baby?"

She uses a finger to draw the blanket away from the infant's face, revealing a tiny seashell ear. Having confirmed her suspicions, she frowns at me, searching my face for answers. I don't blame her. I'm holding a baby. On a freezing cold mountain. Where multiple fatalities have been reported.

"I found her not far from where the decedents were discovered," I explain. "Her and the dog." I give a half turn so she can see the canine in my backpack, wishing someone would step forward and help me already. "They might have belonged to the family."

"Oh my God! How tragic. The poor things."

"You're with the unit state police dispatched, then?"

"Yep, me and the doctor, here."

I shift my gaze to the short lady. "Maggie Riley, Coyote Cove Police Chief. Thank you for the quick response."

"Dr. Erika Ricky." She casts a sideways glance at the statie, mirth still dancing on her lips. "It's a true pleasure."

I unzipped my jacket during the introductions, preparing to hand the infant over, but as I try, Dr. Ricky takes a step back, staring at the child like she's a leper. I hold the baby out closer to her. "She needs a doctor."

The woman looks as panicked as I feel. "I'm not that kind of doctor."

"But you have medical training."

"I work with dead people."

"And I work with criminals. I think you're better equipped—"

Brigette swoops in and saves us both, holding her arms out for the infant. She coos to the child as she checks her over. "She's cold. And lethargic. Probably dehydrated. She needs to be treated for exposure, but I'm not seeing anything that has me too concerned. Babies are tougher than you think."

Thank God for that.

"There's an ambulance on the way," I say, gently slipping the pack off my back to check on the dog. "That's why I was on my way down. To meet them."

"Wait a minute. If you're here, then who's guarding the crime scene?"

I turn my attention to the red-faced statie with the bristly mustache and say, "No one."

"Excuse me?"

I straighten my spine, pulling myself up to my full height. Return his glare down the slightly crooked bridge of my nose. I'll be damned if I'm going to let some peon from state come onto my turf and disrespect me. "No. One."

"That's unacceptable," he sputters.

I don't feel the need to defend myself, but I reply anyways. "I felt it was more important that I seek care for the survivors of this incident than to keep watch over remains that weren't going anywhere."

"That's not your decision to make."

"And you are?" I ask.

"Officer Kevin Miller, State Police. I'm the one sent to oversee this circus."

I raise my eyebrows. "So, no detective, then?"

"Not necessary. My unit is perfectly equipped to handle this on our own."

I seriously doubt that.

"Or, at least, we were until you botched our scene."

"Well, officer." I give him a smile that could melt plastic. "Welcome to Coyote Cove. I surveyed the scene and the victims. Cause of death isn't apparent. Barring the results of a tox screen, the baby and the dog may be our best clue as to what happened. It was a judgment call."

"Poor judgment."

Brad coughs. The doctor clears her throat. Bridgette looks like a kid whose parents are fighting on Christmas morning.

"Given your obvious lack of experience and mishandling of the investigation thus far, I'm going to have to request that you be removed from the scene and that Officer Peterson here becomes our Coyote Cove liaison."

Brad coughs again. This time it sounds like a choke. His cheeks pinken like a cooked shrimp as his eyes dart back and forth between me and Miller. "Uh, actually—"

"Don't be bashful, son. This is how men get ahead in their careers. If it wasn't for those ridiculous equal opportunity laws, the job would probably already be yours."

"No, really," Brad stutters.

The statie gives the group an imperial look. I roll my eyes so hard I strain a muscle.

"I'm afraid I really must insist," he says, giving one end of his mustache a tweak.

"Actually, *Kev*," the doctor says. Her eyes meet mine. She lifts her chin, gives me a barely perceptible nod before she continues. "It's my understanding that Chief Riley's expertise was expected to be relied on in lieu of a state detective. As the senior member dispatched on this investigation, I've been charged with requesting that she stay on with this investigation, if she'll be kind enough to do so."

"That's ridiculous."

She turns dagger eyes on him. I've received the same look myself decades ago for goofing off in class as a kid.

"Is that so, Mr. Miller?"

"It's officer."

"Yes, it is, isn't it? Which means you aren't qualified to be the lead investigator on a case involving a suspicious death. And while I'm sure that Brad here would—"

"I'm not a cop." Brad's eyes flit around the group, finally

dropping to his boots. "I'm just a hiking guide. I never said otherwise."

"Well, then, there you have it." Dr. Ricky gives the statie an insincere smile, and I realize it's a good thing I like her, because I suspect that we're stuck in this together now. And I doubt we'll be getting much help from Miller and his friends. "So, Chief Riley. Will you be willing to accommodate the state's request? After we secure the necessary medical attention for our survivors, of course."

I've got a full plate already. A police department to run. A lieutenant to hire. A wedding to plan. There's no way I can juggle another ball without letting one drop. And yet, I find myself saying, "You can count on it."

16

STEVE

I feel like I'm halfway to a heart attack, but I can't stop now. Like an old steam engine, I chug away, trying to ignore the pain and the doubt and the worry. Trying not to remember how much easier this was the last time I did it a couple of decades ago as an undergrad. Or to wonder if I'm as old as I suddenly feel.

It doesn't seem fair, how it sneaks up on you. How one day you wake up and you're forced—whether by your aching joints or your foolish attempt to be a hero—to confront your own mortality as you realize you've stopped growing older and started growing old. Especially when you still feel, well, maybe not like a kid, but certainly not like an adult of an age where you need to consider drawing up a will, which this hike is making me do.

I'm overwhelmed with relief when I see a cluster of men on the trail ahead, at a standstill, and I know I've reached the staties sent to help Maggie with this case. The only question is, are they going to mind if I leapfrog ahead of them?

It took me forever to get here, like some cosmic force was working to keep me away. First, I'd gotten caught behind a logging truck driving the centerline, blocking me from passing as it went agonizingly slow. Then, I'd had to park so far down on the road because of all the police vehicles that I had to hike a quarter mile just to get to the trailhead. Even with all that, I managed to beat the ambulance here, but now this.

I scramble up the steep stretch of trail separating us, preceded by white clouds of condensation as I huff and puff. Loose talus shifts under my boots, trickling down behind me. I wipe my nose with a gritty wrist, the crease already chapped from the constant drip of my half-frozen sinuses. I can't even imagine what I must look like, so I'm only half-surprised when one of the cops notices my approach and places his hand on his holstered weapon, ready to draw.

"Halt."

I freeze, one foot in the air. My ankle buckles and I lose my balance against gravity, landing painfully on a knee.

"This trail is closed, sir. I'm going to have to ask you to turn around."

Several of his companions crowd behind him, forming a barrier across the path. I don't know how I'm going to pull this off. I need to tread carefully.

"Yeah, I know, but, um, my name is Steve." I push up to my feet. "I'm here to meet Chief Maggie Riley."

"Who?" he asks, pinching a corner of his mustache.

"Chief Riley. Of the Coyote Cove Police Department. She's the one who secured the scene for you guys."

"Can you believe this?" he asks, turning to the officers behind him. "Inviting friends up for a looky-loo. I've never even heard of such a lack of professionalism before."

"That's not—"

He holds a hand up, cutting me off as they confer in low tones, random words drifting in my direction, none of them good. I'm feeling a little nauseous, and now that I'm holding still, my sweat-soaked clothes are starting to chill me to the bone. I shove my hands into my pockets. Four pairs of eyes immediately narrow at me.

"You can call her to check," I suggest. "I'm sure whoever's in charge here was given her number. Or I can give it to you." I close my mouth because I don't think my attempt at being helpful is doing me any favors.

And then the clouds part and a ray of light shines through. Only you can't actually see the clouds because the sky is just a uniform shade of wintry gray, and the light is actually Maggie hustling down the trail behind the staties, but same thing. I see her and I know that everything's going to be all right.

"What's going on here?"

She uses her cop voice, which is loud and firm and instantly lets you know who's in charge. I'm not going to deny that I kind of like it.

The staties split their focus between us, Mr. Mustache keeping his hand at the ready on his firearm. "Listen, whatever liaison you had planned with lover boy here's gonna have to wait."

Maggie cocks an eyebrow. She takes a step closer to the men, then another, until it seems she's decided to not let them slow her descent. I have no doubt she'll bulldoze straight over them if they don't get out of her way.

"Excuse me?" She's only fifteen feet from them now. "I'm the chief here." Ten feet. "This is my town." Five feet. "And you're interfering in an official investigation. Step aside."

Like a bucket of boiling water poured into a pile of snow, the men melt off to the sides of the path, clearing the way. As soon as she's past them, her face crumples. Her lips tremble. Tears shine in her eyes. I can see how much strain she's under.

She closes the distance between us. We hold a silent conversation as she presses the bundle she carries into my arms. I look down into a pair of eyes that seem unfathomably sad.

"She saved the baby," Maggie says in a low voice. "She has to live."

But I'm not sure that she will. She doesn't look good. As I hold her cold body against my own, I can barely feel the beat of her heart. Yet still, I do something incredibly stupid. I make a promise I'm not sure I can keep. "She will. She'll be fine. I'll make sure of it."

Maggie smiles like I knew she would—like she believes me. Then she turns and yells, "Why isn't that baby on her way down to the ambulance already?"

Two officers hurry toward us, one carrying the infant.

"You should hike down with them. I have to stay here and help." Maggie's tone is apologetic.

I nod, having suspected this was the case. We step aside for the cops to squeeze by. When they pass, the dog lets loose a high-pitched whine. As they draw away from us, she squirms weakly in my arms. I don't think she wants to be separated from the baby. As her struggling intensifies, I'm sure of it.

"I better get going. You'll be all right?" It's as much a statement as a question. It earns me another one of her smiles.

"Will you keep an eye on her for me? Let me know how she's doing?" Maggie asks.

"Of course," I say. "Don't worry about a thing."

Tearing myself away, I speed down the path, in a rush to catch up with the staties and the baby so the dog will relax. It's not until I reach them and Maggie's already out of sight that I wonder—did she mean the dog, or the baby?

17

MAGGIE

I stumble, my mind too busy, racing too fast to pay attention to minor details like my footing. I just can't stop seeing the baby's blue-tinged lips. The dog's sad eyes. The three dead bodies strewn across the trail like they just dropped and died. And I can't ignore the way my gut keeps insisting that something about this doesn't make sense. Because it's right.

Realizing the group in front of me has come to a stop, I look up and catch Brad staring at me. His eyes flick between me and the switchback he's paused at, and it's only then that it registers. We're here.

I hurry to the front of the line, relieved he had the forethought to stop the group before three dozen staties had the opportunity to trample my crime scene. Not that I'm actually sure it is a crime scene, I'm not sure what we're dealing with yet, but I certainly don't need it to get any harder to figure out.

I should have been paying better attention, but I can't stop thinking about the baby. Did she belong to the dead family? If so, how did she survive what they didn't? An image of the dog flashes through my mind and I think of Mowgli from *The Jungle Book*, suspecting I have my answer.

Brad steps aside once I've reached him, which is probably more an act of self-preservation than anything else. The sea of faces I find looking at me are mostly hostile. Officer Kevin Miller, in particular, appears to be trying to burn me with his searing glare. Catching my eye, he holds my gaze while he elbows the man next to him and whispers something that makes the guy smirk.

I fight the urge to roll my eyes. I've dealt with his kind before, and I don't have the time or the patience for his juvenile pissing contest. Instead of offering him a withering look of my own, I seek out the few friendlies among the bunch and give them a weak smile.

Then, clearing my throat, I take a deep breath and say, "The decedents are just around the next bend. At this time, I'd like to ask the doctor and Ms. Parsons to accompany me. I'd prefer that the rest of you remain here for the moment. As soon as we collect evidence and get the scene squared away, we'll begin prepping the bodies for transport. With any luck, we'll be back on flat ground before dark."

The thought makes me glance at my watch. It'll be close. Really close. I ignore that fact and forge on.

"Please stay on the trail for the time being, and should you feel the need to relieve yourself," I say, recalling the number of times one of the men had stepped off the path on the way up, an inequality that my own bladder has me resenting quite fiercely at the moment, "then please hike down to the last switchback."

As an investigator, it's my job to work under the assumption that I'm dealing with a homicide until it's proven otherwise. That way, details don't get overlooked, and clues don't get destroyed. There's no telling if this investigation will necessitate the need to search the surrounding area for evidence, but I want to make sure that proper precautions are taken, just in case.

I look at Bridgette, who has taken her camera equipment out of her pack and is ready to get to work, and I get a brief flash of the last case we worked together—a body on the side of the road lit by moonlight, a storm getting ready to break, me resurrecting training from my past life, documenting the scene with my cell phone before it was ruined by rain.

That night was the catalyst that set in motion events that morphed Coyote Cove from a hiding spot to a home. My engagement to Steve. My lieutenant's untimely death.

My chest tightens as I remember the dummy hanging from the tree outside my office this morning. Another reminder of how few allies I have in this world. Of how few people there are to watch my back, which apparently has a very large target on it. I swallow down the grief and the anger and I do what I do best. I get to work.

Which means even though Bridgette's here this time to properly document the scene, I'll still take pictures of my own for reference. I give her a nod to proceed as I slip my cell from my pocket and bring up the camera app. I catch a curious glance from Dr. Ricky as I do.

"I can make sure you get a digital copy of the photos as soon as they're processed," she says.

"I'd appreciate that."

We follow Bridgette as she leads the way, pausing every stride as she snaps photos. I've always liked this part. It's like doing a wedding march. Gives you time to get your head straight, prepare for what lies ahead. For the first time it occurs to me that may be the purpose of the march. Huh. I always thought it was to give people time to admire the bride's overpriced dress.

Should I worry that I still feel such cynicism about weddings? It's going to be pretty hard to plan one if I find every detail ridiculous. Except maybe the cake. I think I understand that part.

"But you're still going to take your own shots?"

"Huh?" I look at the doctor, confused, my addled brain taking a moment to segue from thoughts of societal rituals to those associated with suspicious deaths. I glance back to the phone held out in front of me, thumb poised over the shutter button. I give her a sheepish smile. "Old habits die hard."

But she's correct. As Bridgette steps to the side, starting to circle the perimeter of the scene, I click the button. It's the very thing I refused to let myself do earlier, but, strangely, now it seems so completely natural that I can't imagine not doing it.

I wonder what's changed, besides the fact that I've been officially invited in on the case. An image of a squinched-up face with chubby cheeks, of a stumpy tail giving a feeble wag, pops into my head, and I find myself worrying about how the survivors are doing. I shake it away, knowing it'll be a while before I'll be able to call and find out.

Bridgette kneels beside the first body, the youngest. I take photographs of the other two while she bags the young man's hands, no doubt waiting to take nail scrapings until she's in a more controlled environment out of the wind. She places a shower cap on him to preserve whatever trace evidence she might be able to comb out later.

I'm impressed. It shows a remarkable amount of forethought. These measures aren't taken at an average scene, with a body found indoors, or in a car. Or even, for that matter, most bodies found outside. Then again, when working a fatality al fresco, many times you're either able to see the cause of death, or you're dealing with remains that are already in an advanced state of decomposition, predation, or both.

But here, the mode and manner of death are a complete mystery. And Bridgette is doing everything she can to make sure any evidence still on the bodies will be able to be recovered.

Dr. Ricky squats beside the young man as Bridgette moves on to the female decedent. Her face is curiously blank as she pulls on a pair of gloves. Her tone is clinical and detached as she says, "I'd put age at late teens, early twenties."

"Quite a gap in years between him and the infant."

She shrugs. "It happens."

Her hands work methodically as she palpates the body. Raises an eyelid to check the sclera. Lifts a lip to check the gums. Sticks her finger in his mouth to check the tongue. Her head cocks to the side. She looks up at me.

"I hope you're as good as Bridgette thinks."

"Why's that?" I ask.

She groans as she stands. Side by side, we look down at the body. Her head barely reaches my shoulder. "There are no signs of trauma. No signs of the victim having succumbed to the elements. No obvious signs of poisoning. To be honest, I'm stymied, and I'm not so sure a tox screen is going to help us out here."

I cut my eyes at her sharply.

"Don't get me wrong, I'm going to run a full panel. Based on the lack of physical indicators, my best guess would be a toxin or poison of some kind, but I don't think we're dealing with any of the usual culprits here—most of those leave some sort of physical evidence if you know what to look for. This might be something that gets missed if you don't know to check for it. A specialized test. Could be, the half-life of whatever it is has already degraded."

Dr. Ricky tucks the sides of her bob behind her ears. Her expression is serious as she says, "I have a feeling that figuring out what happened here is going to come down to some very impressive detective work. On both of our parts. Because I have to tell you—what I'm seeing here? I don't think it was anything natural. Or accidental. I suspect that what we're dealing with is murder."

My stomach goes liquid, and it's not because all that's in it is water. It's because my gut is screaming at me that the doctor is right.

Someone did this. Someone killed these people.

But here's the question that I really need the answer to—did the culprit put some distance between themselves and their victims? Or is the killer still in Coyote Cove?

18
ERIKA

I'm freezing. Exhausted. Coated in a grimy layer of trail dust mixed with my own sweat. Every part of me aches, and I'm pretty sure I smell. But I've never felt so alive.

I've examined all three bodies and have been unable to find any anomalies. Sure, once I have them on my slab I'll be able to perform a more thorough visual examination, but, right now, whatever happened to these poor people remains a mystery.

There's not much I can do here in the field, but I'm doing it. I've taken several blood draws from each victim at different anatomical locations from both veins and arteries. I've drawn urine directly from each bladder. Vitreous fluid from every eyeball. I've swabbed nasal passages, ears, and mouths. I even used some of Bridgette's hinge lifters on the decedents' faces and hands to see if any trace residue was present.

I feel like I'm pulling at straws, but I have to do something, because I've been running through a mental checklist as I work, and I'm drawing a blank. Poisoning, exposure, environmental factors—it seems highly unlikely that all three members of the family would have succumbed to any of these variables so quickly that they would be found in such close proximity to each other—especially when the most vulnerable among them, the infant, survived.

At this point, we don't even know who they are for sure—there's no identification on any of the bodies. Chief Riley says that it's not uncommon for hikers to leave their valuables locked in their cars while they're hiking, but that doesn't do us much good at the moment. It's clear that the only answers we're going to have at present are the ones I can give. But I've got nothing.

The father's pack still contains food, water, and extra cold weather gear. That leads me to rule out dehydration and hypothermia. I'll have an analyst test the water when I get back to my lab to rule out the possibility that they filled the bottles in a stream and were exposed to toxic algae, parasites, and bacterial toxins.

Could they have come in contact with a soil toxin like anthrax? Maybe the spores of some rare and deadly plant? The ones I know of would present with skin lesions or other irritation of the dermis. There are none.

There's also no red livor or jaundice present, no abnormal discoloration of the skin at all besides that caused by death. That rules out a freak carbon monoxide accident and several health issues that could have resulted in sudden death.

Most poisons have predictable side effects. There are no signs of vomiting or other symptoms of gastric distress. No rashes. Hair and nails appear healthy. Bodies are in proportion with no abnormal bowel distention or other irregularities. The ground surrounding each victim is undisturbed. Skin, clothes, and shoes have the same proportion of trail dust as my own—there's nothing to imply that any of the victims had even the smallest seizure. Visually, every aspect is unremarkable.

It appears as if they all just simultaneously laid down and died. I've never seen anything like this before. None of it makes sense. I have to figure this out.

I have to know what happened to this family.

I glance over at Chief Riley, who's been examining every inch of the trail and surrounding area with a fine-toothed comb. At Bridgette, who's taken so many samples that she's not going to be able to carry them all down the mountain by herself. At least I'm not the only one who's gone Ahab on this. But I suspect I am the only one who has nothing else going on in their life to distract them.

I finish with the final body, fold the woman's hands over each other on her chest, give them a soft squeeze before I let her go. It's never easy when you're processing an untimely death, but this? I'm not even sure if they have anyone left to mourn them. And I can't decide if that's a good or a bad thing.

Standing, I clear my throat, drawing the attention of my companions. I force myself to turn my back on the decedents. "I'm done for now. I've done all I can out here. Do either of you ladies need more time?"

Both look regretful as they shake their heads no.

"Then let's get them packed up and bring them home."

19

STEVE

I'm in the passenger seat of the ambulance, one arm holding the dog as we weave along the mountain roads, the other braced against the dash to steady myself as I twist to watch the paramedic attending to the infant. An IV taped to her tiny arm provides fluids. The blue tinge has disappeared from her lips. Her vitals are strong.

Her hazel eyes flutter open as we round a sharp curve. And I swear she looks right at the dog in my lap.

Don't ask me how I managed to pull this off—a canine in an ambulance. When we reached the trailhead lot, and I tried to take her to my car, she started struggling again, harder this time, yelping in my arms as she fought to get free. She refused to leave the baby.

I was afraid she'd injure herself, more than I suspect she already is, so I insisted we accompany the infant to the hospital. The driver's initial refusal was overturned when he learned that the dog had saved the child. I guess no one can refuse a hero, even one with fur. One of the staties who carried the baby down even offered to follow us to the hospital in my vehicle.

But I can't shake the guilt that's worming its way under my

skin. I'm not sure I'm doing the right thing. The paramedics assured me that the baby appeared in good health besides being cold and dehydrated. The same cannot be said of the dog. She's been asleep for most of the journey, her breaths shallow, her ribs barely moving under the palm I'm using to support her. She needs medical care.

We leave the winding mountain road, slowing as we approach the town of Lincoln and encounter traffic. The driver blips the siren to alert the motorists around us to make way.

The noise wakes the dog. She opens her eyes, meeting my gaze. A soft whimper sounds from the back of her throat as she stretches her head, nose lifting as she scents the air. Smelling the baby, she relaxes. Her actions reassure me that I've made the right decision. I'm fairly certain that if the dog could talk, this is what she'd want.

The ambulance slows as we reach the hospital. It pulls around the side and backs into an unloading bay. I gently gather the pup in my arms, preparing to get out.

"They won't let you bring that dog in there," the driver says, noticing.

I give him a hopeful smile as I zip my jacket up over her. He presses his lips together, gives me a frown of disapproval, but doesn't say anything as I jump out and join the fray surrounding the baby.

I have to jog to keep up as they rush her inside, doctors and nurses gathering around, each with an important job to do, each intent on making sure this infant receives the best treatment possible. Pressing my back against one wall of the room they wheel her into, I will myself invisible. Promise myself that I'll leave and take the dog to the vet as soon as we know for sure that the baby is okay.

"Steve?" I turn at the familiar voice, surprised to see Sue bustling toward me at full speed. Her eyes flick down to my jacket front, noticing the bulge. Positioning herself in front of me as a human shield, even though she's half my size, she turns her head sideways to continue the conversation. "What are you doing here?"

"They needed a guardian to stay with the baby."

She arches an eyebrow at me. Busted.

"We had to make sure the baby was okay."

"We?" She harrumphs as she gives me side-eye.

"What are you doing here?" I counter.

"Lincoln social services couldn't assign an advocate for the baby on such short notice." But her nose twitch gives her away. We're both caught out. I should have known that Sue would insist on overseeing the care of the baby herself. She and Maggie are two-of-a-kind that way.

But if we're both here, that means Maggie is all alone. And since what happened to her lieutenant, she has fewer allies than ever in the already hostile town of Coyote Cove.

"I wouldn't have come had I known—" she starts, at the same time that I say, "One of us should—"

"Which one of you is with the child?"

We both straighten up. Sue shoots me a quick look before saying, "I am."

"I'm Dr. Oaks, the emergency pediatrician. Overall, given the circumstances, the infant is in good health. Besides some slight dehydration, I don't see anything of concern. I expect that she'll make a full recovery. I would, however, like to admit her for observation and to run some additional tests."

The dog sighs loudly under my jacket. Sue spins, giving me a stern look. "You can go now. I'll give you a call if anything changes."

I turn, thanking the doctor over my shoulder as I leave. Rubbing the bulge under my coat, we slip outside. I expect the dog to protest, but for the first time she seems to be okay with leaving the baby. I hope that's not a bad thing.

20
MAGGIE

It's a relief to be back on flat ground. I eye my Jeep, wanting nothing more than to climb inside, blast the heat, and head on home to a hot bath. But I can't. Not yet. Instead, I stalk back and forth across the trailhead lot, impatiently waiting for the staties to finish packing up and leave.

As I pace, I check my phone, hoping to get an update on how the survivors are doing, but the X on the top right of the screen remains constant, dashing that hope. I'll have to wait until I get closer to town and can get a signal again. Even more of a reason why this needs to wrap up quickly.

The chaos ratchets down a notch as the two vans transporting the bodies leave the lot and hit the road. The remaining staties lean against vehicles rubbing sore muscles, congratulating each other on a job well done—the treacherous task of carrying three weighted stretchers down a mountain, switching out carrying crews every fifteen minutes, successfully completed without injury.

Bridgette catches my eye and gives me a wave goodbye. I return it and exchange nods with Dr. Ricky, who's climbing into the passenger seat beside her. The doctor made it clear that this case was her number one priority, that she'd be starting the postmortems as soon as she could. I gave her my number and told her to call day or night. I hope to be hearing from her soon.

Several more vehicles leave the lot, and that's when I see him. Officer Miller preens the end of his mustache with one hand, clapping one of his men on the shoulder with the other. I hear a growl and tell myself it was my stomach. I'd been hoping he left already.

Lifting his head, he catches my eye, stares right at me. And smiles. But it's not a friendly gesture. Neither is the wave he gives me. There's something eerie about it, something that unsettles my already frayed nerves.

He turns, taking his time as he saunters to one of the powder blue patrol cars and ducks inside. I watch as he slowly steers out of the trailhead lot, waiting until the glow of his taillights has disappeared before drawing a deep breath and releasing it in a sigh of relief.

That man had me worried. I've met his type before, and I fully expected him to cause more trouble. Now that he's gone, I can focus on more important things.

Slowly, the remaining men retreat to their vehicles, eager to sit, ready to be home already as the adrenaline wears off. Farewells are shouted. Doors slam. A few even give a nod in my direction.

As the lot clears, I spot Brad, sitting on his car off to the side. I close the distance between us, lean against the battered navy hood by his feet. "I thought you would have taken off a while ago," I say.

He shrugs. "I was blocked in."

"You aren't now."

"Guess I wanted to make sure that everyone made it out all right."

I give him a weary grin. "That's my job."

He smiles back, the wattage not nearly as bright as it had been this morning. "You can keep it."

"Really? 'Cause I need a new lieutenant." It's a joke, but only partly. Because he did good today. He stayed calm, level-headed, did what was needed to get the job done. There's no denying I could use the help, and he has promise. But the moment the words have escaped my lips, I regret it. "Just kidding," I rush to say. "But I really do appreciate your help."

"Any time."

"And please bill the department for your hours."

"I'm not worried about that."

"You sure? The state's paying."

Brad smiles again, a little brighter than before. "Nah. Believe it or not, I actually kind of enjoyed myself. Not the dead people part. But the rest of it was... interesting. Really cool to see how it is in real life versus what they show on TV." He leans forward, closer to me, his eyes locked on mine. It looks like there's something else he wants to say.

I hurry to fill the silence. "You should go home, grab a hot shower and a cold beer."

He points at me, says, "I think I'll do exactly that."

We say our goodbyes and a moment later the dust stirs as his vehicle leaves the lot. I watch him go, a cloud of exhaust following in his wake as he speeds down the road, a portrait painted in shades of gray.

Dusk has fallen. Night's arriving quickly. And I'm out here all alone.

I hurry back to my Jeep, a case of the creeps suddenly taking hold, tapping like fingers up my spine. I close myself in and lock the door. Shiver. Duck down low so I can take a last look at the mountain looming in the twilight like a slumbering giant.

Cranking the engine, I turn the heat to max. Wiggle my half-frozen fingers and toes while I wait for the warmth to kick in and defrost them, glancing around the now vacant parking area as I do so. And that's when I realize.

I really am all alone. My vehicle is the only one left behind. We're almost twenty miles and a half-hour from town. So then, how did that family get out here to hike the mountain in the first place?

21

CHERYL

Cheryl knows what she told that cop, but she can't risk staying. She's got to get out of here, fast, before anyone finds out the truth. All she has to do is buy herself a bit of time, not much, just enough to put some distance between herself and Coyote Cove, and, by then, if anyone comes looking for her, it'll be too late. She'll be gone for good.

Her hands are trembling so badly it takes her multiple tries to open her motel room. Finally, she manages and spills through the door. Draws to a sudden stop. Glances around, imaging how the space would look to someone else, her belongings strewn carelessly around, covering the bed, the dresser, the floor. A bottle of vodka and the empty bag of potato chips she ate last night for dinner on the side table. Toiletries carelessly abandoned on the dingy bathroom countertop.

This does not look like the room of someone trustworthy. Not someone who can be believed. But none of that matters, not now.

She squeezes her eyes shut, shakes her head against the image of the woman's face, the empty, accusatory stare burned into her memory. She feels a brief moment of remorse, which is quickly replaced by desperation. She has to move.

Flopping her suitcase open, she scoops handfuls of clothes and shoves them inside. Uses a still-damp towel to collect her soap and lotions and cosmetics and dental hygiene items and shoves them unceremoniously on top. Curses as she struggles with the zipper.

She slips the bottle of vodka into her purse and gives the area a last check, then grabs her suitcase by the handle and wrestles it out the door, the bag banging against her leg, no doubt leaving bruises as she manhandles it to her car.

Cheryl stops in front of the vehicle, frowning at the way it sags on the driver's side. She tilts her head, shocked by the angle necessary to bring it even in her field of vision. Something's not right.

Then she sees it. The way the tires puddle at the bottom. Flat. The rims almost touching the ground.

She just can't catch a break. It feels like the universe is conspiring against her.

Hot, angry tears seep from her eyes and trail down her cheeks. She can't drive the car like this. Who knows how long it'll take to get it fixed.

Fishing her phone out of her purse, she runs a search. There's not even a cab company in this godforsaken backwoods town.

She's not going anywhere. Stuck with no escape. And she can't even be surprised. Isn't this what she deserves?

22
STEVE

I send Maggie a text, updating her on the baby as I look for my car in the lot outside the emergency room. I find it parked under a streetlight, the door unlocked, the keys tucked under the floor mat as I'd requested. Unzipping my coat, I gently lower the dog to the passenger seat and tuck her in, trying to make sure she's comfortable. I watch her for a moment, giving her a few pets.

I had expected her to put up a struggle when we left the baby's side, but she hadn't. I don't know whether it's because she knows the baby is safe now, or because her energy is waning. Swallowing a lump of worry, I close the door gently, hurry to the other side and slide behind the wheel.

I had texted our local vet during the ambulance ride to let her know of the change in plans, and she had responded with a recommendation to one of the local vets in Lincoln, the one she refers clients to when they need the most comprehensive array of tests available. I text her again now to tell her we're on our way, so she can let them know to expect us.

Pulling up to a stop light, I glance over at the passenger side, at the dog bundled in my jacket. Her eyes are closed. Her breaths are shallow. She doesn't move under the palm I've kept on her the entire drive to keep her steady on the seat. And to let her know that she's not alone.

I urge the car in front of me to move as the light turns green. "Hold on, little girl. We're almost there."

As I steer around a corner, the veterinary clinic appears up ahead. Two women in scrubs are out front waiting for us, bundled up against the cold. I barely slow for the deep dip into the parking lot, wince at the screech of metal on pavement as something on the SUV bottoms out.

The vet tosses the passenger door open before I even have the car in park. Her eyes meet mine for a brief second as she scoops the dog up into her arms, already whispering a steady stream of comfort as she hustles her patient inside. I jump out and race after her on trembling legs, following her into an over-heated room.

She ditches my jacket, letting it drop to the floor as she lays the pup on an examination table, barking orders to her assistant. I watch as she peers at the dog's gums and eyes. Runs her hands over its body. Plugs her ears with the stethoscope from around her neck and listens to the dog's chest.

"Get out if you care about radiation exposure," she says, gaze never leaving the dog as she lays her out and pulls a machine on wheels closer, adjusting a flat panel over the table.

"Ready," she yells.

There's a click as an X-ray is taken.

"Develop that, stat."

She shaves a bare patch and grabs a catheter off a side tray, expertly inserting it into the dog's forelimb. She tapes the line down and draws several vials of blood, handing them to me one by one as they fill, then connects an IV drip. She grabs a warming blanket off the counter, tucks it around the dog, and then snatches the samples from me.

"Watch her. Shout if there are any changes."

I chew my lip as I stare down at the dog, suddenly reluctant to be left alone with her. She looks so fragile lying on the table. Reaching out, I gently lay my hand on her head.

It might be my imagination, but I think she might have pressed against my palm. I know what Maggie's dogs—my dogs by proxy—enjoy. And though I have no experience with canine companions besides Maggie's terriers, maybe this pup would like the same. It's worth a try.

I stroke her head, check over my shoulder, make sure that we're alone. Lower my face closer to hers and start softly singing to her under my breath. There's movement under the blanket as her tail gives a weak thump. I sing a little louder, a song I make up on the spot about a brave young puppy who's going to be just fine.

I check her collar, but there's no tag, no name. It seems wrong to have nothing to call her.

"Laurel," I whisper. Like the mountain flower, which is pretty and delicate yet still hardy and tough. "How's that?"

Her eyes open and find mine, and in that instant I know. This dog needs me right now like no one else does. Or ever has before. I drop my nose to hers as I caress and croon. I'm so wrapped up in my efforts to make her feel better that I don't even notice when the vet comes back into the room.

"Don't let me interrupt," she says, smiling softly, but the expression doesn't reach her eyes.

I straighten but continue stroking the dog. "What are we looking at here? What's wrong with her?"

Her lips press into a thin line. She gives the pup a few pats of her own. "The poor girl has several fractured ribs. My best guess is that she was kicked."

I rest my hand on her paw, so she knows I'm still here. Wondering who on that mountain did the damage. One of the dead people? Or someone who's still walking free? "Will she be okay?"

"Well, the fractures alone won't kill her. But the conditions you described surrounding her discovery. Have there been any new developments? Any updates on what killed the people up there?"

"Not that I'm aware of, no."

"It's quite possible that she's just suffering from exposure and the rib injury, maybe even a mild case of shock. That all we need to do is hydrate her and warm her up and keep her calm while her fractures heal."

"But?"

The vet shakes her head. "I don't know what she was exposed to up there. I've run all the tests I have at my disposal, but it's going to take some time to get the results. I'm hesitant to give her any sedatives or painkillers until I do. I just don't know what her system can handle right now. I'd like to keep an eye on her in the meantime. Would you mind leaving her with me for a night? Maybe two? Just until we get some answers?"

I glance at the dog. Her eyes are open, watching me. Waiting for my answer.

"Would you mind if I stayed here with her?"

"Not at all. We'll keep her out here, then, instead of putting her in a kennel in the back. Just let one of my staff know if you need anything."

"I appreciate it," I say, following her out of the room. I pause in the doorway, glancing back at the dog before lowering my voice and asking, "In your honest opinion, do you think she's going to be okay?"

The vet sighs. I remember an article I read that said that veterinarians have the highest suicide rate of any profession. I'm glad I'm not in her shoes, but they sure are noble ones. "I hope so."

Her steps whisper across the floor as she retreats down the hall. I return to the room, moving the chair beside the examination table before settling into the hard plastic seat for a long night. As I watch the dog sleep, I'm struck by how much I need her to survive.

Not because of Maggie. Not because she saved a baby's life. Not even because my heart will be broken if she doesn't. It's because I suspect that this world is a better place with her in it.

23

MAGGIE

Long shadows cloak the mountains as the winter day fades to night. Of all the many differences between my homeland of Florida and this corner of northern Maine—the cold, the landscape, the people—it's how early it gets dark this time of year that's been the biggest adjustment. I turn my high beams on and tighten my grip on the wheel as I round a sharp corner.

The road opens up before me, a straight stretch cut by nothing other than the lonely glow of my headlights. My phone buzzes with a series of alerts, letting me know I've got service again. I grab it from the drink holder, mutter a silent prayer when I see the bars I've been waiting for. Mutter a not-so-silent curse when I see a text from Sue informing me that Lincoln Social Services was unable to take custody of the baby and that she'll have to act as the child's advocate until the next of kin is found.

I hit the phone icon next to her name and jab the speakerphone button. As the sound of the call ringing fills my car, the back of my neck prickles with the same uneasy feeling I've been unable to shake all day. Even the sound of Sue's voice on the other end of the line, a beacon of my return to civilization, isn't enough to chase it away.

"Any word on the victims' identities yet?"

"Hello to you too." I hear a garbled announcement being made over an intercom in the background. "Wasn't there anything in their car?"

"There wasn't a car." Which means no IDs, no vehicle registration, not even a random receipt to go on.

"Huh. Then how'd they get out there?"

"That question nears the top of my very long list."

"Well, good luck with that. Nobody's reported any hikers missing yet, so I called state HQ, made sure you're the first call they make if one comes in."

"You're the best."

Sue sniffs. "I know."

"I really mean it."

"I know that, too. I wasn't sure how this would affect your day tomorrow, so I only scheduled one interview. Most promising candidate as far as I can tell. Figured two o'clock would be a good time. Late enough for you to get some work done first, early enough for me to cancel Monday's interviews if the guy works out."

"What would I do without you, Sue?"

"Probably work yourself into an early grave."

The reference to death sends an involuntary shudder down my spine. I clear my throat and change the subject. "Any word on how the baby's doing?"

"Just that she's stable. They're treating her for exposure now, running a bunch of tests, making sure there are no long-term effects from whatever she went through up there." She drops her voice and adds, "Besides a lifetime of therapy."

"You ask them to run a drug and chem panel?"

"Wouldn't be the best if I hadn't."

"That's true."

"Anyways, rumor is, barring any unforeseen discoveries, she'll be released tomorrow afternoon. I'll probably just stick around here until then."

"Sure." I drum my fingers on the wheel, wanting, selfishly, for her to be here with me instead. "Just get receipts for anything you need, we'll expense account it."

"Uh-huh. What about you? You going to be okay with both me and Steve out of town?"

"What?"

"Steve. He was here at the hospital when I arrived."

"Steve's there? With you?"

"Well, not anymore. He's taken the dog to the emergency vet over here, I imagine. You didn't know?"

I did not. But should I have? Should I have predicted that Steve would stay with the baby? Should I have read his messages before Sue's?

I clear my throat. "No."

"Huh."

It's not the slight undercurrent of judgment in her tone that bothers me. It's the idea of returning to an empty house that has my stomach feeling kind of fluttery. Usually, it wouldn't be a big deal, but, for some reason, the idea of being alone tonight is making me uneasy.

I'm not the type of woman who needs a man to take care of her, but still. I wish he was here. With both Steve and Sue gone, I'm officially on my own without an ally in this town.

"Anyways," I say. "It's getting pretty late. I think I'm just going to head home, get an early start tomorrow."

"Mm-hmm."

She knows me well enough to guess the game we're playing. I round another curve and am finally able to see the scant lights of town in the distance. "Seriously."

"You all right?"

"Of course." This lie makes me feel guiltier than the last. "Why wouldn't I be?"

"Can't have been easy."

"It never is."

"True, but..."

"But?"

I screech to a halt, just in time to avoid the figured cloaked in black who just stepped out into the street in front of my Jeep. He pauses, swinging his head toward me, scowling into my headlights, and I see that it's Eddie Diaz. Pulling his hood forward, closer around his face, he continues walking.

"Maggie?"

"Yeah. Sorry, Sue." I drive on, stashing the unsettled feeling the encounter has caused with all the others I'm harboring right now. "You were saying?"

"You sound tired."

"I am."

Her voice is thick with concern as she asks, "You sure that's it?"

I rub the back of my neck, still unable to dispel the strange sensation that's wrapped around me and crept under my skin. "What else would it be?"

A child's scream carries through the phone. Several adults yell. Sue's surrounded by the chaos of an emergency room, and she's worried about me. Maybe I'm not as discreet as I thought.

"You tell me," she says.

"I climbed my first mountain today. Parts of it twice. The only thing that's wrong with me can be cured by a long bath and a tall drink."

"If you insist." She sounds doubtful.

"I do." I try to sound convincing.

"Guess I'll see you tomorrow then."

I turn right and pass the last of the streetlights, heading

down the pitch-black road that will take me home. I flick my high beams back on.

"Sue?" All the things I can't bring myself to say jumble in my mouth, threatening to choke me. This woman has children and grandchildren of her own. I'm just her employer. She doesn't have to care about me, and yet she does.

She goes out of her way to make sure I'm all right when my own parents don't even bother, and haven't for years. They probably don't know—or care—if I'm even still alive. "Thanks. For everything. I really do appreciate it."

I end the call and peer through the windshield, finding myself once again swaddled in a thick blanket of silence. I can't see the town anymore, not even a faint glow of the lights, but I still feel... I don't know. Like I'm being watched, maybe. Or that I'm missing something. Something that makes me wish I wasn't heading home to an empty house.

24
ERIKA

A jolt awakens me. I open my eyes reluctantly, expecting to find one of my cats mere seconds from launching an attack on me in my sleep. So I'm shocked to discover instead that I'm not in my bed, or even in my house, but slumped against the window of a vehicle, the seatbelt sawing against my neck.

"Sorry," Bridgette says from the driver's seat, yawning into her fist. "Wish they'd fix that pothole."

I peer through the windshield at the bleak façade of the state crime lab building. We jounce over the rest of the pitted blacktop as we approach the department parking spots, and she pulls into a space. I'm surprised by how many cars are still here, gathered in the darkness at—I check my watch, discover that it's just past nine. I guess it's not so late after all, only feels like it.

"Whew, I'm going to sleep well tonight." Bridgette grins as she turns the car off. Pulling the keys from the ignition, she says, "I'm just gonna hand these in, then I'm off. I feel like I could hibernate for the next month. How about you?"

I roll my shoulders, checking in with my body. I feel stiff, muscles burning with lactic acid, but other than that, I feel... good. Sharp. Surprisingly refreshed and alert. I suppose I should feel bad about abandoning Bridgette to navigate back on her own while I napped, but I don't. Because I'm ready to get to work.

I ignore her surprise as I say as much. Thank her for her help today and promise to keep her in the loop, because she really is a nice person. Nice enough not to chuckle behind my back as I hobble across the lobby and over to the bank of elevators, unlike the night deskman.

I'm alone as I descend into the bowels of the building. Alone as I make my way down the empty hall, footsteps echoing loudly off the plain block walls. Alone as I scan my ID card and push open the doors to the autopsy suite.

I stand still for a moment, taking in my familiar surroundings, alone no more. I study the door across from me—oversized, cold, unwelcoming—and imagine the people lying on the gurneys within, their lives stopped in the same way that the industrial cooler stops their decomposition. Each has their story to tell, and I'm just one of the devices they use to tell it.

Some keep their secrets better than others, but not if I can help it.

I pass into the locker room, take the world's quickest shower, appalled by the dirty gray water swirling around my feet, then throw on a pair of clean scrubs and the tennis shoes from my cubby, eager to begin. My skin bubbles with goosebumps as I step into the cooler, the damp fabric beneath my wet hair instantly chilled as I locate the decedents from the mountain.

You might think it would be a difficult decision, choosing who to start with, but it's not. This time, it's easy. Because there was something I noticed back when we were still on the mountain, something I was reluctant to mention even though I'm quite sure it's true. And if I'm right, which I know I am, it's going to change everything that's been thought so far about this case.

25
MAGGIE

I wake face down on the couch in the dampness of my own drool. Open my eyes to find a dog nose mere inches away. Groan as I try to move only to find my muscles seized up from my poor choice of location. Why didn't Steve wake me and get me into bed?

I'm halfway convinced we must have had a fight, which is strange because we almost never argue—ignoring our problems is more our thing—when my phone starts buzzing on the coffee table, and I get the déjà vu sense it's what woke me in the first place. I make a half-hearted attempt to grab it, but I can't reach.

Everything hurts as I push onto my side. I let loose a string of expletives that earns me happy grins from both dogs as they jump up, tails wagging, thinking it's a game. Either that or they're enjoying that I've been adequately punished for taking their sleeping spots.

My phone starts yet again, and I manage to snag it with my fingertips, knocking it onto the ground where I can reach it. I test my voice with another curse word, make sure I don't sound like I just woke up, then answer.

"Morning, sunshine. Did I wake you?"

It takes me a moment to place the voice. When I do, the memory of the previous day crashes over me. "Sue? What happened? Is the baby okay?"

"Everything's fine. I'm sitting beside her right now, haven't taken my eyes off her all night."

I flush hot with shame, hurrying to get off the couch, trying to not make it sound like I can barely move, but yeah, I can barely move. I grab my tactical belt from the coffee table, holstered weapon still clipped on, and shuffle to the kitchen, various joints popping, tight muscles tugging. I feel like I've been tortured on one of those medieval rack things.

"I figured you'd probably need a wake-up call after the day you had yesterday," Sue says. "I was half worried you'd fall asleep in the car and freeze to death."

"Oh, no. I'm fine," I lie.

Sue snorts.

"Really. It's like I've hiked mountains every day. For a hundred years. As part of a fiery sentence of punishment in hell."

"That sounds pretty accurate," she laughs.

"So... any news?" I ask, filling up the coffee pot and hitting the brew button. I let the dogs out, do a little dance while I watch them, promising my own bladder it will only have to wait another moment.

"You fully awake yet?"

"Of course."

"Good."

The tone of Sue's voice has changed. I rub at the goose-bumps on my arms as I follow the dogs back into the house. Prop myself on one of the stools at the kitchen island and watch the coffee brew, wishing I could snag a cup before it finished without making a mess. "And?" I prod.

"The baby was drugged. She's fine, don't worry about that, but they found lorazepam in her system."

"Drugged," I repeat, dazedly. "Lorazepam? That's a sedative, isn't it?"

"Yep."

"I'll ask the medical examiner to test the mother for it."

"That's the first thing I thought of when they told me. That it must have passed to the baby through the mother, but the doctor here says even if the mother was taking it, the level that would pass through into her breast milk would be significantly lower than the levels found in the baby's system. Said she was given it directly."

"But why would her parents sedate her?"

"That's a very good question."

It's too soon to know what really happened, too soon to pass judgment, as much as I'd like to. My job is to remain impartial and collect the facts until the evidence provides us with a picture of what took place. But I can't help but wonder what kind of people would sedate a baby just the same.

The coffee maker slurps as it finishes brewing. I stand up to pour a cup, remember how badly I have to pee and sit back down. "They wouldn't drug their own baby just because they wanted to hike a mountain, would they? I mean, wouldn't hiring a babysitter have been easier?"

I'm asking Sue because she knows these things, at least more than I do. She's raised two kids, and I? I hold up a hand, signaling for the dogs to stop whining and be patient for their breakfast, and even that makes me feel a bit overwhelmed with responsibility this morning.

"Eh. Who knows with people these days?"

I'm floored. I think about the couple I saw the day before, the type of life I had imagined they'd had when I saw them. I'd taken them for more of the brunch and museum kind than the drug-your-infant type. Just goes to prove that Sue is right, as usual. I clear my throat, hoping I don't sound as shocked as I feel when I say, "Can they tell if this was a one-time thing?"

"Hold on, the doctor just walked in. I'll ask."

I listen as Sue relays my question to the physician. His response is too low for me to hear.

"No," Sue says. "It doesn't build up in a concentrated dose like that."

I consider all the unknowns that pockmark this case. Anything I can learn at this point will be progress. "Can you ask him if he can give us a best guess on when she was dosed based on the level in her system?"

"Tell you what. Here."

There's a series of muffled noises that carry through the phone, then a soft-spoken doctor is on the line introducing himself. I pose him my question.

"The half-life of lorazepam is generally about twelve hours. That means the amount of the drug's active substance will reduce by half in that time. Based on that knowledge, and the levels still in her system when she was tested, I'd say her last dose was received approximately ten to fourteen hours before that."

Which narrows down the range for time of death for me. I do some quick math. The officers who took the baby down the mountain probably reached the parking lot around two o'clock yesterday afternoon. Add at least a half-hour for the ambulance ride to Lincoln, maybe another half, max, for the baby's blood-work to be drawn, and I have at least one person who was still alive and drugging a baby between one and five yesterday morning.

I thank the doctor for his time and say a quick goodbye to Sue, eager to end the call. My mind is reeling.

Dr. Ricky had said it would be near impossible to use algor mortis, the change in temperature a body undergoes after death, to help give us an idea of when our decedents met their demise. The freezing temperature and our victims' thick layers of cloth-ing, coupled with the elevated body temperatures you'd expect from someone undergoing the exertion of hiking a mountain, would skew the fairly predictable rate of cooling that occurs after death.

But now I have a timeline—and even though it's much more recent than I think any of us imagined—something's not adding up. I'd have to check the logbook to see the exact time Sue took the call from Cheryl Patton about her grisly discovery, but it was quarter of nine at the latest. Cheryl said she'd started her hike before dawn. Glen said he'd started his when the sun was just barely up. I do a Google search for when sunrise was yesterday: 7:14 a.m.

It took me just over two hours to make the hike up to where Cheryl and Glen were. Granted, as I'd painfully discovered, I'm out of shape. And I'd never climbed a mountain before. So could Glen have reached the same point in a half-hour less than it took me? Yes.

But could a family with a baby? And would they really have started their hike when it was still dark? Of that, I'm not sure.

I'd had a funny feeling yesterday that the man was hiding something. That there'd been something he wanted to say that he hadn't. Or couldn't. Almost like he was scared to. But of what? Or who?

Cheryl had already discovered the bodies when he stumbled onto the scene. But she hadn't called it in yet. How long was she alone with them before he came along? What was she doing in the time between? And what cause was there for the delay?

If she started hiking before sunrise, how far had she been behind the family? Were they just ahead of her? Was she close enough to hear them? Is it possible, even, that she had been a member of their group? That would explain the missing vehicle.

One thing is clear. I need to speak with both witnesses again. Soon.

26

GLEN

He hadn't gotten much sleep. Not that he had expected to. Somehow, he'd known that every time he closed his eyes, they'd be there—the bodies from the mountain. In particular, the face of the kid he'd worked so hard to find. And every time he managed to blank his mind and make them disappear? The questions came.

What did the police think had happened to them? Had they been identified? And most importantly, was he a suspect?

It's this last question that's bothering him the most, for obvious reasons. He's been driving himself crazy, so much so that when there's a knock early in the morning, and he peers through the spyhole to see the police chief standing on the front porch, her breath fogging in the cold morning air, it's almost a relief. Tossing the door open wide, he beckons her inside.

Leading her into the kitchen, he pours her a cup of coffee without asking, then tops off his own mug before dropping heavily into a chair. Not that he needs any more caffeine. There's already a slight tremor in his hand, and his heart feels like it's going to break through the walls of his chest and go galloping down the street, but the hot liquid is a comfort, and he has a feeling he won't be turning down anything that provides that for a long time to come.

"Sorry to disturb you so early in the morning," she says as she takes the seat across from him. If she notices the stains on his T-shirt, the hole in his sweatpants, his filthy socks, or his morning breath, she's polite enough to pretend she doesn't.

"Wasn't sleeping anyway."

Her fingers rest atop a leather folio on the table before her. "I won't take much of your time. I just wanted to run this summary of your statement by you, make sure I got everything correct." She opens the folder and removes a sheet of paper. As she slides it across the table toward him, she says, "Or see if there's anything you might want to add."

He looks up at this, startled. She offers him an unreadable smile and he glances away.

"After a shock like the one you had, it's not uncommon to remember certain details after your brain's had a bit of time to process."

He pulls the paper closer and busies himself with reading over what it says, buying himself time to think. Because he wants to tell her everything. But he can't.

"Nope, that's it," he says, holding the paper out to her.

She doesn't take it. Her eyebrows raise slowly as if pulled by an invisible thread. "Are you sure?"

He licks his lips, trying to find moisture somewhere in his arid mouth. "Yep. I'm sure. You've got it all right here. Everything that happened."

"And you maintain that the woman, Cheryl, was the first to discover the scene?"

He covers his mouth, swallows hard, feeling like he needs to be sick. "That's what happened," he says, weakly.

"Are you sure? Seems like there might have been a little confusion about that yesterday."

"No. No confusion."

"Okay, then." She holds his eyes as she reaches inside her jacket. His pulse tics in his neck as he wonders what she's reaching for. Handcuffs? A gun?

"Oh, by the way..."

He stiffens and drops his eyes to the hand still in her coat.

"Did you notice any vehicles when you parked in the trail-head lot yesterday?"

"No." His heart thrashes so wildly that he's sure it's going to give out, that he'll have a heart attack right here, in this chair, in this cabin, in this microscopic Maine town that he wishes he'd never heard of.

Hold on. What is it she's just asked? "Wait. Actually, there was, sorry. A white SUV. A Toyota, maybe?"

He's blowing it. Being too obvious. But he can't concentrate, can't take his eyes off her hand. He's worked himself into such a panicked mess that he almost laughs when she pulls out a pen and offers it to him. "If you wouldn't mind adding a short description about the car you saw and then signing down there at the bottom?"

Glen scribbles his name quickly, drawing in a deep breath of relief as she tucks the statement sheet back into her notebook. She slips a pair of winter gloves on, takes her pen from the table, and stands. He tries not to seem too eager as he trails her to the door. Bites his lip painfully as she stops halfway across the threshold.

"What are you really doing here in Coyote Cove, Mr. Coffrey?" she asks him.

"I already told you," he stutters, eyes widening. "I'm meeting some friends. We're going fly-fishing."

"Did you book a guide?"

"Don't need one," he assures her. "We know what we're doing."

"Mm-hmm. Well, I wish you the best of luck with that.

Kind of hard, fishing with flies this time of year. You all might decide to try ice fishing right now instead."

His body trembles. This time, it's not from too much caffeine.

"And, Mr. Coffrey? I'm going to need you to remain in Coyote Cove for the duration of the stay indicated in that statement you just signed. Let me know if you have a change of plans. Anyways, have a good time fishing with your friends. I'm sure I'll see you again soon."

He stands in the open doorway, letting out all the heat as he watches her get in her Jeep and back down the driveway. But it doesn't matter. He doubts he'll ever feel warm again.

27

ERIKA

It isn't until my coworkers start showing up that I notice how late it is. Or rather, how early. Somehow, I've worked through the night and now it's time for my shift to begin without the prior one technically having come to an end.

The insides of my eyelids feel like sandpaper. My tongue feels—and tastes—like I've been licking the dirty pavement out in the parking lot, and I've never noticed before quite how annoying my fellow employees are in the morning. I mean, the autopsy tech, JoAnn, normally wears too much perfume, and the other pathologist on duty, Tony, always speaks too loudly, but they've only been here five minutes and I already feel lost in a haze of floral and musk at an ear-splintering concert.

I escape to my office under the guise of dictating some notes, but really it's because I've realized that it's finally a decent enough hour that I can call Chief Riley. As I sink into the chair, and fatigue hits, I know I need to make it fast. I don't think I have enough adrenaline to keep me going much longer.

Kicking off my shoes, I rotate my ankles as I make the call. Each movement brings a new pain with it that I use to keep myself awake while the line rings. I'm debating whether I should have grabbed some caffeine first when she answers, and I launch right in.

"Are you sitting down?"

"Um... With whom am I speaking?"

"It's Dr. Ricky. Well, are you?"

"I'm driving, so yeah. Do you always have this much energy in the morning?"

"Haven't slept yet." It sounds like she's chewing on her end, which reminds me I also haven't eaten. "Listen." I raise my voice to be heard over my stomach. "I noticed something yesterday. About the decedents. Only, I didn't want to say until I was sure, but now I am, so, well, they weren't a family. At least, not biologically."

The chewing noises on the other end cease.

"You still there?"

"Yeah. I'm here. Will you take me through your line of reasoning? From the first thing that caught your attention yesterday until whatever confirmation you've achieved since then?"

Closing my eyes, I remember my initial impressions of the scene. "Well, as you know, the first body we reached was that of a male that I posited in age between late teens and early twenties. The decedent that we assumed was the son."

I pause, then start again, approaching my explanation from another angle. "Part of my process when I perform an autopsy is to perform a visual inspection. Observe what's discernibly apparent. Some of these things might be related to the cause of death, like a wound, or, say, how a certain coloring would indicate carbon monoxide poisoning. But others are just things that grab my attention, like a birthmark or an inheritable trait, like a cleft chin."

I wait for Chief Riley to let me know she's following. After a stretch of silence, she says, "Okay," drawing out the word.

"You are aware that there was nothing indicative of cause of death."

"Yes."

"But when I was looking, a couple things did catch my attention."

"Like a cleft chin."

I can tell by the way she says it that she remembers that the young man had one.

"Yes. And attached earlobes."

"Which means one of his parents should have presented phenotypically with each of those traits."

"Exactly!" I'm thrilled that she understands. "But I've got news for you."

"Neither did."

"Neither did," I repeat.

"But there could be an explanation for that. A stepparent, an extramarital affair…"

"Which is what I thought, so I drew some blood to send off for DNA. But since I figured you wouldn't want to wait until the lab got around to testing the samples—"

"Which I don't."

"I went ahead and blood typed all three decedents to see if I could tell to which parent he might have genetic ties."

"And?"

And I'm grinning too hard to say. I'm not sure why, exactly, except maybe it's been a long time since I worked a case that really piqued my interest. At some point, I just started going through the motions, though I couldn't say for how long. I rub a hand over my mouth to wipe the smile away. "Neither."

Chief Riley clears her throat. When she speaks, her tone is filled with the same intensity that I feel. "That's—very—interesting. And how did you make that determination?"

"How much do you know about serology?"

"Let's pretend nothing."

I suspect that's a lie, but I give her a primer anyways. "There are four blood types. A, B, AB, or O. Your blood type is determined by your parents. Two As can make an A or an O. Likewise, two Bs result in a B or an O. An A and a B can have an A, a B, or an AB. Same if one or both parents is an AB."

"So how can you tell that neither adult was related to the younger victim?"

I wind the phone cord around my finger, the same way I used to when I was a teenager. "Because both adults were type AB, and the young man was type O. Two ABs can't make an O."

I don't think she means for me to hear the word she just said. "I'm going to have to call you back."

"Wha—"

But the line's already dead. I stare at the phone in my hand, wanting an explanation that never comes. Start dialing Chief Riley back to give her a piece of my mind, but I'm interrupted by a knock.

"Dr. Ricky?"

I recognize the young woman who pokes her head around the door as one of the new interns. She looks so timid that she reminds me of myself at that age, and I'm too sympathetic to chew her out, changing my terse, "What!" to "Yes," mid-word, making it sound like, "Why, yes."

She takes it as an invitation, which is the last thing I intended. I watch as she takes in my appearance, eyes traveling from my discarded shoes to my disheveled hair to the phone cord knotted around me. I allow her to gape at me for a moment before I force out a tempered, "What is it?"

"You're the one working the triple fatality from that mountain out by Coyote Cove, right?"

"I am."

"There's something you should see."

28

MAGGIE

I brush granola bar crumbs off my chest, realizing too late that I should have waited until I got out of my car. Guess I have too many things on my mind to exercise common sense. Like a trio of dead people who aren't what they appeared to be, a baby who's been drugged, witnesses who are keeping secrets, and the fact that I forgot to ask Dr. Ricky if she's determined cause of death yet.

I'm slipping. In more ways than one.

I type a quick text to Sue, asking her to find out the baby's blood type. It's funny how we as a society are hardwired to jump to certain conclusions. You see a man and a woman of similar age together and assume they're a couple. They're accompanied by someone who might be young enough to be their child, and you assume it is.

Even as a detective, even after years of training, it's impossible to not be swayed by preconceived notions. But you try. Or, at least, you're supposed to. But I guess I've been out of the game too long, because in this case I was unsuccessful. One person—a possible suspect, no less—made an incorrect statement and I ran with it.

I assumed the people on the mountain were a family, when they might not be related at all. They might not even have known each other. But then what were they doing up on that mountain together?

Of course, something as simple as adoption would explain our younger victim's uninheritable blood type. But the couple would have had to have been very close to the likely age of the young man—late teens to early twenties—when he was born. Who adopts that early in life?

No, something else must be at play here. Babies exchanged at birth, maybe. Or the much more likely explanation that they just weren't a family. Maybe he was their guide, like Brad was mine. Still, why were they up there with a baby? And a drugged one, at that?

Spotting a pedestrian I don't recognize walking by, I crane my head to get a better look. We get plenty of tourists up here. I usually don't give them a second glance, but now? I don't know. Something strange happened on that mountain, and until I figure out what, everyone and everything seems wrapped in a cloud of suspicion.

My phone buzzes and I read Sue's reply. The baby is blood type B, so no help there. Any of our victims could be a biological parent. She lets me know that there's still been no missing person reports filed that match the descriptions of our hikers. I wonder if there's some friend or family member out there being given the runaround about having to wait forty-eight hours.

But she also mentioned that the baby will be released later today, which is wonderful news. And according to Steve the dog is also doing well, though she might not be released as soon. Both are victories that should make me feel good about the job that I'm doing here in Coyote Cove.

But as I look up and catch Mrs. Perkins, the organist and choir director at the local church glaring at me through the windshield as she shuffles by, any feelings of accomplishment I have crumble. Does everyone in this town hate me? I suspect I don't want to know the answer.

It's one thing to have criminals want to see you burn, but when even law-abiding citizens are standing by with a stake, some rope, and a match, well, it's not a good feeling. Then again, being vulnerable never is. But I have more pressing concerns at the moment.

I'm reaching for my door handle when a flash catches my eye. I turn just in time to see someone ducking around the corner of the trading post. Someone who was wearing powder blue, the same color as the state police. And though I barely caught a glimpse of them from the corner of my eye, it looked like that someone had a mustache.

I tell myself I'm just being paranoid. It's not like I don't have just cause. And I can't deny that I haven't been able to shake the feeling of being watched since I got back to town yesterday. But I'm being ridiculous. Officer Miller might be a jerk, but I'm sure he has better things to do than prowl around town like a stalker.

My body complains as I climb out of the Jeep, my thigh muscles tight and tender from yesterday's hike in a way they've never been before. I pretend it doesn't bother me, pushing aside thoughts of getting older and ignoring the fact that I'm horribly out of shape, as I cross the lot and enter the motel's office. Margot looks up, her shrewd raisin eyes watching my every step as I try to walk normally.

"What happened to you?"

Apparently, I've failed. I release a small, involuntary grunt as I lean on the counter. "I finally met my arch nemesis in life. Its name is mountain. I think I lost."

Her face cracks into a spider's web of wrinkles as she grins. "Oh, yeah. I heard about that. Welcome to the North Country."

I groan, mostly because I shifted my weight. "Any trouble keeping our guest around?"

"Nothing a couple of flat tires couldn't cure."

I shake my head in disapproval, but the truth is, I don't. Disapprove, that is. Whatever gets the job done and, right now, I'll take whatever help I can get with that.

"Don't think she's too fond of us, though," Margot says. "Doubt she'll ever decide to visit the Cove again."

"Are we sad about that?" I ask.

"I don't think that we are."

"What can you tell me about her?"

Margot grabs a printout she already has waiting for me and slides it across the counter. "Cheryl Patton. Revere Beach address. Likes include hotels with room service, spas, and heated pools, none of which we have. Dislikes include me, you, and," she makes air quotes, "'this whole entire white trash town.'"

"Wow. That hurts."

"I know, right?" Margot grabs her chest and feigns injury as she rolls her eyes. "Think there'll be any cause to haul her out of here in handcuffs?"

"There's only one way to find out." I take the paper with Cheryl Patton's information off the counter, fold it, and put it into my pocket. Feel another piece already in there, this one balled up, and the memory of the dummy hanging outside my office yesterday morning resurfaces. I feel a momentary pang of guilt, then hold my breath as I add that vendetta to the already overwhelming weight of tasks on my back. Breathe a sigh of relief when I find myself still standing. Not crushed yet. Carry on.

"What room?"

"Number eight."

I nod and take a step toward the door. Then, just to be thorough, even though I know Margot would have brought it up, I ask, "I don't suppose you had any guests matching the descriptions I emailed you?"

"Nope."

"What about any vehicles not registered to guests in your lot?"

Margot arches an eyebrow at me. "What kind of a place do you think I have here?"

She wouldn't like the answer, so I don't respond. But the truth is, despite the somewhat seedy reputation of her motel, Margot runs a tight ship. Not much escapes her attention.

As if to prove my point, she says, "But before you go," she waves another sheet of paper at me, "I caught a guest on the security cameras acting suspicious night before last. Micah Jenkins. Guy left around midnight, didn't come back until almost six. The image is crap 'cause I'm too cheap to invest in better equipment, but the way he was holding himself, looked like he could have been injured. Long as the room's paid for and doesn't get damaged, it's no skin off my teeth, but I thought you'd want to know."

"That is strange," I mutter, frowning down at the details of the guest who just happened to be skulking around at the same time three people died mysteriously, which seems an awfully improbable coincidence. Trying not to think about the skin on Margot's teeth, I add, "I'll definitely ask him a few questions. Thanks."

"He's not here right now. Left just before eight. Want me to give you a buzz when he comes back?"

"Sure, that'd be great." I purse my lips, wondering if I should keep my question to myself, but curiosity gets the better of me. "Do you always check the security cameras to see what happened overnight?"

She shrugs. "It gets boring sitting here all day. Besides. These people? I don't trust a one of them."

I can't blame her there. We've all got something to hide, don't we? "Well, thanks for the intel."

"Not a problem." She gives me one of her slightly creepy

smiles, nicotine-stained teeth worn down to corn kernel nubs. "Now go git 'er, Chief."

I give a nod and a wink, then I'm on my way, moving a little less stiffly with each step as I shuffle down the corridor. This is a leave no stone unturned, hound every witness kind of situation, because I need answers. And if there's one thing my past life as a detective taught me, it's that you have to keep a sharp eye and an open mind, because you never know where you're going to find them.

29

MICAH

Micah Jenkins isn't sure he's ever been so exhausted before. He can't wait to get to his room and crash. Besides a quick nap early yesterday afternoon, he's been up for almost forty-eight hours.

But it's not like he's had much of a choice. Not if he's going to salvage the deal.

He considers calling a friend, someone who's helped in the past, but decides against it. This is something he should probably do on his own. He doesn't have time for distractions. Although, to be honest, even on his best days, he's never been the most focused. That's probably part of the problem.

He suspects he should have been able to foresee the flaw in his plan. The complications. The mistakes. No part of this has gone as he'd anticipated. And now look at the mess he has on his hands. Quite literally.

His arm is killing him. He holds it gingerly across his chest as he hobbles down the street, stiff and sore and defeated. Wondering if maybe he's out of his league this time. Facing consequences steeper than ever before.

But none of that really matters, does it? He can't afford to lose.

Micah rounds the corner, and the motel comes into view. He can already feel the sagging mattress under his aching body, the lumpy pillow under his head. It will be such a relief to close his eyes, if only for a while. His need for sleep right now even trumps that for food, though he'd never thought he'd ever say that.

He quickens his step, his gait awkward. Braces himself against the pain radiating through his body. It's not like he hasn't been banged up before. He's broken more bones in his body than he can count, all in the name of his career goals. It's just that, usually, he has more to show for it. This time, he has nothing.

Yet.

But he's not done trying. He refuses to go home empty-handed. He still has a few tricks up his sleeve.

Approaching his destination, he rubs at his tired eyes with his good hand. And keeps right on walking. The bed, the pillow, the rest, all forgotten the instant he sees the police decal on the Jeep in the parking lot.

They couldn't have possibly found him already, could they? Because that could seriously complicate things.

He limps down the sidewalk, toward the diner at the end of the street. He needs to think. Regroup. There's got to be a way out of this.

He's determined to get what he wants. And not pay the consequences. No matter what it takes.

30

MAGGIE

The woman who answers the door is almost unrecognizable. Had I been looking for her on the street, I might have missed her. But there's no missing the glare burning from behind those reddened eyes. Cheryl Patton pushes a lock of greasy hair away from her puffy, tear-streaked face and continues to scowl at me.

"May I come in? I'd like to ask you a few follow-up questions from yesterday."

"I have nothing more to say."

She crosses her arms and widens her stance. This isn't going to be easy. Nice cop isn't going to get me anywhere with this one.

"We can do this here or down at the station, your choice." I mirror her body language.

She stares at me for a long moment before taking a step back. "Fine," she huffs. "But make it quick."

I enter to find the room dark. All the lamps are off. Only a sliver of sunlight has managed to sneak in around the edges of the curtains. Balled up tissues litter the floor. An almost empty bottle of vodka lays on its side on the nightstand. I take all this in as I lean my back against the wall and wait for her to settle into the sole chair in the room.

"Is that your white Pathfinder out in the lot?" I ask, gesturing toward the window with my head.

"You mean the one with two flat tires?" she asks me pointedly. "Yeah, why?"

"Ms. Patton, did you notice any other cars in the lot when you got to the trailhead yesterday?"

She shakes her head but doesn't look at me.

"Are you sure?"

"What kind of question is that?"

I don't like her attitude. "The kind you get asked during an investigation where three people are found dead. The kind you get asked when you're the one who discovered the bodies, and the second witness on the scene attests that your vehicle was the only car in the trailhead lot when he got there. I'm trying to determine how the victims arrived at the mountain, Ms. Patton."

"There were no other cars in the lot when I got there. I'm sure."

"Did you drive anyone else in your vehicle with you?"

"No."

"Do you remember passing any vehicles on your drive there?"

"I wasn't really paying attention."

"Ms. Patton, what were you doing up on that mountain yesterday?"

She looks at me like I'm an idiot. "Uh, hiking."

"Why that mountain?"

A flash of fear briefly breaks the stony façade of her face. "What do you mean?" she asks warily.

"I mean, what made you choose that mountain to hike. And, more specifically, that trail?"

"Nothing. I mean, there was no particular reason. Just bad

luck, I guess."

But her eyes dart hard to the side as she speaks. She can't hold still, repeatedly fidgeting and shifting her weight in her seat. And a small bead of sweat has bubbled up on one of her temples. She's lying.

"Have you ever been there before?"

"No."

Another lie. Her body language is giving her away, practically screaming that she had, indeed, been up that trail before. "What were you planning to do up there?"

She avoids my eyes, hands balled tight into fists. "I don't know. I just wanted to go up there. To think."

Her words don't ring true. The way her voice trembles makes me think that she knew exactly why she was there. Unfortunately, she's not sharing that reason with me.

I don't have grounds to charge her with a crime. And I'm not making any headway with this interview. I need to go over her background with a fine-toothed comb until I find a weakness that I can leverage to make her more cooperative.

"One last thing. Are you sure that Glen Coffrey arrived at the scene after you did?"

"What do you mean?"

"I mean, is it possible that he was already there, before you? Could he have maybe been hiding in the brush somewhere along the trail? Maybe he doubled back, after you passed?"

She gives me a blank look for a moment before saying, "I suppose so. Why? What happened to those people?"

"We're still trying to find out. I'm going to need you to stay in town until we do."

I ignore the hatred burning in her eyes as I turn to leave. But hatred for what? Impeding her escape from Coyote Cove? Investigating the murders she's committed? Or something else entirely, something I'm missing?

31

CHERYL

She watches through the spyhole as the cop leaves. Waits until the police chief disappears from view before collapsing to the floor, her back pressed hard against the door. God, what a mess. Just one more thing that's all his fault.

Elbows on her knees, she cradles her head in her hands. She knew she should have just left yesterday. Nobody knew who she was. No one knew why she was there. She could have just turned around, made her way back down the mountain. But then that guy had shown up, and she couldn't think straight. She'd panicked.

She hadn't always been like this. Such a basket case. There was a time when she had it all together. But that was back when she had it all. Or, at least, she thought she had it all.

There's no telling how long her husband had been cheating on her before he left. No way to know how long he'd been with the other woman before he divorced Cheryl to marry her. How long had she played the fool? Since the day she said, "I do?"

Twenty-one years of marriage gone in the blink of an eye, like the flush of a toilet. That is what her ex had done, isn't it? Discarded her like waste?

How do you reconcile that and move on?

The truth is, you can't. At least, she couldn't. Not when he was free to live his life, happy and unpunished.

All she'd wanted to do was even the score. Was that so bad? Hadn't she at least deserved that much?

And now here she is, all alone.

Alone and hiding a very big secret. One that she can never let that cop find out. The real reason she was up on that mountain. Revenge.

32

ERIKA

Reading over arrest rap sheets isn't part of the normal scope of my work duties, but I have to admit, it makes for some interesting entertainment. It's not as thrilling as locating the blood vessel that burst inside someone's brain, or tracing the path of a bullet that ricocheted off multiple bones, but it can be almost as telling.

Take, for instance, a teenager who first appears on an arrest affidavit as the victim of domestic violence. And whose next appearance is as the perpetrator.

The medical records from the first occurrence suggests an ongoing history of abuse. That the victim had just turned eighteen, and therefore no longer had their name shielded from the record, is akin to finding a cheeseburger among the stomach contents of a heart attack victim. You can't prove that wasn't the first burger they ever ate, but the evidence is there to draw the conclusion that other burgers—or beatings—preceded the event at hand.

But it's not my job to leap to conclusions. It's not even my job to connect the dots to see if a picture starts to emerge. And usually, I don't even want to. I've always been more than happy to stay in my comfort zone, performing postmortems and reporting my findings. To let others make the intuitive leaps.

I'm the voice for the dead. Once I've revealed the secrets their bodies contain, my work is done. I've never been interested in negotiating the bridge between the deceased and the living or investigating how those facts can be used to make the connections that solve crimes and build cases. That's what detectives are for.

Only, something's personal about this case. Maybe it's because I went out into the field, saw the deceased in situ. Maybe it's because I feel myself drawn into the mystery of what happened. Or maybe I'm just evolving into the type of forensic pathologist you see on TV, the kind who wants to take part in the investigation from beginning to end. Because, this time, I care.

Which makes my job harder. I still haven't performed the autopsy on the female victim. Every time I raise my scalpel, I think about who she was. Who she left behind. And how they'd feel about me slicing into her body, searching her deepest, darkest, most private corners for answers.

But I can't put it off any longer. Any of it.

I attach a copy of the file to an email and hit send. I check the time and begin the count down. *Three. Two. One.* Actually, a full four minutes goes by before my phone rings.

"What is it that I'm looking at?"

I can't resist smirking. "I thought that might get your attention."

"Seriously." A scratch of static hisses across the line between us.

I'm glad I requested that I be the one to forward our youngest victim's arrest record to Chief Riley. Maybe the tiny thrill of vindication I feel is petty, but it doesn't stop me from enjoying it.

"I'm sorry, I didn't realize you were interested in speaking with me after the way you hung up earlier."

I can feel her cussing me out in her head. I think. I'm pretty sure I would be if the situation was reversed.

"I apologize for ending our call so abruptly. I wanted to make sure we had a blood type on our baby Jane Doe before she left the hospital."

"You're thinking you could narrow down which of the victims she belonged to?"

"Something like that. She had blood type B, though, so she could have biological ties to any of them." I hear the telltale sound of a printer, then the shuffling of pages. "Am I correct in assuming that this belongs to our younger male victim?"

"Otherwise known as Justice Panettiere," I reply. "Violent offender, burglar, trespasser... there's a whole slew of charges here."

"And at the ripe old age of twenty. Jesus, I feel old."

"Doesn't look like the poor kid stood much of a chance in life."

"That's bull. There's always a choice. Plenty of people are born into bad situations. I'd like to think that most of them don't use it as an excuse to become scum."

I'm a little surprised by the vehemence of her reply. "Please, tell me how you really feel."

"I'm sorry, I just—I'm frustrated. Do we have any idea what cause of death was yet?"

"I'm still waiting for the results of the bloodwork. Postmortems of both males were unremarkable other than some visceral congestion, which is the obstruction of normal blood flow within the vessels of the internal organs, in this case the right side of the heart, and cyanotic changes, or a bluish discoloration, to the blood. I haven't autopsied the female decedent yet."

"What are those findings indicative of?"

"They're non-specific, but could be attributed to some form of asphyxia."

"They suffocated?"

"I can't say for sure at this time. They lack other indicators you'd expect, like petechiae. And both could be caused by other pathology, like poor circulation or drug use. Until I get the results of the blood work, it's all just speculation."

"And I'm assuming you would have forwarded any pertinent information about the two older victims if they'd been IDed."

"That's correct. Still no hits on their fingerprints."

Chief Riley sighs loudly. "No guarantees they're in the system. Which leaves us with three dead from unknown causes, one of whom has a rap sheet the length of my forearm, and a baby who survived whatever happened."

"So. What's our next move?"

"I've got to go over this arrest record and see if it's worth requesting the case file details on any of these charges. And we need to ID our other two victims."

"How will we do that if we don't get a hit on the prints?"

Chief Riley snorts. "If they didn't tell anyone where they were going hiking? Luck. And I have a funny feeling that they didn't. I think that whatever they were up to on that mountain? They didn't want anyone to know."

We both fall silent at that, because if I had to guess, I'd bet she's right. Sometimes even good people do bad things. And sometimes, cases never get solved.

33

MAGGIE

You expect to hit roadblocks during a case like this, but, to be honest, I hadn't anticipated quite so many so soon. I finish my request to the National Crime Information Center for background records on Glen Coffrey, Cheryl Patton, and the elusive Micah Jenkins. There's something just a bit too coincidental about the way he was sneaking around overnight at the same time that the three hikers' mysterious deaths occurred.

I knew that policing in a small town was a far cry from working in a large metropolitan area, but I hadn't realized exactly how much of a disadvantage I'd have in terms of investigating suspects. Probably because there hasn't been much need for it before now.

Part of the allure of Coyote Cove was its lack of major crime, and the state police's responsibility to investigate if and when a major crime occurred. But realizing that I couldn't even access the NCIC database without filing a formal request—complete with signing a statement that the information is for use in an ongoing investigation, and that the records I receive will be destroyed when the investigation is over—is unbelievable. It's like being expected to knit a sweater while I have my hands tied behind my back.

But my efforts so far haven't been a total loss. When I entered the names of my suspects into the local database I have access to, it was a complete surprise when I got a hit for Cheryl Patton. She's been in Coyote Cove as least one time before, something that she strangely failed to mention.

There's a big leap between being ticketed for running a stop sign twenty-one years ago and a triple homicide, but keeping this minor previous offense to herself shows a propensity to deceive. I've contacted her local police department to see what they have on her, but I'm still waiting to hear back.

Then there's Glen Coffrey. His fly-fishing trip is an obvious cover story. But is it to conceal murderous tendencies, or something else? When I reached out to my neighbor who owns the cabin, he said it was rented in Coffrey's name only, and that Glen had told him he'd be staying on his own. Besides that lie, though, neither I nor his local police have been able to find anything on him. Yet.

But, so far, it's Micah Jenkins who has drawn my suspicion the most. Maybe it's because I still haven't actually met the young man. Or maybe it's because the more I learn about him, the more parallels I see between him and Justice.

Micah is twenty-two—a similar age. He has an arrest record, mainly for petty crimes like trespassing and criminal mischief, but it's another thing he and Justice have in common. And the local police from the town he lives in were quick to respond to the request I sent earlier. Turns out they're no strangers to his house. They'd been there a number of times responding to complaints.

Any of them could be guilty. Then again, they could all be innocent. I don't know enough about any of them yet. It's too early to tell.

I'm trying not to get frustrated, keep reminding myself that it's barely been twenty-four hours since I responded to the scene on the mountain, but it's little comfort. Three people died mysteriously in my jurisdiction, leaving an infant behind. I want answers.

As I pull the printout of Justice's arrest record closer, hoping that a thorough read might provide a link between him and Micah Jenkins, a sudden gust of cold sweeps inside. I look up in surprise and see Brad juggling two flimsy Styrofoam cups of coffee from the gas station, struggling to maintain control as he closes the front door.

"Hey." He gives me his print ad smile. "Just wanted to check and see how you're doing after yesterday. I brought caffeine."

Standing, I round the desk to take one of the cups from him. "You're a godsend. I appreciate it. And thanks again for all your help yesterday. I'm not sure I could have done it without you. I wasn't kidding when I told you to bill the department for your time."

He brushes the suggestion away with a flip of his hand. "I was happy to do it. Besides. I don't like the idea of something like that going down on one of my mountains."

"But your boss—"

"I told him it's good PR and he seems to agree."

I've met Horace before. He's not one of my biggest fans. I can't believe that he and Brad are on the same page about this, but what's the point in arguing?

"Okay, well. If you're sure..."

"I am."

"Then thank you. Again."

His smiles reappears, but this time it seems tense, awkward. It makes me wonder the real reason why he's here.

"You know, yesterday, um," he begins. His lips twist into a knot while he thinks of his next words. "I know you had your hands full, so I didn't want to say anything."

"About?"

"It's probably nothing." He makes brief eye contact, then lowers his gaze like he's embarrassed. Taps a finger on the Styrofoam cup lid, like he's working up his nerve. "But I thought I should tell you. Just in case it's not."

I wait, keeping my expression blank.

"Anyways, that lady, the one who discovered the bodies? She was acting really weird on the hike down. Like, a complete one-eighty from the way she acted in front of you. She was aggressive. Hostile, even. It struck me as really suspicious, especially considering the circumstance. So I took a video on my phone of some of the things she was saying."

"May I see it?"

Brad pulls the cell from his pocket, then leans against the desk next to me. His arm brushes against mine as he cues up the recording. When the short clip is over, I say, "I appreciate you bringing this to my attention. Would you mind sending me a copy?"

"Yeah, sure. What's your number?"

I turn, grab a business card from a holder and hand it to him. A moment later there's a buzz as I receive the file.

"Well," he says, tucking his phone and the card into his pocket as he straightens, "I should probably be on my way. I'm sure you've got a million things to do. But if you need anything, even if it's not hiking related, you know where to find me."

I follow him to the door, watch through the slats in the blinds as he treks down the sidewalk, thinking about the video he showed me. Given the timeline, it's possible Cheryl Patton was on the mountain at the time of the deaths. Not to mention that the lack of trauma on the bodies suggests some form of poisoning, which is most often attributed to female killers. And she was lying to me when I questioned her earlier today—she's definitely hiding something.

But so is Glen Coffrey. And who knows what Micah

Jenkins was up to when Margot's surveillance camera caught him roaming around on the night that the deaths took place. It's still too early to rule anyone out. I still have more questions than answers. Like if there could possibly be a legitimate reason to give lorazepam to a baby.

I wait for Brad to turn the corner before stepping outside into the cold and locking the door. I rub the back of my neck, unable to shake the feeling of being watched as I walk down the steps. And not the normal keep-track-of-the-cop stare I'm used to getting. This feels different. More uncomfortable.

Are the eyes I feel on me those of the killer? Are they keeping tabs on what I'm doing?

Usually I'd make the short trip across town on foot, but I find myself opting instead to drive today. And it has nothing to do with the bitter cold.

Only a few short minutes pass before I'm looking for a space along the curb. Finding a spot down the block, I exit the vehicle, hunching my neck down farther into my jacket as I backtrack down the street.

I shiver as I reach the landing to the Cove's only doctor's office. Even though I'm eager to get inside, I pause, unable to resist the urge to check behind me. I turn slowly, trying to look nonchalant—and see him loitering outside of Frank's Hardware across the street. Scowling from beneath the brim of a black hoodie as he stares at me. Eddie Diaz.

I don't know much about the kid. Don't know why he's skulking on the street in the cold when he should be in school. Then I remember the call I responded to earlier this year, the pocketknife he'd had on campus, and realize the principal must have carried through on his threat of expulsion.

Eddie had said that he'd been using the Swiss Army to cut his line while fishing over the weekend, that he hadn't even real-ized it was still in his pocket when he'd woken late and pulled his dirty pair of jeans on that morning. It's possible the story was true. God knows it's easy enough for a kid to get their hands on something more dangerous than a three-inch blade, if that's what they have a mind to do. Then again, every criminal starts somewhere.

I fight a second shiver as I stare at the space where his dark eyes should be. Like Justice Panettiere, the kid comes from a bad background. They both found trouble early. And I can't help wondering what else they might have in common.

I'm debating whether I should walk across the street and talk to the kid, ask him a few questions. Like if he's keeping himself out of trouble. Or if he realizes how creepy his little lurking act is. But before I can decide he trudges off, shoulders hunched high under his ears, hands shoved deep into his pockets.

Freezing, I continue inside before anything else can stop me, the soft parts of my head—cheeks, nose, lips, and earlobes—burning from the cold as I step into the overheated waiting room. Karen Edmunds, receptionist, nurse, and town selectman, greets me with a curt smile.

"Morning, Chief. You here for our business or yours?"

"Mine."

"The doc should be out in a minute if you'd like to wait."

I nod and start toward the waiting room.

"Nasty business up there on that mountain, huh?"

Stopping, I turn back to face her. I don't think Karen's quite made up her mind about me. Or maybe she's just trying to squeeze me for more gossip to add to her rumor mill. Either way, I close the distance between us so no one can listen in. Propping an arm on the counter, I drop my head in a conspiratorial manner and ask in a low voice, "What'd you hear?"

She leans toward me and whispers, "That an entire family... you know." Louder, she adds, "Hiking's a dangerous sport. We're always getting tourists in here with injuries. Why, just yesterday there was a fella waiting out front for us to open. All bruised up. Had a nasty gash on his arm, don't know how he managed to get it. You ask me, you should have to pass a test before you hit the trail."

My pulse quickens a notch. "Did he say where he'd been hiking?"

"Nope. He was pretty quiet about the whole thing. Refused to say what had happened. Think he was pretty embarrassed, to tell the truth. Doubt he'd even have come in for treatment if his arm hadn't been in such bad shape. Took me twenty minutes to debride the wound. Doc put in over a dozen stitches."

I chew on the inside of my cheek, trying to maintain my poker face. Because there are other reasons to keep your mouth shut besides embarrassment. Like self-incrimination.

HIPAA laws prevent me from asking to see this man's file, but I need to find out if it's Micah Jenkins. As long as the violation isn't mine, though...

I roll my eyes and huff a laugh out my nose. "Sounds like this real winner I ticketed the other day. The guy sure did think a lot of himself. Mickey or Michael or something."

"Could it have been Micah?"

"You know? It just might have been." I let my gaze drift casually to the clock on the wall. "Oh, shoot. Is that the time? I have to run."

"What about speaking with the doc?"

"I'll have to come back."

"But... You're coming to the next council meeting, right?"

"I'll try my best," I shout over my shoulder, already halfway out the door, in a rush to get back to my office. Because it's the second time this morning that I've come across something that makes this guy look suspicious. And what I need to do now is find out what Mr. Micah Jenkins has been up to, and what—or who—injured him.

34

BRAD

He's rewatching the video he sent Chief Riley when the bell on the door rings as someone enters the store. He straightens a little, makes himself look a bit more presentable on instinct, before he sees who the customer is.

Some local kid he's seen lurking around, a dark-eyed brat, always glaring at the world like he hates it. Like he's the only one who's ever had a hard time. The only one who's ever been too broke or too dumb or too short or too whatever to get the smooth sailing pass some chumps are lucky enough to get.

No doubt he's here to help himself to some merchandise at a five-finger discount. Brad slumps back down into his thinking position, resting his chin on his hand. If the kid wants to shoplift the whole damn store, let him. He can tuck it all under that black hoodie he's wearing. Brad doesn't get paid enough to care. And he's got more important things on his mind right now.

Like finding a new place to live. He sighs, frustrated. Glances up and catches the kid looking at him.

No. Not looking. Staring.

"There a problem?" he asks.

The kid shakes his head, tugs his hoodie forward, shrouding

his face in shadow. He pushes a hanger to the far end of a rack, then another, like he's browsing, but Brad can tell he's still watching him.

"You planning on buying something?"

He's answered by a shrug, before the boy says, "You were one of the hikers up on the mountain yesterday. You know, when they found those bodies."

"What's it to you?"

Another shrug. "I was just wondering, is all."

"About what?"

"What they think happened."

"Honestly? No one's got a clue."

The kid grunts. "But they're investigating it as murder, right? They've got to be."

"Why are you so interested?"

"Just curious."

Brad leans forward, slips his phone beneath the counter under the guise of shifting his weight. Taps the phone on, the camera button, video, record.

"Seems kind of suspicious if you ask me," Brad says.

"What do you mean?"

"Your interest in what happened on the mountain. All the questions you're asking. Almost like you're trying to figure out if the cops are onto you or not. What's your name, anyways?"

The kid drops his hand from a hanger and turns to leave.

"Hey, I'm talking to you. I'm serious." Brad gets off his stool, wends his way around the counter, stalks across the store after the kid. "What's your freakin' name, kid?"

The teen pushes out the door, the bell jangling violently at his departure. Brad catches it before it has a chance to close, his palm smearing a large handprint that he'll have to clean off before he closes up tonight.

The figure in the black hoodie is already halfway down the

block. Shaking his fist at the retreating form, Brad yells, "Don't you come back here again, you little shit."

"Whoa, hey, what's going on here?"

Brad spins around, teeth bared, fist still raised. His arm drops limply to his side as he finds himself face to face with Officer Kevin Miller.

"Oh. Hey."

"That kid causing you problems? He take something?"

Brad considers telling the officer about the questions the teen was asking, to see if the statie finds it as suspicious as he did, but something makes him think twice. "Nah. Just don't feel like putting up with the punk's attitude today. Don't get paid enough for that, you know?"

"You'd think your chief would have a better handle on the town than that."

Teaching manners doesn't seem like a job for law enforcement, but Brad doesn't say so. Instead, he forces a smile and says, "Didn't think I'd get the chance to see you again. Figured you'd be out of here the first chance you got."

"You'd think. But no. Figured you all could use a little help sorting this mess out, so I stuck around. And no hard feelings about yesterday, huh? Innocent misunderstanding."

Brad nods, a wave of relief loosening the tightness in his chest. "So you're working with the chief, then?"

A brief flash of contempt sours the statie's expression before a nasty smile curls the lips under his mustache. Something about it makes the skin on the back of Brad's neck bristle. "Yeah, something like that. And I could use your help."

In an instant, the tension is back, wrapped tight around Brad, making it hard for him to breathe.

35

MAGGIE

I hurry down the ramp from the doctor's office, jogging along the street to my car. Climbing into my Jeep, I buckle myself in and start the engine. I've just thrown the engine in gear when my cell rings.

I fumble it from my pocket, praying the call is serendipitous and it's Margot calling to tell me Micah Jenkins has returned. Icy fingertips shock the skin of my cheek as I raise the phone to my ear.

"Chief Riley."

I pull out on the road, waiting to turn my lights and siren on until I'm off the call.

"It's Dr. Ricky. I finished the postmortem on the female decedent," she says. "Amanda Marsh."

"You IDed her?"

"I did. She's a teacher in Massachusetts. Her prints were on file."

"What about the unknown male?"

"Her husband, James Marsh. No prints on him, but we were able to make a visual confirmation using his driver's license photo."

"That's excellent. Can you send me the information you have for them?"

"I will. I'm also sending you a copy of my report on her so far, but I wanted to discuss my findings with you."

My brakes screech as I'm forced to a sudden halt, a string of tourists stepping out into the road and crossing with the same disregard to safety as a brood of baby ducks.

"She appears to have a nulliparous cervix."

I grit my teeth as half the tourists stop walking, deciding that the middle of the road with traffic waiting is a suitable spot to hold a conversation. Two start returning to the side they started from, then go back and join the others. "What?"

"She lacked the cervical changes typically indicative of a postpartum woman. Her symphysis pubis joint, the cartilaginous tissue between where the left and right superior rami of the pubis articulate, also does not appear to have undergone the relaxation that one would expect to find."

I feel like getting out of the car and threatening to arrest any pedestrian who remains in the road after the count of three. I take a deep breath to temper my frustration.

"In plain English, doctor."

"The anatomy of the decedent does not suggest a recent pregnancy. Or any pregnancy at all, really. I feel quite confident in my determination that she did not give birth to that baby."

"What! Do we have a cause of death yet?"

"Not yet. I'm still waiting for the results of the lab work, but the physical examination on all three decedents is inconclusive."

"But she didn't give birth?"

"No."

Who are these people? What killed them? And where does the baby belong in all of this?

I eye the people on the sidewalks warily as they walk by.

Could one of them be behind this? Could I be looking at the killer?

Then there's the question that's bothering me the most. If the woman on the mountain didn't give birth to the baby... "Then who on earth did, and where are they?" I mutter to myself.

Dr. Ricky's voice startles me. I'd forgotten she was still on the line. "That, I imagine, is the million-dollar question."

36

MICAH

Micah's not quite sure what he'll need yet. He wanders the aisles of the hardware store, scanning the shelves, looking for inspiration. Grabs a coil of rope, checks the tensile strength, making sure it'll withstand a couple hundred pounds, then slips it over his shoulder. Selects a tarp from a rack. Stops in front of a bin of carabiners and rummages through for the size he wants. Slowly, a plan is starting to form.

It's going to be tight. He's not sure he has enough left on his credit card to pay for it all. He eyes the convex mirror mounted in the corner of the ceiling, debating whether he should risk shoplifting a few of the carabiners.

The clerk isn't watching, isn't even facing the right direction. All he has to do is time it right. He palms several of the fasteners, preparing to slip them into his pocket as he rounds the corner. Keeps watch on the mirror as he steps around the end of the aisle.

"*Oof.*"

"My bad." He puts a hand out to steady the lady he just ran into, but she steps back, out of his reach, glaring at him like he was reaching for her throat. Her eyes are red and swollen, bloodshot. Her lips press together in a thin, hard line as she adjusts her grip on her own coil of rope. He decides she has worse things going on in her life than some stranger running into her.

"Sorry," he offers, rounding the endcap into the next row, right into the path of a state police officer barreling down the aisle toward them in his powder blue uniform. *Shit.* He retreats back around the corner, sidestepping around the angry lady to duck into the aisle he just came from. Stares hard at a can of lighter fluid on the shelf before him and draws deep breaths in an attempt to steady his pulse.

Micah had chosen Coyote Cove because it was supposed to be a sleepy little town. But if that's true, why are there cops everywhere he looks?

He cranes his neck until he can see the mirror. The statie appears deep in conversation with the lady he'd bulldozed just a moment before. He watches as she crosses her arms over her chest, head shaking adamantly at whatever the cop's saying. Her reflection turns and walks away, toward the front of the store, leaving the cop behind, tugging at a corner of his mustache. Micah has a feeling he should follow suit.

But first. He leans his weight against the display to his left, reaches across himself to adjust his grip on the tarp tucked under his arm. Extends two fingers of his reaching hand and uses them to lift the bottle of butane off the shelf, tucking it into his jacket pocket, along with the carabiners.

You never know what will come in handy. Fire's a great way to cover your tracks. Especially if you need to destroy evidence.

37

CHERYL

Cheryl pulls up the picture on her phone. How many times has she looked at it? Inspected the faces of this seemingly happy family, with their bright smiles and their loving embrace, each with one arm looped around the other and one cradled around the baby held between them.

A baby that isn't hers. And never will be.

How many times had she pled to be a mother with her ex over the years, begging him to consider having a baby? How many times had he insisted that he didn't want children? Had he changed his mind? Or had he meant just not with her? Because he looks pretty damned pleased with himself and that infant he's holding. His daughter.

And now it's too late for Cheryl. She'll never have children of her own. Never have his child.

She runs the rope through her fingers, thinking of how she plans to use it. Plotting her next step. She needs to get the hell out of this town. No matter what it takes. She has to find a way to escape without the use of her car, even if it means stealing a vehicle.

But she's too distracted. Can't focus. Can't stop looking at the picture, imagining what the expression on their faces would have been if they'd realized what they were responsible for. If they'd been given the chance.

But they hadn't had that opportunity.

If he'd known how things were going to turn out, would he have done things differently? Maybe the better question is, after everything she's seen and done, would she?

38

MAGGIE

I drive back to the station, eager to find out more about James and Amanda Marsh. Needing to find out how they ended up on that mountain. And, most importantly, where the baby came from.

But when I get to my desk and open the email from Dr. Ricky, all I find are the bare bones of who they are: Their names, ages, and home address. I need more than that. Much more.

I look up the information for the Marshes' local police department and contact the Springfield PD, requesting that they coordinate with me once they locate the next of kin to make the death notification. I'd like to speak with the family while the officers are there to help ensure I get some answers to my growing list of questions.

But I'm not known for being the most patient person. And I don't have time to sit around, waiting for answers. Especially not when there could be a killer in my town.

So I do what most people do. I type Amanda Marsh's name, city, and state into the search browser on my computer and hit enter. Skimming through the results, I choose one for a Facebook profile. I click the link, holding my breath as the page loads. It's her. The dead woman.

Her profile picture shows her and James standing in front of a boat holding hands, looking at each other instead of the camera, smiles wide. They look genuinely happy.

But as I scroll through her page, looking at her photos, searching for clues, each appears to be a perfectly curated moment. There's not a grin at half-mast. Not a hair out of place. This is not reality. This is what Amanda wanted people to believe—not the truth.

So what was? Were she and her husband not as content as she wanted everyone to think? Or was she hiding something else? Perhaps something to do with the baby, who is noticeably absent from the pictures.

Dr. Ricky determined that Amanda Marsh had never given birth to a baby. There are other explanations, though. She could have had a surrogate. It could be her husband's from an affair. They could have adopted. But there's no point wasting time with speculation.

Speaking of wasting time... I type out a lengthy text to Sue. Then I delete what I've written about the acumen of hiring a potential new lieutenant that I already want to fire, and replace it with a text asking how she and the baby are doing. I'm assuming they've left the hospital by now, but I also assumed someone who wanted a job would be professional enough to show up on time, so it's not like I haven't been wrong before.

I turn back to my computer, trying to focus. Usually, I keep the door to my office closed, but since Sue's gone I don't have anyone to run interference for me right now if someone— perhaps even a new-hire candidate—should walk through the door. So I keep it open, which makes it nearly impossible for me to concentrate. Instead of tackling anything from the mountain of tasks I need to accomplish, I find my attention drifting out the window.

The sky is gray. Low-hanging clouds threaten snow. And I can tell by how clear it is and how far I can see that the temperature is dropping.

Across the street, someone in a black hoodie skulks in the shadows cast by the bank. Eddie Diaz. Geesh, that kid is starting to give me the creeps.

I remember hearing about his family when I took over as the Coyote Cove Chief of Police. A father in jail for shooting a gas station attendant while robbing him, several towns over. A mother in jail for neglecting, abusing, and defrauding an elderly patient she was hired to provide homecare for. An aunt living in a trailer on the outskirts of town who—I hope—has kept herself on the right side of the law. She'd returned to the valley a few years ago after finishing up parole for drug charges. As far as I know, Eddie's been living with her since she got back.

I remember when I'd been called to the school when he'd had the knife. He'd had such a stricken look on his face when Principal Bartz mentioned expulsion. At the time, I'd believed him when he said having the knife in his pocket was an oversight, and I'd told the administrator as much. But now? With the way he's been skulking around town in the shadows? I'm not as sure as I once was. It's possible I was wrong.

I'm so lost in thought that I'm taken by surprise as the door opens suddenly. A draft of icy wind swoops in, swirling around my ankles and sending goosebumps sprouting up my legs. I gasp, earning a smirk from the man who enters my office uninvited and drops into the seat across from me.

Clearing my throat, I look at the application in front of me on the desk and say, "Mr. Greer, I presume."

"Yep."

"You're late."

This earns me a one shouldered shrug. "It's a long drive."

There's no arguing with that. And it wouldn't be fair to not give the guy a shot just because I don't like the look of him, with his narrowed eyes and cockily tilted baseball cap, or even the fact that he's wearing a baseball cap at all. I decide that I need a lieutenant more than I need to be judgmental, so I do my best to overlook the bad beginning and launch into the interview. "It says here that you graduated from the academy in Vassalboro almost two years ago. May I ask what you've been doing since then?"

Another shrug. "A little of this, a little of that."

"Which would be?"

"Pay looks pretty low."

"It's the same starting rate as in the rest of the state. Commensurate with experience. I'm still trying to establish whether or not you have any."

"Seems like it should be higher. You know. Like a hazard incentive."

I didn't like the guy from the start, but now I'm starting to actively dislike him. "And why's that?"

He makes a distinctly unattractive noise in the back of his throat. "Everyone knows what happened to your last lieutenant."

Make that hate. I hate him and I hate that I'm desperate enough to continue this conversation. I lean forward, propping my forearms against the edge of my desk. Interlace my fingers. Stare hard into his eyes until he has the sense to look away.

"Are you planning to kidnap a teenage girl and hold her hostage at gunpoint?" I ask.

He grunts. "Not likely."

"Then you shouldn't have anything to worry about. For the most part the job is tourist patrol and domestics, parking tickets, shoplifting, minor infractions."

"Oh, yeah?"

"Yes."

"Well, I heard about the case you're working now and I

gotta say that this town doesn't sound too sleepy or innocent to me. What do you have to say about that?"

"That it doesn't appear that you're the right candidate for the job, Mr. Greer. But I thank you for making the drive up for this little chat."

I wait for him to get up and leave, but he doesn't. Instead, he sprawls out in his chair. Loops his arms around the back. Gives me a long up and down look that makes my skin crawl and my anger boil.

"Listen. Maggie. Let's level here. Obviously this is an example of affirmative action at its finest. And I do mean fine."

His gaze lingers too long on my breasts, and I can't help crossing my arms over them.

"But let's be honest. You need me more than I need you. It's obvious this town's spiraling out of control without a man to keep watch."

I laugh. "Well, Derek. I hate to burst whatever bubble of delusion you're living in, but this town doesn't need a chauvinistic goon with no experience."

"Your negotiating skills need work."

"Then how about this? If you leave right now, I won't tell anyone about this conversation. And if you leave quietly, I won't feel the need to look into why you left the only job you've ever held in law enforcement after only five weeks."

If looks could kill, I'd have to place this guy under arrest. But he's smarter than I thought he'd be. After a long, tense minute, he gets up and slinks silently to the door. He can't resist mumbling a nasty word on his way out, but at least he's gone.

How did he know about what happened on the mountain? Who's he been talking to?

I realize, as I watch him peel out of the parking lot, that I should have grilled him and found out. I'm halfway tempted to jump in my car to follow and give him a ticket, really earn that name he called me, but I decide to let it go. I have enough to handle already. And I'm starting to worry that I'll never have anyone to share the workload with.

Fishing my phone from my pocket, I find I have two missed calls, one from Steve, and one from Margot. Skimming the text Steve sent in lieu of leaving a voicemail, I sigh. The vet wants to keep the dog, who he has apparently named Laurel, another night. He'll be staying with her.

I know that dog probably needs him by her side more than I do. And I love that he's the type of man who cares so much about an animal he just met. But still. I wish he were here with me instead.

I play the message Margot left. It's only five words, but they have me jumping to my feet and racing for the door. I stop at Sue's desk and switch the phones over to call forwarding before turning off the lights and locking the door. I need a hug, a hot shower, and a beer. But I'll settle for talking to Micah Jenkins.

39

MICAH

Sometimes you have to cut your losses. And sometimes, you have to get out while you still can. Which, for him, is looking like ten minutes ago. He stares through the windshield at the old woman standing in front of his car, scowling at him with her arms crossed, the room key he'd just handed back to her clutched in her gnarled hand.

"Listen, lady, you need to move."

"What's the rush?"

"The rush is, I'm ready to go." He tries to return her glare but knows he's outmatched. "You can't do this." His voice gets higher pitched, whinier with each word. "Isn't there a law about holding people against their will?"

"I don't know. Let's ask, shall we?" She lifts her pointy chin toward the Jeep turning into the lot, a Coyote Cove Police Department decal on the door.

He swears. Hits a hand against the steering wheel, cursing his luck as the cop pulls up, blocking him in. Tries to push his face into some semblance of pleasant as she exits the vehicle and approaches him.

"Good evening, officer."

She gives him an insincere smile as she nods at the old lady, who salutes the cop with the room key he'd given her. He realizes what's going on too late, and now he's trapped. Had he guessed earlier, when the lady was blocking his car, he would have abandoned the vehicle and ran. Or, at least, hobbled.

"Is there something I can help you with?"

"Are you Micah Jenkins?"

A knot forms in his stomach. It's worse than he thought. She wasn't just looking for someone—she was looking for him in particular. Even if he somehow managed to escape, she knows who he is. His voice sounds young and feeble as he says, "Yeah."

"May I ask what you're in town for, Mr. Jenkins?"

"Um, just visiting."

"Anyone in particular? Or maybe one of our local sites?"

"Just, you know, in general."

"Well, it's a great little town for that, isn't it?" Before he can answer, she asks, "I was wondering if I could ask you a few questions?"

"Here?"

"We can go down to the department if you'd prefer."

"That's not—I mean, no. Here's fine."

"Are you okay? You look a little..."

Sweaty? Terrified? Guilty? She trails off so he doesn't know what she was going to say.

"Just a little sick. Stomach virus."

"Oh, that's a shame. You should get that checked out. We've got a great little clinic one street over. You ever been there before?"

Swallowing hard, he nods, swiping at the perspiration that's rolled into his eyes.

"Really? What for?"

"Stitches."

"Ouch. What happened?"

"I fell. Hurt myself."

"On your vacation? That's unfortunate."

He nods again, realizes that he hasn't stopped nodding, and forces himself to stop.

"How'd you do it?"

"What?" he asks, chest constricting as he feigns innocence. She's fishing. She has to be. She can't possibly know.

"Fall bad enough to need stitches? I mean, most of the injuries our local doctor sees are from hikers."

"Yeah."

"Yeah, what?"

"I was hiking."

"On a mountain?"

"Yes."

"Which one?"

"I don't remember the name."

"Huh. You really *must* be sick. Well, there's still time to catch the doctor before he closes. Want me to follow you over there so we can get you checked out?"

"That's really not necessary. I just need to get home. Get some sleep."

"Hmm. I bet you're tired. Heard you were out during the wee hours night before last."

His shirt is soaked now, sticking to the small of his back as he shifts in his seat. How the hell did she know that?

"Mind if I ask what you were doing?"

"I was just, you know. Driving around. Sightseeing."

"Overnight?"

There's only one plausible excuse he can think of. "Best time to see moose, right?"

Her face twitches almost imperceptibly. He gives himself a silent cheer. But she misses only a fraction of a beat. "See any?"

"A few."

"Take any pictures."

His mouth goes dry. "Uh-uh."

"Well, that's a shame. I don't suppose there's anyone who can corroborate your story, is there?"

He shakes his head, draws a hand down over his mouth.

"That was the same night you hurt your arm, wasn't it?"

Micah nods, swallowing hard.

"You see, the reason I ask is that we had an incident up on one of our local peaks the same night you were out and about. Rattlesnake Mountain. You ever been there?"

"No." The tremble starts in his feet, works its way up his legs.

"You sure? Might have been the mountain you were hiking when you hurt your arm."

Micah licks his lips, his mouth gone dry. "Yeah. I'm sure. I'd remember a name like that."

"Three people lost their lives up there."

His ribs vibrate. His elbows. "I hadn't heard."

"I was hoping maybe you'd be able to help me out with some questions I have about what happened to them."

"I really wish I could, but I don't know anything."

"No?" Her eyebrows raise as she stares at him. "You didn't see anyone while you were out on your night hike?"

"I, um. Night hike?"

"You said you hurt your arm when you fell. While hiking on a mountain. The nurse said your wound was fresh when you came in first thing yesterday morning to get it taken care of. Means you must have been hiking in the dark. During the same time that something happened to those hikers up on Rattlesnake. And that you were out all night looking for moose."

"I told you. I don't know anything about that."

"Mm-hmm. Well, listen. I know you need your rest. Margot said your room was all paid up through the weekend. But you were trying to check out early? Is that right?"

"I'm si—"

"Sick. Yes, I know. But I'm afraid I'm going to have to ask

that you stay in town for the next couple of days and complete your stay. Do you think you can do that for me?"

He nods, not trusting himself to speak. He clenches his jaw against the quaking that's taken hold.

"Fantastic. I'm sure Margot will be happy to give you your room key back. I really do appreciate your cooperation, Mr. Jenkins. I'll be in touch."

He watches as she gets back into her vehicle and drives off. Then he turns his car off. Climbs out, pulling his duffel bag after him, and limps to the motel office to get his key, outrage brewing silently in his gut.

She can't get away with this. She won't. He just has to figure out what he's going to do about it.

40

MAGGIE

There'd been no mistaking Micah Jenkins' physical reactions to my questioning. The kid was scared. He's hiding something. And I will find out what. He's officially moved to the top of my suspect list.

But I don't have the evidence I need to detain him. I don't even have actual proof that this is a homicide investigation yet, just my gut feeling. Legally, he doesn't even have to stay in town like I requested. None of my suspects do. Let's hope they don't figure that out before I discover what happened up on that mountain.

I check my phone, refreshing my email, hoping to find some communication from Dr. Ricky, but there's nothing from her. There is, however, a quick note from the officer who made the death notification to Justice Panettiere's family.

I check the time, wondering if I'll be able to catch her before shift change, decide to make the call anyway. I dial the number, put the call on speaker, and start the drive home.

"Officer Kelly here."

"Yes, this is Chief Maggie Riley from the Coyote Cove Police Department. I'm calling because I received your email. I believe you informed the Panettiere family of the passing of their son, Justice."

"Yes, thank you. I hadn't expected to hear from you so quickly."

"Well, your message piqued my interest."

"The family piqued mine."

She sounds older, seasoned, and I feel my pulse pick up a notch. If this officer believes there was something notable about her interaction with Justice's family, she's probably right.

"May I ask who you spoke with?"

"I had the distinct pleasure of speaking with his mother and stepfather," she says, the sarcasm in her tone not lost on me. "Or perhaps I should say the pleasure was theirs, because I've never had a family respond in quite such a way to a death notification before."

"How so?"

"They seemed relieved."

"That he was dead?"

"Yes."

What kind of parent wouldn't be devastated by the loss of their child? Or maybe the better question is, what kind of person would you have to be for your parent not to mourn your loss? I think back to Justice's colorful arrest record and realize that I never finished reading through all the charges. It's obvious that I need to take a closer look.

"But I suspect that there'd been some issues between them," Officer Kelly continues. "They didn't know where he'd been living. Had no idea how long he'd been in Maine. Said they hadn't heard from him in a while. And, to be honest, I don't think that they were surprised to find out that he was dead, either."

"Why do you say that?"

"They never asked what happened. Most families, they want to know how they lost their loved one. I got the distinct impression that these people thought they already knew. But on the paperwork I received, the cause of death was listed as undetermined?"

"Yes, that's correct."

"Strange, don't you think?"

"Very." My turn signal clicks loudly in the silence that's descended, accentuating the point. "I really appreciate you taking the time to let me know all this. Would you mind sending me the contact information you found for his family? Everything you have?"

"Anything I can do to help."

I pull into the driveway as we say our goodbyes. Ending the call, I stare at the empty house before me. Even if a kid was a bad person, you'd still imagine the mother would be saddened by his death. Then again, maybe it was that apathy that helped form Justice into whatever it was that he had become.

It really makes you think. And appreciate the people who would care if you were gone. It's been a long day. I need to hear Steve's voice.

41

STEVE

I'm balancing a paper sack of takeout Chinese, struggling to unlock the hotel room door, when my phone rings. I barge my way inside, set the food down, then free my wrist from the stranglehold of a plastic bag full of toiletries before I fumble the cell from my pocket.

I answer as I step back outside, aiming my key fob, watching for the telltale double flash of the headlights as the alarm arms. I give a cursory glance to the two guys huddled in the corner of the parking lot beneath a broken streetlight, before stepping back inside and flipping the deadbolt to the locked position.

"Hello?"

"Hey, it's me."

"Maggie." I'm surprised to hear her voice. She isn't exactly the phone call type. I'm not sure whether to be pleased or worried. "Is everything okay?"

"Yeah, fine."

But I can tell by her tone that something's wrong.

"How's the pup doing?" she asks.

"Good. Alert. They're keeping her mildly sedated right now. They don't want her too active until her ribs get a chance to mend a bit. But it's looking like I'll be able to bring her home tomorrow."

"That's great news."

"It is. I was really worried for a while there."

"Me too."

I know now's probably the time to broach the subject of where this dog is going to live, and how I'd like for her to become a permanent part of our lives, but I chicken out. Instead, I change topic.

"How's the case going?"

"Ugh, don't ask."

"Okay, then how did the interview go?"

Maggie groans. "You want to hear about the case?"

"That good, huh?"

"I don't know what I'm going to do. I desperately need a new lieutenant, but this whole process is ruining my faith in humanity."

"Ha! Ruining something you don't have. Tell me how that works," I say, unpacking small white cartons of Mongolian beef, dumplings, and fried rice.

"Okay, but still. The guy was ridiculous. The scary part is that he was supposed to be one of the better choices."

"I'm sure you'll find someone soon." As soon as I say it I feel bad, because I'm not sure. The truth is, I'm kind of doubtful about the quality of the candidates who are willing to take a position in such a remote corner of the state. The citizens of Coyote Cove were extremely fortunate to get Maggie, although not all of them realize it.

They say that lightning doesn't strike twice, which leaves me to believe that the whole lieutenant thing is going to be a major headache. And the only reason I'm not saying so is because I'm hungry and I want to eat my food while it's still halfway warm, which makes me feel horrible and selfish because I bet she hasn't had anything to eat all day. Though I haven't said anything, I've noticed she's lost weight recently. Enough to worry about.

"Have you eaten?" I ask, walking across the room so I can't smell the aroma of the delicious Chinese food awaiting me.

"What's this thing you call eating?"

"There's a box of the frozen enchiladas you like in the freezer."

"What would I do without you?"

A tiny thrill puffs up my chest. I push it down deep and say, "Well, starve is a good probability."

She laughs. "Seriously, though. I miss you."

"I miss you, too."

"And the pups miss you."

"Give them cuddles for me?"

"Of course. Promise me you'll be home soon?"

I do. But as we say our goodbyes, dark thoughts crowd each other in the back of my mind—would she be in such a rush to get me back if her life wasn't easier with me in it? And if she knew the truth about my past, would there be room for me at all?

42

MAGGIE

Steve sounded weird. Almost like he wasn't happy to hear from me. A variety of scenarios run through my mind, starting with my cop thoughts—is he guilty, hiding something, up to no good —and segueing into my woman thoughts—is he guilty, hiding something, up to no good?

He certainly has the opportunity, alone in a strange town, and the means, an anonymous motel room, but does he have the motive? Steve isn't like that. He wouldn't risk what we have just to see if he could get away with it. He's happy in our relationship.

Only, as I think all these things, I wonder if I'm really right. How many other women have thought the same about their partners only to be proven wrong? There's no denying that things have been different between us lately. Strange. Tense. Something's changed, and I'm not sure either of us quite knows what it is—or what to do to fix it.

But even if I am wrong, it's not like I can do anything about it across all the miles between us. And it's not like I haven't had my life implode on me before. I've survived worse.

The loss of my baby brother. My career. My parents.

There wasn't even a falling out. I seem to have simply ceased to exist to them. Once Brandon was gone, so, apparently, was any desire they'd ever had to be a family.

Is it possible that, like Justice's parents, they'd be relieved to hear of my death?

We haven't spoken in years. They don't seem to mind. Why would they? It's their choice. And though I thought I had gotten over it, ever since Steve and I got engaged, it's been bothering me again. What would the wedding be like?

Me with Sue and Margot and a scant handful of other misfits on my side, and Steve with, what? A whole church full of people? Would we even get married in a church? It seems like this is something we should have talked about by now. Poor Steve doesn't know what he's getting into.

Or maybe I'm wrong, and he does. I was mostly honest when I told him about my past, yet he still chose to fight his way through the layers of scar tissue and hurt that shrouded my heart until he found his way inside. It wasn't easy progress to make. And I can't imagine him being callous enough to risk it lightly. Even if he hasn't been entirely honest with me.

Because that's a game we're both playing. I know he's hiding something. But I'm the one who outright lied. If his reason is half as good as mine, well, who am I to judge? And all that has to do with our pasts, anyways. This is our present. Our future.

I decide that I'm worrying for nothing, I think. Besides, I have my hands full enough at the moment with what's right here in front of me. Quite literally.

I squat to give the two squirming bodies rubs, then buy myself a few free minutes by feeding them. As the sound of crunching kibble fills the kitchen, I grab a beer from the fridge, twist off the cap, and take a long swig. Rummage through the freezer until I find the frozen enchiladas and pop them into the microwave. Sigh with relief as I remove my bra.

The microwave whirs as I power on my laptop, intending to

skim the applications from the candidates that Sue scheduled interviews for on Monday, but before I can an email from Dr. Ricky snags my eye. The one she sent earlier containing Justice Panettiere's arrest record.

This is one of the things I used to love about my job when I was a detective. The math of an investigation. Does one plus two equal three, or do we somehow wind up with five, C, or a killer with a penchant for wearing his victim's skin. I've never actually worked a case where the killer wore his victim's skin, but I once arrested a suspect after tracing the prints left by his prosthetic hand, which seems like it would be almost as unlikely.

Opening the file, I read through the listed charges, skimming past the ones I read earlier. Battery, trespassing, burglary, criminal mischief, kidnapping... I stop, the word drawing my attention like a theater marquee. Kidnapping.

I glance over the rest of the pages, but there are no details surrounding that kidnapping charge. He never served time, so it might not be relevant to my case. It could have been the pissed off parents of a seventeen-year-old girlfriend, for all I know.

And there's a big leap between battery and stealing a child. Two entirely different MOs are at play. Two entirely different victim pools, not to mention probable motives.

But still. I've got a known kidnapper, a sedated baby, and a woman who had never given birth, all up on the same mountain together. Two of them, along with the woman's husband, mysteriously dead. I'm not entirely sure how the pieces fit together yet, but a hazy picture is starting to emerge. And I suspect that Justice Panettiere is my smoking gun.

It would certainly help narrow the focus of this investigation if he'd stolen a baby before, but there's one very important thing that I can't forget. In the end, he ended up dead. Whether this indicates an accomplice, or simply an instance of being in the wrong place at the wrong time, I don't know yet, but the particulars of this past arrest could help point me in the right direction. I need the facts.

Finding the details for the arresting officer, I send him a quick email, asking for the full file for the case. I hit send as the microwave beeps. Grabbing my dinner from the tray, I wonder what this discovery could mean. Mystery solved, or expanded?

The doorbell sounds before I can decide.

I follow the two barking dogs to the front of the house while I struggle back into my bra without removing my shirt. Then I grab my service weapon from the holster on my belt, hanging from the coatrack with my jacket, and tuck it into the waistband at the small of my back, because you never know. We don't exactly get a lot of kids selling Girl Scout cookies and raffle tickets out here.

I nudge the pups back with a foot and crack open the door, find myself staring into the vaguely familiar eyes of an older woman. "May I help you?"

"You must be Mary."

I don't miss the quick up and down glance she uses to appraise me. Nor how she finds something about me distasteful, signified by the slight wrinkling of her nose.

"Where's Steven?"

I'm so stunned that when she pushes a hand against the door, I fail to stop her. The dogs run out, circling, sniffing, jumping up. She shrieks and pushes them off her, brushing at an invisible spot on her white corduroy slacks. Apologizing, I herd them into the guest room off the hall and shut the door, their frantic barks barely muffled by the wooden slab. When I turn back around, she's already inside.

"Steven?" She walks down the hall like she owns the place, leaving me trailing in her wake, and as I take in her profile while her heads swivels from left to right, searching for Steve, I realize what's familiar about her.

Her journey stops at the kitchen, where she turns to face me. "Where is he?"

It's half-accusation. In other circumstances I might make a joke, probably something she'd consider crass and ill-mannered, but fortunately I rein myself in. This is already a bad enough way to meet your future mother-in-law.

"Steve's out of town right now. Just for the night."

"But this is his house, is it not?"

I can see what she's thinking. It's etched clear as day on her heavily made-up face. If I wore that much makeup, I'd look like the kind of hooker who turns cheap tricks in the back of a laundry mat, but somehow the dark eyes and red lipstick works for her, looks classy even. Maybe it's the pearls.

My voice is weak, I can barely hear it myself as I say, "It is."

She takes a step closer, her scrutinizing gaze boring into me. "And where do you live?" *And why aren't you there right now?* remains unspoken between us but is duly heard.

I straighten my spine, rising to my full height until I'm towering almost half a foot over her. It's a petty move, I know, but I don't exactly feel like I have much going for me right now.

"I own the house across the street," I say. I try to fix my sweetest smile on my face, though I'm out of practice and it feels like it might not be a smile at all but more of a grimace or a scowl. I add, "But since our engagement I've been spending most of my free time over here."

"Even when Steven's out of town?"

I want to explain that he left unexpectedly. That I make a comfortable living and don't need her son to support me. That she doesn't intimidate me, which just might be a lie. Instead, I simply say, "Yes."

"Hmph." She looks around, runs a finger along the top of the range hood. "At least it's cleaner than he usually keeps it. I hope you didn't go to too much trouble on my behalf."

I have no reply to that.

"Still, it would have been nice if he'd have let me know he wasn't going to be here when I arrived. I was expecting to see my son tonight, not, well..."

It's a miracle she doesn't finish the sentence. I shove my hands into my pockets to hide my trembling fists. The dogs howl behind their door.

"Do those... things live here too?"

"The dogs? Well, yes. Of course."

She sniffs. "And my son is okay with that? He really *must* be smitten."

I'd known that Steve had never had a pet before, but it had never occurred to me that might have been because he didn't like them. But who doesn't like animals? Apparently, this lady right here. If I had to guess, I'd say she actively hates them. I could totally imagine her driving out of her way to run over baby bunnies—she's giving complete Cruella de Vil vibes.

I swallow hard, trying not to jump to any conclusions that might make the situation worse. I had imagined that meeting Steve's mother would go better than this. Although, when I imagined it, I knew she was coming and wasn't blindsided by her arrival.

"So he knew you were coming?" I ask, managing to keep my tone civil.

"Of course. Didn't he mention it?"

"He must have forgotten."

We fall into an uneasy silence, the woman who used to be number one in Steve's life and the woman who's supposed to be number one now. I think we're both a little disappointed. I suspect neither of us feels much like making nice.

Tension crackles like heat lightning, filling the kitchen with the potential of a storm. I get the impression she expects me to leave. I'd prefer if she did. Before either of us can make a move, my phone buzzes on the counter. As I turn to grab it, I hear, "Is that a gun?"

I pause. If she can't even get my name right, chances are she didn't bother to pay attention when Steve told her what I did —*if* he told her at all. I could point out the uniform that I'm still wearing. But that would require more effort than I feel like making right now. It's been a hard day.

I give her a smile, and while I'm pretty sure this time it might actually look like one, I'm fairly certain that it's coming off as creepy. So I own it. "Why, yes," I say. "It is."

43

GLEN

When Glen looks through the peephole and sees a state police officer standing on the front porch, he thinks, *this is it*. Obviously, he's been found out. They must know. And now he'll probably never get to finish what he's here to do.

He briefly considers ignoring the knock, pretending to not be home. So what if his vehicle is here? He could have gone for a walk. It's possible. But what if the cop sticks around, waiting for him to return? That would make him look even worse than he already does. Reluctantly, he decides there's no use putting off the inevitable.

He opens the door, head hanging low, fully expecting the statie to escort him to the squad car parked in the drive. So it's a surprise when the man, who introduces himself at Officer Kevin Miller, asks if he can come inside for *a little chat*.

He steps back, watching as Miller takes a seat on the couch without being invited, spreading out and tossing an arm over the back, making himself comfortable. Looking like he owns the place as he requests a cup of coffee like he's ordering from a restaurant. Under normal circumstances, it would have riled Glen, but these aren't normal circumstances. He's grateful for this man's arrogance, for the opportunity to retreat to the kitchen to get his head straight.

He wonders what charges he'll be facing as he pulls a mug from the cabinet. He's been fighting the urge to ask Google since he got down off the mountain; if they checked his phone and found the search, it would make him look even guiltier. So he's been watching the true crime channel on cable instead.

It hasn't been much help. All it's done is clue him in to what he should have done, which is leave before the police had an opportunity to respond that first day. Because obviously, being discovered up on the mountain with the bodies proves he had the opportunity. And his motive is unmistakably clear. He wonders if they've discovered the means yet. And if there's a way he could use that to help himself.

He realizes now that he should have had a much better plan before coming to Coyote Cove. Not that the insight will help him now. But maybe if he cooperates, it will buy him some leniency.

He carries the coffee to the living room, offers it to the cop with a trembling hand. Officer Miller takes it and draws a long sip, watching over the rim as Glen settles in the armchair across from him. Glen fights the urge to squirm under the man's scrutiny.

Finally, the cop speaks. "Heard you had the displeasure of meeting the local police chief."

The statement is not at all what Glen was expecting. His first thought is that he heard wrong. His second, as the man sets the mug on the coffee table between them and remains leaning forward, his elbows on his knees, is that the cop is bugged and it's a trap. He struggles to think of a safe reply, but Miller continues before he does.

"On behalf of the state of Maine, I apologize for that. That's why I'm here."

Aware that the conversation might be recorded, Glen says, "I don't understand."

"It's easy. You see, a little birdie told me that you were one of the witnesses who discovered the bodies up on that mountain yesterday. I imagine that must have been quite a shock. And I imagine that shock must have been made even worse by Miss Riley's mishandling of the situation."

Glen swallows hard, not daring to hope. Waiting for the catch.

"I believe there's grounds to file a complaint about the way this investigation has been botched. And I'm hoping I can count on you to help."

He studies the statie, watching as the man strokes the sides of his mustache. He appears completely serious, an Oscar-worthy portrayal of contempt etched across his face. Maybe, Glen decides, his situation isn't as bad as he thought.

44

MAGGIE

I shift from foot to foot, trying to stay warm, but it's a hopeless cause. The stars in the night sky shine brightly, but their heat does little to keep the frigid air here on earth from chilling me to the bone. I eye the French doors as I end the call, longing to go inside, but I don't. Not yet. Besides, it's not all that much warmer in there with Steve's mother.

I'd rather brave the cold than more one-on-one time with her. I'm aware that makes me a coward, but the truth is I'd prefer to be facing off with a criminal, someone with whom I could solve our differences with a gun or a show of force, rather than with that woman. I can't believe Steve did this to me.

I try his phone again, but the call rings out to voicemail. I tell myself he's asleep. And that he didn't know his mom was coming. That he would never intentionally blindside me like this. It doesn't make me want to throttle him any less.

The first text I type is too unpleasant, so I delete it and settle on something simple.

Your mother is here at the house. Surprise??!!

Then I head on inside before I end up frozen solid.

I find her perched on the sofa, both dogs at her feet, staring up at her. Tempest shifts impatiently, and I know we're only seconds away from catastrophe. You don't sit on a terrier's couch without becoming their property. And this woman does not look like the type to welcome—well, anything. But especially not a woolly dog butt on her lap.

I cluck, drawing their attention. Unfortunately, I gain hers as well.

She pins me with a stony gaze. Her left eyebrow arches up so high that any questions about Botox use are ruled out. I'm rescued by the doorbell.

"Who's that? Are you expecting someone?"

I pretend I don't hear her, chasing after the dogs to the front of the house. I'll take whatever diversionary tactics that come my way. Two visitors in one night is straight up unheard of out here, but this, this is serendipity. And it took her long enough to get here. Tossing the door open, I fight the urge to fling myself at her. Sue's arms are already full.

"*Brr.*" She stomps her feet on the mat and comes inside. "Hell of a night to have my heat go out. Sorry to... oh. I didn't realize you had company."

She gives me a questioning look as I take her bag from her. I may have forgotten to mention Steve's mother when Sue called to tell me that her furnace had died. I was too busy thanking the freezing climate and telling her to come over.

But now that she's here, all else is forgotten. My focus is solely on the baby as I scan her features. No cleft in her chin. Earlobes distinctly detached. I'd checked the pictures Sue had sent me of the baby multiple times, but nothing beats seeing with your own eyes—she doesn't share any of the physical genetic traits inherited by the young criminal whose body was found so close to where she was. It doesn't actually prove anything about her parentage, but it's still a relief.

A relief that fizzles as Steve's mother approaches, standing at my elbow like the invisible electric fence that was crackling between us only moments ago has vanished. "Is this your child?"

Sue laughs. If she's noticed that the voice coming from beside me is colder than the polar vortex we had last year, she doesn't let on. I give her a desperate look, and we hold a silent conversation with our eyes that results in her straightening until she's standing at her full five foot two. Despite her lack of height, she's an imposing figure.

"This is the baby Chief Riley rescued yesterday."

"Chief?"

Sue gestures at me with her head. "I don't think Maggie here just wears the uniform because it's cute. 'Cause it's really not."

I feel Steve's mother dragging her gaze over me once again. Is she seeing me with new eyes? Is she finding me any less wanting this time?

"We're going to get out of your hair," I say, trying to think of what I'll need to bring with me. There's a second set of food and water bowls for the dogs at my house, but I'll need toiletries and a clean uniform to wear tomorrow.

"Where are you going?"

"To my house. Across the street."

"When will my son be back?"

"Should be tomorrow."

"And you expect me to stay here? All by myself?"

I open my mouth, but I have no response, because yes, I do, and apparently that's not what she wants to hear.

"That's ridiculous. You're both already here. Let me see her. Why don't you warm up?"

She takes the baby from Sue, carries her over to the couch. "Oh, you're just precious, aren't you? You don't want to go back out into that nasty cold, do you? No you don't."

Watching her with the infant, I can almost imagine her without the prickly edges. Then she turns her stony gaze back to me and the vision vanishes.

"Rescued how? What happened to her?"

Sue sits beside her like she's fearless, a lion tamer without a whip or a worry. "Maggie responded to a call up on Rattlesnake Mountain yesterday. That's one of our local peaks. Three fatalities. Such a shame." She *tsks* and shakes her head. "While she was up there waiting for the state police to arrive, she heard a noise and investigated. Found this little sweetie here and a dog about frozen half to death. Carried them both down for medical attention."

I don't add that I only had to carry them halfway. Or that the dog I rescued is the reason why Steve isn't here right now.

"Well, that's a true miracle, isn't it?" A smile cracks the granite of her face. It doesn't look nearly as out of place as I would have imagined. "I'm Steven's mother, Diane."

"Sue."

"And you work with Mary here?"

"Maggie. And yes. I've worked for the last four police chiefs we've had in this town, and she's by far the finest."

They fall into an easy conversation, fast friends, and it's decided that we'll all spend the night bunking at Steve's like some kind of slumber party, which, in my mind, is on par with the very scariest of horror movies. But that's probably just my opinion. Because despite what the movies tell us when all those coeds get slaughtered onscreen, there's safety in numbers. Right?

45

ERIKA

I scroll through Facebook on my phone while I'm waiting for my frozen dinner to cook, even though I don't like that social media platform. I don't have enough connections on there to make it interesting, but Bridgette sent a request, so here I am, wistfully looking at what everybody else is doing on a Friday night. Dinner, drinks, movies—it all looks so much more appealing than the "Thanksgiving feast" I have to look forward to.

I don't even like turkey, but I wanted to do something special for my cats to make up for my absence. They don't like the dry, cardboard slabs of poultry that come in the vacuum sealed container, either, but they're strangely fond of the stuffing, so here I am, the scent of candied cranberries the highlight of my night while everyone else has fun.

And all for what? I don't think the cats even noticed I was gone.

I exit the app, swearing that Facebook's true aim is to make people think nasty thoughts. In my defense, what's supposed to come to mind when you see one of your frenemies from high school post a selfie that she only *thinks* looks flattering?

I shake my head, trying to erase the image like my memory's an etch-a-sketch, suddenly thankful that I spend so much time in scrubs that I haven't been faced with the challenge other women of my generation seem up against—to embrace appliqué or not?

The microwave beeps and I remove my meal, peel the plastic film off. I'm supposed to stir and put it in for more time, but then it'll be too hot for the cats, and, anyways, after seeing the congealed mess of gravy, it's all theirs.

"Here, kitty, kitty, kitties."

I set the container on the floor and walk away, not even waiting to see if they come get it. Humans can play the disinterested game, too. I've got the opposable thumbs and the ability to open food containers—if I can hold out long enough, I'll win eventually.

Dropping onto the couch, I open my email on my phone, pleased to see that I've received the bloodwork results from my mountain decedents. Guess I'm not the only one with nothing better to do on a Friday night. I turn the TV on while I'm waiting for the PDF to load. Scan the results while also scoffing at a commercial showing cats that actually crave their human's attention.

Please. I wonder what kind of cat crack they used to get that kind of reaction. The poor actress probably has tuna juice all over her hands. I refuse to sink that low.

"Nope, not that desperate yet," I call to the invisible felines lurking somewhere inside my house. Although that head nuzzle to the cheek looks nice. And that sweet-looking kitty seems happy to do it.

"Maybe you guys are broken. I wonder if I could trade you in..."

Then suddenly I'm not thinking about affectionate cats or ungrateful cats or any cats at all. I lean forward, spreading my fingers on the screen to enlarge the image, making sure I'm seeing this right. Hold my breath as I exit the older male's lab work, download, and open the younger male's, and then the female's.

I've seen results like these before. Once. On the labs of a ten-year-old boy who died during an appendectomy due to an error made by the anesthesiologist. I absolutely shouldn't be seeing anything like that here.

I get up and head for my home office, everything else forgotten. I find my dusty copy of the *Physician's Desk Reference* on the bottom shelf of my bookcase, which only answers a fraction of the questions I have, so I boot up my computer and run a quick search. My blood chills as I scan the results.

My hands shake as I pat my pockets down. Empty. Cursing, I search the house for my cell, finally finding it twenty minutes later on the shelf where I'd taken the book from. Figures.

I'm so keyed up that it takes me three tries to enter the right passcode, two more to access my contacts to find the right number. I run nervous fingers through my hair, the roots damp with sweat, as the phone rings. The call goes to voicemail. I try again, same result.

I stare at the time on the microwave. As the digital readout claims another minute, I make my decision. I'm not sure what help I'll be. She's the one with the gun, but I'm the one with the intel. I've got to do something. Chief Riley needs to know that she's dealing with a very dangerous situation.

46

STEVE

A door slams. Angry voices exchange terse words that should probably be kept private. It takes me a minute to realize I'm not in a dream, to recognize my foreign environment, and remember the reason why I'm here.

I'm stiff and groggy, fully dressed on top of a scratchy, multicolored quilt. Rubbing my eyes, I smear a sticky substance that smells like soy sauce onto my face. I sit up, spilling a half-empty carton of cold rice. Under normal circumstances, I'd be grumbling by now. But not today. I'm looking forward to going home, to sleeping in my own bed again, next to the woman I love.

Stumbling to the bathroom, I take a long leak, then turn on the water in the shower, cranking the heat. Strip as I wander back into the room, looking for something to drink. Spot my phone peeking out from under the bed, grab it to pop it on the charger, then remember I don't have one. I suppose it'll have to wait until I'm in the car.

I press my finger to the sensor to check how much battery I have left and see a text from Maggie.

Your mother is here at the house. Surprise??!!

Oh, shit. How could I have forgotten? And I thought *I* had a bad night.

I press call. Rack my brain for what I can do to make this better. Gifts, apologies, favors—nothing seems like enough. Because it isn't.

I'll be the first to admit that my mother is not an easy woman. She's blunt and judgmental and if she doesn't like you she has no qualms about making it known. And Maggie? Maggie has no patience for people who play games and can be brutally honest when she speaks her mind.

While I believe Maggie loves me enough to take a heaping serving of my mother's abuse for the sake of our future together, she has her limits. She's not going to just lay down and be a doormat. If anyone could make her lose her cool and snap, it's my mother. Which is probably why whenever I've imagined the two of them in a room together, even my most optimistic visions of them meeting have not gone well.

I love them both. My mother from a distance and Maggie with a grain of salt. I hold no hopes that last night went well. And since Maggie isn't answering her phone, I'm slightly concerned about their welfare.

But I can't decide who my money's on to have survived the night. Maggie has a gun, sure, but bullets are no match for my mother's barbed tongue and poison dart eyes, the pitchforked tines of her wrath. I've done nothing to prepare Maggie for this. Whatever's happened, it's all my fault. I need to get back home, and fast.

47

MAGGIE

I've never felt like such a third wheel before. Don't get me wrong, I'm both relieved and grateful that Sue and Steve's mom are getting along so well. I can't even imagine how last night would have gone without Sue's intervention. And if she hasn't quite turned Diane into a fan of mine yet, it's not for lack of trying.

But I've got a million things I've got to do and none of them include trying to find a way to get out of the house without being rude. Just because they've found common ground, fussing and doting on the baby, doesn't mean that's the way I can spend my day.

I peek through the window, hoping they'll finish in the kitchen and move on before the dogs are done outside. When I spot Diane preparing to brew a second pot of coffee, my hopes are dashed. I retreat, pressing my back against the wooden side of the log cabin before she can see me.

It's Saturday. I have three suspicious deaths to investigate, along with the mystery of the baby and who she belongs to. I need to follow up on my request with the NCIC. Track down the details of Justice Panettiere's kidnapping arrest. Check in with Dr. Ricky to see if we have a cause of death yet. And I'd like to speak with the Marshes' next of kin.

Instead of making calls and reading case files while sitting on the couch with my dogs, who I don't get to spend enough time with, I'm forced to go into the office for some privacy. Which, under these circumstances, I'll gladly do. I just don't want to have to run the gauntlet before starting what should be the more challenging part of my day. Who has the energy for that? I wish Steve would hurry up and get back already.

Shouldn't I have heard from him by now? Unless he went into hiding when he saw my message that his mom was here. He's probably halfway to the border right now, haggling over the purchase of a new identity.

I snort a laugh at the thought, drawing the dogs' attention. Now they want inside. And since I just realized that I probably haven't heard from Steve because I don't have my cell, and I can't remember the last time I actually saw my phone—aka the town of Coyote Cove's after hours and emergency number—there's no way I can put it off any longer.

I open the door and slip inside after the dogs, hoping to remain unnoticed, but no such luck. Diane spots me immediately, closing the distance between us like a shark zeroing in on a seal. At least there's a baby between us.

"There you are. Here."

She holds the infant out to me. I stare at her. She stares back, hazel eyes large and curious.

"Well? Aren't you going to take her?"

I know this shouldn't be a big deal. It's not like I haven't held the baby already. I carried her halfway down a mountain. But now, when there's no dire need, when there are other, more qualified arms around, it just seems unnecessary. It's a bad idea. One that dredges up too many unwanted memories.

"Here, I'll take her."

Sue swoops to my rescue and I make a note to give her a

raise. Diane hands the baby over, but not without that eyebrow arch that I hope I don't have to get used to. The curiosity is plain to read in her eyes, but there's something else there, and I can read that, too.

What kind of a woman doesn't want to hold a baby?

This kind. The kind that sees terrible things, who lives immersed in a world of the horrors people inflict upon each other. The kind that worries she'll sully an innocent child just by taking it in her arms, like all the evils I've witnessed will seep into the baby by osmosis. The kind who's had her heart irreparably broken by the loss of a child already.

My throat tightens at the thought of Brandon. The empty space inside me he's left behind. The vengeance I long for, and what I plan to do to get it if I'm ever given the chance.

I'm not ashamed of the way I feel, but it's not something I care to explain, either. And I imagine it's probably not a desirable quality to find in a future daughter-in-law.

"I don't suppose you have any baby shampoo?" Diane asks.

I scan the countertops, shift a stack of catalogs. No phone. "I have some dog shampoo you can use."

Her look of shock is priceless.

"It's organic. All natural ingredients. Plant-based cleaners. Doesn't have any of the chemicals most shampoos are full of."

She's still gaping at me like I suggested throwing the baby in the dishwasher during the rinse cycle.

"It's human grade. I use it myself all the time." I clench my jaw, pinning my tongue firmly in place before I say something I can't take back, and move into the living room. Check the coffee and end tables. Run my hands between the couch cushions, searching. I find two peanuts and half a cracker. The dogs are slacking.

But this is serious. Worst-case scenarios of all the emergency calls I might have missed run through my imagination—a child wandering off, a multi-car pileup, a fire, a burglary, a murder. I draw a shaky breath, duck my head back into the kitchen and say, "I have to go to the office for a while. I can get some baby shampoo on my way back if you'd like."

"That won't be necessary. I'm sure I'll have taken care of the issue well before then."

I count to five in my head. Count another five. Realize I could count to a billion by fives and it still won't change anything.

I've got to get out of this house and do my job. But first, I have to find my phone. Even if that means asking for help. "Well, I'll be off then." Reluctantly, like it's an afterthought, I add, "I don't suppose either of you has seen my phone?"

"Oh, I put that in your purse last night for you."

I swivel to face Diane. Swallow down some anger, chase it with a shot of rage. Fight to keep my voice steady as I say, "What? Purse?"

"The one on the coatrack by the door. I assumed that was the one you were using. Was I wrong?"

She isn't. That is the purse I use. The once or twice I year that I actually carry one.

Anxiety claws at my chest as I rush into the hallway, my eyes briefly meeting Sue's on the way past. She knows what a big deal this is, the fact that the phone has been out of my possession, unmanned, all this time. This could be a disaster.

Then again, it might not. I might be getting ahead of myself. Last night could have been like the three hundred and thirtysomething days a year that the phone remains silent after hours.

Even if it was, my negligence is unacceptable. This isn't like me. I can't believe I let myself get thrown off my game so badly. And why? Because my fiancé's mother showed up and decided not to like me? So what? I usually don't succumb to my petty first world problems.

Okay, that's a lie. I'm human. I totally do. But there's a time and a place, and it's not while handling an investigation of this nature.

I find the purse Diane was talking about and plunge my hand inside, both eager and dreading the discovery. Four missed calls.

My teeth throb from being clenched, a sharp pain lancing up behind my left eye as I scroll through the call list. One from Steve. No biggie there. And the other three, two from last night and one from this morning, placed just minutes ago, are all from Dr. Ricky.

I give the pups a quick pat and yell a goodbye toward the kitchen as I blink away the black spots encroaching on the edges of my vision. I think I was halfway to a panic attack. This is bad, but it could have been so much worse. If Dr. Ricky's calling, it's probably about the case, which means no one new is dead. At least, I hope.

48

CHERYL

She'd had a plan. She'd had this whole grand idea of what she was coming back here to accomplish. To the town where they'd spent their honeymoon. To the place where they'd once been happy.

And she had been so close. All she'd needed was another twenty minutes, maybe thirty. Instead, she'd been forced to switch gears.

Even so, if she'd only been able to able to get out of Coyote Cove right away, put some distance between her and what had happened on the mountain, everything would have turned out so very differently.

But those flat tires had thrown her. Not one, but two. They'd made escape an impossible task. She suspects she has Chief Riley to thank for that. And more.

All the extra time has forced her to rethink her next step. Now she's suspecting that it's a good thing that she got trapped in this tiny, claustrophobic little town. Because she has a new plan brewing. And it might actually be better than the first.

There may be another option. Maybe not for her to get everything she wanted, but for her to move on from this. Escape with a new lease on life. The more she thinks about it, the more she likes this new idea.

But she needs to take her time, do things right. Really think her steps through this time. The only way to successfully put this behind her is to be thorough and make sure she doesn't leave anything to chance. And that's just what she intends to do.

49

ERIKA

I'm staring at my phone when it goes off, yet I'm still caught by surprise. I fumble the device and it falls into the passenger side footwell. I groan as I chase after it, the crick in my neck falling into spasm, tightening in protest against the stretch. I'm left slightly breathless by the whole ordeal.

"Hello?"

"I'm so sorry I missed your calls, I, my... There's no excuse."

Chief Riley sounds strange. Much less composed than I've become accustomed to.

"Is everything all right?"

There's a long pause even though it seems like that should be an easy answer. Though I suppose I wouldn't have asked if I wasn't slightly worried that it wasn't. And I certainly wouldn't have driven halfway across the state overnight.

"Never mind," I say. "Listen, where are you?"

"At home. I'm getting ready to leave for my office. Why?"

"Is there any place around where I can get a cup of coffee?"

"Uh... around where? Where are you?"

"In the parking lot outside your office."

"What! Why?"

"Long story, and I need coffee to tell it." I scan my surroundings for the dozenth time this morning. Coyote Cove is tinier than I thought it would be. As in none of the stores have websites, and zeroing in on my location using the GPS app on my phone reveals no local businesses of any kind.

I hear the hesitancy in her voice as she invites me to her place. The regret as she gives me her address. And though I could be polite and provide her with an easy out, I choose not to. Because I'm tired, I'm cranky, and I don't feel safe—I'd much rather keep company with someone who has a gun than be alone right now.

I'm wondering why anyone in their right mind would choose to live in a place so remote as I drive out of town. I decide the easy answer is they don't, and Chief Riley is crazy. Then I round the corner and gasp. Breaking to a sudden stop, I drink in the view.

A hazy mist paints the mountains before me in pastels. The whitecapped peaks spread as far as the eye can see to the horizon, an endless, undulating blanket of beauty. Shades of rose and tangerine have yet to be burned away by the rising sun. I think I'm beginning to understand.

I continue down the road, struggling to find the almost hidden turnoff to Loon Lane. Finally locate the road on my second pass and make the turn. Come to a halt once again, this time as a family of deer cross right in front of me. I'm about ready to pack up my bags and my cats and start searching property listings until I remind myself why I'm here, which is all the impetus I need to hit the gas and hurry on my way.

She must have been keeping watch for me, because the front door opens as soon as I pull up. I grab my bag and dash across the yard. It's much colder than it was a couple of days ago. The air has the thin, crisp feel of impending snow. God, I hope I'm out of here before then. The last thing I need is to get stranded by impassable roads with no place to stay.

Chief Riley ushers me inside the house and leads the way to the kitchen, where she pours me a steaming cup of coffee. I take a long sip, burning my tongue in the process, but it's worth it—it feels like a layer of fog lifts off my brain.

"You have a lovely home," I say, trying to be polite. And it is nice. It's just that there's an empty, abandoned feel to the place.

"Thank you. Although I spend most of my time at Steve's. My fiancée's."

That would explain it. "That's the guy who hiked up to get the dog?"

"Yes."

I try to think of an appropriate thing to say, but the truth is, I've never been good at small talk. It's like a wood-boring insect slowly drilling a hole into my brain—complete torture. I need to tactfully find a way to broach the reason for my visit.

"Why are you here?"

Or Chief Riley can do it for me.

"I needed to talk to you about the case."

"Why? Have you determined the victims' cause of death? What was so important that you had to drive all the way up here to tell me in person?"

"Geesh, you'd know already if you'd just let me talk." I slap a hand over my mouth, appalled by my rudeness. "I'm sorry, I—"

"No, don't be. It's my fault. I've never been very patient."

"Neither have I."

"Please." She gestures toward me. "I'll keep my mouth shut. I promise."

I nod. Draw a deep breath. And say, "I've discovered the probable cause of death for all three victims. And through cause, the manner. We're dealing with a very dangerous drug here, and whoever administered it is a very dangerous person."

Chief Riley lied. She didn't keep her mouth shut. In fact, it's hanging wide open.

50

MAGGIE

"Hold on. Say that again?"

"All three decedents recovered from the mountain were drugged. I believe they were victims of homicide."

I rub a hand over my mouth like I'm the one who said it and the words tasted foul. I mean, I was ninety-nine percent positive, but having those suspicions confirmed? Let's just say there's not always a thrill in being right.

"Is there any way their deaths could have been accidental?"

"None." Dr. Ricky adjusts her glasses. "I'm ruling the cause of death as asphyxiation due to succinylcholine, a powerful, fast-acting paralytic only used during surgery or to assist in intubation, and only then in conjunction with a respirator since patients can't breathe on their own once their lung muscles are paralyzed. There's absolutely no recreational use. Once administered, it's a matter of minutes before a patient is fully incapacitated."

"How's it given?"

"It's injected. Either intravenously or intramuscularly."

The last thing I want to do is hike back up that mountain. "I didn't notice any needles by the scene."

"Neither did I."

"How far could they have gotten once injected?"

"Not very."

I stare down at my boots, tapping my foot impatiently while I think. Notice for the first time a stain on the left toe in the shape of a bird. "Did you find any injection marks on the bodies?"

Dr. Ricky shakes her head. "No, but that's easy enough to miss, especially if you don't know to look."

"Do you think one of our victims would have had time to inject themself and then toss the needle in the woods?"

"Well, anything's possible. But I have to say, succinyl-choline paralysis would not be a pleasant way to die. In essence, you'd be conscious, aware of what was happening as your lungs stopped working and you slowly suffocated to death. I can't imagine anyone choosing to do that to themselves. Can you?"

"People do plenty of crazy things that I don't understand, but no."

"That's why I'm here." She gets up and helps herself to another cup of coffee.

I look down at my own cup and notice it's empty. Something tells me we're going to need another pot. Or three. "We still can't rule out suicide, though. We can't rule out anything at this point."

Dr. Ricky leans against the counter, facing me. Holds my gaze as she asks, "You want to hike back up the mountain and look around?"

I'm embarrassed by the sound that comes out of my mouth. "Not in this lifetime. Besides, if they gave the syringe a good toss? I'm pretty sure finding a needle in a haystack would be easier than on a mountain."

"Quite possibly true."

"I think the best way to proceed would be to assume that there was a fourth party up there, one who administered the drug to the deceased, until we can prove otherwise." Which is exactly what I've already been doing.

"That's what I thought, as well. And I have to stress that if there is a fourth person that we're dealing with, they're extremely dangerous. It's not even a question of their mental state. It's a matter of how easily it would be for them to strike again. Undetected."

A shudder runs down my spine as I consider what she's said, because she's right. An intramuscular delivery means a quick needle jab is all it would take. You'd think you got stung by something, or bit, and by the time you knew something was wrong it would be too late to tell anyone what was happening to you.

For all we know, there's no connection between Justice Panettiere and the Marshes. The attacks could have been random. This could have been some sick psycho's trial run. They could just be getting started.

Whoever did this could find their way into the middle of a crowd and just start poking. A wave of nausea crashes against me, makes my head spin. Because an even more terrifying thought just occurred to me—what if this drug has the same effect when ingested?

My voice wavers as I ask, "Are there any other ways this drug could be administered?"

Dr. Ricky frowns. "I didn't see anything mentioned in the literature. That's not to say there's not, but none that are used medicinally. Why?"

"I was just wondering if it could be used to poison someone's food or drink."

"Oh, God. I certainly hope not."

This is one of those cases that every law enforcement officer dreads. If you issue an alert, let people know what's going on, you'll cause a mass panic. If you don't, you're leaving them unaware and defenseless. It's a tough decision and I'm not going to claim that I haven't made the wrong one before.

"So. What are we going to do?" she asks.

"We?"

Dr. Ricky shrugs. "I couldn't help but notice before that you're a little understaffed. I'm not a detective, but I have forensic training, I'm meticulous, and I'm here to help."

"Thank you. I appreciate it." I really do.

I get up, pace to one side of the kitchen, turn and head back, again, and again, and again, while I think. What I want most is to call Steve and tell him not to come back yet. But that wouldn't be fair, would it?

Finally, I stop and return to my seat. "There are two things that will tell us more about this case. One is the victims. We need to determine whether they knew each other. And their possible assailant. Which is going to be hard considering that they can't actually tell us."

I fall silent, staring at my hands folded on the table. How many times lately have I wondered what my left will look like with a ring on it? Seems kind of ridiculous right about now.

"And the other?" Dr. Ricky asks.

I swallow hard, not wanting to say what else is on my mind. But sometimes being the good guy also means being a villain. I clear my throat and voice my darkest thought, even though doing so makes me feel like I'm spitting up my insides. "The baby. It's possible that she's what this was all about."

I do my best to ignore the horrified expression on Dr. Ricky's face as I continue. "She's the piece of the puzzle that makes the least sense. If you're killing everyone, why leave her behind? Alive? Unless you couldn't find her. Or," I swallow hard as I think about the drugs found in the infant's system, "you didn't know she was there."

It's been bothering me since I found the child, where she was, how she was hidden. Would the dog have been capable of all that, instinctually knowing that the baby needed to be protected? Or was she placed there on purpose, by human hands, as a means of keeping her safe?

I rub my neck, unable to dispel the feeling of being watched. Were the victims merely killed? Or were they hunted?

51
ERIKA

I forgot how cold it was while we were in the house. It makes me pause as soon as I'm out the door, wanting to run back inside. I turn to do just that, but Chief Riley is blocking the way.

Her nose twitches like an animal scenting the air. Something about the slow way she scans the woods around us makes my skin crawl. It's like watching a predator tracking its prey.

"Everything all right?" I ask.

"Fine." She flashes a sorry excuse for a smile my way, then locks the door, effectively sealing off my escape route. Now there's only one way, and that's forward.

I fall into step beside her, giving my car a wistful glance as we continue down the drive on foot. Flurries drift lazily from a sky the color of a frozen lake. I have a million concerns about what will happen if it snows heavily and I get trapped up here, but I'm hesitant to voice them. After all, aren't I getting what I wanted—in on the investigation?

As if she can read my mind, Chief Riley says, "Don't worry, we've got plenty of emergency supplies in case the weather turns."

"I suppose you have to be prepared when you live this far north."

"It helps."

I want to ask how she found her way here, to this tiny town that appears to be perched on the edge of the Arctic Circle, because even though she's never said that she came from elsewhere, it's obvious. It's more than her lack of a New England accent. More than the way she looks even more miserable than I am from the cold, or the suspicious way she eyes the sky, like it's an enemy she doesn't trust.

There's a story there, I'm sure of it. Just like I'm sure that, since we've reached our destination, the chance to ask has passed.

She stomps her boots heavily on the front steps then wipes them on the mat before entering. I follow suit, trailing seconds behind her, along with a couple of terriers, as she leads the way into a dining room where two women sit, fussing over a baby in a carrier. They both look up in surprise at our entrance.

"That was fast." The woman who speaks gives me a curious look.

"Never left. Sue, this is Dr. Erika Ricky. She's the pathologist assisting with the case. She drove up to lend us a hand with the investigation."

I can tell by Sue's expression that she knows this is highly unusual. Her smile grows strained as she darts a glance at the woman beside her, obviously reluctant to speak freely in front of her.

"Well, that's... excellent news," Sue says, standing and beckoning for me to join them at the table. "Welcome. You look cold. Can I get you some coffee?"

"That would be wonderful, thank you." I drop into the offered chair.

"And this is Diane," Chief Riley gestures to the mystery woman. "My, um, fiancé's mother."

Which explains any reluctance to talk shop in front of her. But it's probably the disapproving wrinkle of her nose and the way her eyes harden every time they land on her future daughter-in-law that explains why Chief Riley is already backing her way out of the room.

Sue returns and sets a mug in front of me. I smile gratefully, wrapping my hands around it and letting the steam rising from the top warm my face.

The chief rubs her lips together as she darts a glance at her future mother-in-law. Her expression is tense as she says, "Sue, could you please give the state police a call and request some additional assistance, perhaps a detective or two?"

I notice the look they exchange, the silent conversation that's taking place. "Of course. What should I tell them?" It's clear she's asking more than that.

"Just that we'd appreciate it if they could send some backup. As soon as possible."

"Mm-hmm. I'll get right on that." Sue's obviously censoring what she really wants to say. Instead she asks, "Is there anything else?"

The chief stares at the infant, frowning. "At this point, we have one key that doesn't seem to fit into any of our locks. I'll speak with the victims' families, see if anyone knows anything about her." She gestures with her head toward the child.

"In the meantime, I'd like you to upload pictures of the baby and contact the missing persons databases. And if you could cross-reference the victims, see if you can find any connection between Justice and the Marshes, maybe check their social media accounts, that would be helpful. Any answers we can get are more than we have now."

She stops her retreat and crosses the room, dropping to a squat beside Sue. Her voice is muffled as she rustles around by the floor. "Don't hesitate to contact me. For any reason. And be careful." Her knees crack as she rises. "I'll be back as soon as I can."

Diane looks relieved to see her go, but Sue doesn't. If anything, she looks spooked, and I don't blame her. I saw what Chief Riley gave her before she left. A small firearm from an ankle holster that had been strapped above her boot. And though, in theory, I realized that I was putting myself at risk by coming here, it was just that—theory.

There'd been none of the physical symptoms that you associated with fear. No rapid heartbeat or aching stomach or lightheadedness. Nothing. But that was a minute ago. Because now? I have them all.

52
GLEN

His heart pummels against the walls of his chest. His pulse rages in his ears. And as Glen pushes his body harder against the trunk of a pine, willing himself invisible, he doesn't even dare breathe. Until he has no choice.

He released the stale air in his lungs slowly, careful not to move. Inhales just as cautiously. As the spots around the edges of his vision fade and his brain reoxygenates, he's sure he must have been mistaken. He must have imagined it.

He's paranoid, that's all. What did he expect after spending all that time isolated in the rental cabin, thinking of dead people and prison sentences? It's no wonder that when he'd finally forced himself out into the cold for some exercise, he panicked.

The explanation allows his heartbeat to return to normal. The sound of his rushing blood subsides. He listens hard, hears nothing but the soft rustle of his coat against the tree; the last of the dead leaves clinging to the birch behind him rattle in the wind.

But he has to be sure.

He inches his head forward, the rasping noise as his cheek scrapes painfully against the bark ridiculously loud in his ears.

His skin stings as he peers around the edge of the tree. His eyes widen and his body freezes.

There she is. The police chief. Maggie Riley.

He wasn't imagining things at all.

His sinuses leak from the cold as he watches her walk up a driveway with another woman beside her. A slow trickle of snot trails down his upper lip, tickling him, threatening to make him sneeze. His nose twitches. He wills it to behave.

He only has to remain still and quiet for a few more seconds. He's not sure he's going to make it.

The women climb up the front steps of a cabin and disappear inside. The moment the door shuts behind them, Glen grabs his nose, his body lurching as he stifles the sneeze with his hand. When he's done and he's satisfied his body isn't going to betray him, he pushes his back against the pine, eyes closed, and processes what he just learned.

That cabin must be Chief Riley's home. The cop had led the way. The other woman seemed hesitant and unfamiliar with her surroundings.

What are the odds that he'd wind up renting a place two doors down from the chief of police?

Glen pushes away from the tree and retraces his steps back to his rental. Part of him is nervous to discover his proximity to the police officer. But the other part thrills at what he's discovered. Because now that he knows where she lives, he knows where she's the most vulnerable. And that's an advantage that he might need to leverage.

53

STEVE

Maggie's coming down the front steps of the cabin just as I arrive. I wish it was solely to greet me, but I have good reason to suspect otherwise. I knew my mother was here, but who else? I pull into what's beginning to look like a parking lot and exit the car.

Cocking an eyebrow at the other vehicle, I ask, "Full house?"

Maggie releases an exasperated sigh. "If only you knew. But hey. You're home."

She closes the distance between us. As much as I long to hold her, give her a kiss, whatever she has in mind, I don't. Who knows who's watching?

My reluctance to show affection stops Maggie short. A hurt expression flashes across her face, is gone so quickly I can tell myself it was never there, even if we both know otherwise. She turns to the car instead and peers through the window.

"How's the patient?"

"Fine. Good. I mean, the vet expects her to make a full recovery."

"That's great."

"How's the case?"

"Potentially more dangerous than I originally thought."

"I don't like the sound of that."

She gives me a sharp look. "And you think I do?"

I glance at the cabin. Lowering my voice, I say, "Let's not right now, okay?"

"That's right. Wouldn't want anyone watching to think we actually know each other, would we?"

This isn't like the Maggie I know, the woman who understands all my odd quirks and loves me anyways. Then again, I did just rebuff her attempt to welcome me home. I'm an adult. Why am I so concerned that my mother might see us together?

"I'm sorry. It's just. It's been a rough couple of days. For both of us," I add, reaching out to wrap my arm around her, drawing her in for a hug, potential audience be damned. Her head tucks into the hollow of my shoulder where it fits so well. She sags against me.

"I'm glad you're home," she says.

"I am, too."

"Now go away."

"Huh?"

She draws away from me so I can see she's not kidding. The tense set of her mouth pulls her whole face down. Dark shadows ring her eyes. "I'm serious, Steve. I want you to pack up and take the dogs somewhere safe."

I exhale with relief. She's not through with me, then. "And leave you behind?"

She nods, looking like she's ready to cry.

I shake my head, letting her know that's never going to happen. Give her a wry smile. "What about my mom? Should I leave her behind? With you?"

Maggie snorts. "She's more Tyrannosaurus than goat, I wouldn't worry about her."

"I don't get it."

"*Jurassic Park?*"

"Ah, gotcha." I give her my best grin until it occurs to me that her words might have a double meaning. "But then who's that make the bait?"

She doesn't answer.

"Maggie?"

"Sue's inside with the mountain baby. Her heat went out last night, but given what's going on, I'd like them to stay, whether her furnace gets fixed today or not."

"And what is going on?"

She ignores me. "The pathologist working on the case is here, too. Dr. Ricky. Her car's parked over at my place."

"The pathologist? Why?"

"And I gave Sue my backup piece."

"A gun? Jesus, Maggie. What have I missed? What aren't you telling me?"

"Just being cautious."

"Why the need?"

She fakes a smile. I watch her struggling to come up with a lie. Her face crumbles as she says, "Not sure there is one, yet."

"Level with me."

"I might have a triple homicide on my hands."

"Might?"

"We don't have enough evidence yet to either rule out or prove murder–suicide."

But I know her. If she's this worried, she has her suspicions, and Maggie's gut is rarely wrong. So I call her out on it. "Then why all the fuss? It's not like you to overreact."

"Because it's my job to work under the assumption that those people were murdered. And if it is a homicide, the drug the killer used is very dangerous. And very easy to administer. But, you know, you could be right. I could be overreacting." She reaches for my hand, slips hers inside my palm. "Until we know for sure, though, I want you to promise me you'll be careful."

"And what about you?"

"Don't worry about me." She squeezes my fingers before she lets my hand drop, backing away. "I'm always careful. Remember?"

I do remember. I remember her waving herself like a red flag in front of a bull, only the bull was her gun-toting, crazed lieutenant and the flag was her lying that she'd killed a man and framed his father to draw his aim. I spin around to call after her, force her to stop, but she's already vanished down the driveway.

Last time was too close. I almost lost her. And I feel like it's happening all over again.

54

ERIKA

Is every day as a detective as frustrating as this? If it is, I don't think I could take it. I like the dependability of my job, the way the inner workings of a body provide concrete answers. Sure, there are cases, people, and bodies where some answers remain unknown, but nothing like this. This is... insanity.

I glare at my phone for letting me down, then shift my gaze to the baby sitting in a car seat on the table. I feel my face soften as I watch her kick her tiny, socked feet. Half her fist is in her mouth. The other half glistens with drool.

But she's not the one pinning me with an intense gaze. I try to give Diane a smile. I'm fairly certain I fail miserably.

"Why don't you pick her up? Hold her for a while?" she asks.

"Oh. No, thanks. I'm good."

"Really. It's not good for her to spend all her time lying on her back like that."

I glance across the table at Sue, but she's reading whatever's on her phone screen with deliberate focus. Steve's outside with Chief Riley's dogs, and the one he brought back from the vet today, Laurel, is curled up asleep on a chair at the table. There's no one to help divert Diane's attention from me.

"Trust me. She'd prefer if I didn't. Babies don't like me."

"I don't get what it is with you professional types. Like kids are infectious or something."

I could point out the truth in that statement, that children are known for carrying and transmitting germs more readily than adults, but she doesn't give me the chance.

"I mean, Maggie acted like she'd rather poke her own eye out than hold the baby."

Sue looks up at the mention of her boss and joins the conversation. "Maggie's issues aren't with the baby, but herself."

Diane's eyes sparkle as they turn toward Sue. I can't decide if it's with curiosity or malice. "What do you mean?" she asks.

Sue looks like she wishes she'd kept her mouth shut, but explains anyway. "She had a much younger little brother. She was already grown, I think she was already a detective when he was born, if that gives you any idea about the age difference. But they lost him. He was taken when he was still quite young. Her department wouldn't let her work the case, the man she knows was responsible was never charged. As absurd as it seems, I think a part of her blames herself for what happened."

Now she's got my interest, too. "Is that why she's up here?"

Sue shrugs. "Maybe at first, but that's not why she's stayed." She glances toward the back door leading to the yard where Steve is still outside. "Anyways, it's understandable if she's standoffish with babies. She might not survive having her heart broken like that twice. But she doesn't let it interfere with her job. As I understand it, she carried that baby halfway down the mountain in her arms."

She looks to me for confirmation and I nod.

Diane reaches forward and caresses the baby's cheek, then says, "Well, I still don't think it's good for her to spend so much time in that car seat. Where's her carrier?"

"She doesn't have one," Sue answers.

"Her sling, then."

Sue's head shakes. "She doesn't have one of those, either. It was my understanding that no baby items were found on the mountain. Just the baby."

"That's correct," I say.

"Not even a bottle? Or diapers?" Diane asks.

"No. Nothing."

"Well, that's crazy. I don't care who you are, there's no way anyone got an infant up a mountain without any of those things."

"None were recovered at the scene," I reaffirm.

"Then someone must have taken them with them."

I search Sue's expression, which only confirms that it's true. Silence descends as we absorb the implications of the statement. We've been working on the basis of assumption, but this seems like pretty clear confirmation to me. There was definitely a fourth person up on that mountain.

The killer. And whoever it is, they're still loose. But where?

55

MAGGIE

The Jeep door opens with a loud creak. My right knee answers with a crack and a pop as I climb inside. I turn the key in the ignition, the engine reluctantly choking to life. I wait for the cloud of white exhaust to dissipate before putting the car in gear, using the time to give both the vehicle and myself a pep talk.

We can make it through the winter. We won't let the cold defeat us. It's almost over. Except it's not, it might, and I'm not sure my poor SUV or my achy joints will last until spring.

To make matters worse, the random flurries drifting from the sky turn into outright snow as I drive into town. I click my windshield wipers to a faster swipe, then faster still as they struggle to catch up with the powder collecting on my car. This is one thing about living in the north that I'm still not comfortable with, and I doubt I ever will be. It's too easy to mess up, misjudge, and wrap your car around a tree, or end up in a ditch. And just as easy to freeze to death waiting for help afterwards.

I'm relieved when my phone trills from the cup holder where I tossed it, interrupting my travels down the rabbit hole of seasonal blues. I glance over quickly, reluctant to take my eyes off the road, but it's facing the wrong way and I can't see if I recognize the number that's calling. I'm even more reluctant to take a hand off the steering wheel long enough to answer, but I do it anyways, because it's my job. Someone could need help. And right now, without a lieutenant, that help means me.

"Chief Riley."

My tires lose traction. I gasp as I skid for a very long second before bringing the vehicle back under control. A distant voice calls up from the phone, dropped and momentarily forgotten in my lap.

"Everything okay there, Chief?"

I know the whiskey-scratched tone instantly. "Margot?"

"Yep. I got a little problem I'd like your help with when you get a chance."

I groan internally because I don't have time for this. I have a mile-long list of things I need to do to make some headway and get some answers concerning this case, and making a pit stop by Margot's Motel isn't on it.

"Could be beneficial to us both, actually. You still looking for a mystery vehicle?"

Or maybe it is.

"As a matter of fact, I am."

"Great. 'Cause I've got one on my lot. Grover Lee's boy found it while he was digging my guests' cars out. Knows I won't pay for any car that's not on my list. Hate to be like that, but the damn kid charges enough, no way someone's getting their car excavated for free. They're lucky if I don't charge them for taking up one of my spots—"

"Margot," I interrupt, because if I don't this call might last all day. "I'm on my way. Almost there. See you soon."

I end the call and crank the wipers up another notch because it's really starting to come down now. I crawl down Main Street, eyeing an approaching snowmobile with envy. I bet it would be much colder on the back of one of those things, and certainly louder, but given the current conditions, I wouldn't mind trading places. They certainly handle the snow much better than my Jeep.

The driver isn't wearing a helmet, giving me a clear view of who's operating the vehicle. I take a long look as he passes. Eddie Diaz. I shake my head as I watch his receding form in my rearview mirror, fairly certain his aunt doesn't own a Ski-Doo. Wonder if I'm going to get a call later about one that's gone missing? But I don't have time to worry about that.

My phone buzzes and I read a text from Sue. The state police have agreed to send several officers our way to assist with the case—tomorrow, after the storm has blown over. My stomach clenches, tightening into a ball of dread.

Because tomorrow might be too late.

There's a killer on the loose, and every neuron lining my gut is telling me that whoever it is, they're still close. And it could be anyone.

Salt crunches under my tires as I pull into Margot's freshly plowed lot. I park in front of the office, am shocked when I realize she's standing in front of me. With her gray beanie, gray jacket, gray hair, and slightly gray pallor, she was perfectly camouflaged against the side of the gray building.

"Now that's what I call service." She ruins the disguise by flashing me a yellowed smile. "It's right over there."

I look toward where she's pointing, see a sedan—already partly concealed by several inches of white powder—parked in the far corner of the lot.

"Anyone touch it?"

"Just enough to clear the license plate. Didn't match any of my guests so he left it alone, told me, I told you, now here we are."

"I appreciate it."

She nods. "I'm gonna go back inside where it's warm, let you have at it."

I wait until the office door is closed behind her before approaching the vehicle. Each step I take across the lot is awkward, partly because the slushy ridges of plowed snow are already starting to freeze.

Shivering, I pause to look around and check my surroundings. I appear to be alone. I doubt many people would want to be out in this weather. And yet, I can't shake the feeling that I'm being watched. I scan the sidewalks again, the storefronts, the shadows, but see no one.

I continue forward, not stopping again until I've reached the vehicle in question. I stare at the car for only a moment before knocking the snow off the passenger door with a gloved hand. I try the handle. It opens.

I exhale heavily. The thick cloud of condensation that appears confirms my guess. Someone didn't just park here leaving their car unlocked while they ran a quick errand. This car's freezing inside. It's been here a while. But it wasn't here yesterday.

I try the glove compartment, am rewarded with a stack of papers. I thumb through them until I find the registration. The vehicle belongs to James and Amanda Marsh. Someone moved their car here. But why? And more importantly, who?

The interior of the vehicle is neat—much cleaner than mine, with none of the detritus you'd expect, especially on a road trip. There are no gas receipts, no fast-food napkins, no snack wrappers.

I walk around to the driver's side and hit the trunk release, then make my way to the back of the sedan. Nothing. Not a suitcase, not a backpack, not even a change of shoes.

What's not here is perhaps even more telling than what is.

Because there's also not a diaper bag, a car seat, a stray sock tugged from a tiny foot.

I glance around the lot, the vehicles parked there already shrouded by a fresh coat of snow. It's not making my job any easier. I trudge through the slush back to the office. Margot looks up from the book she's reading as I come inside.

"Can I ask a huge favor and get a copy of your surveillance footage from last night?"

One grizzled eyebrow twitches like a live wire as she grimaces. "About that."

"Yeah."

"I just checked the recording, and it fizzled out around midnight. Looks like a snowball or something hit it, but that shouldn't have knocked it out all night."

No, but it probably bought whoever threw it time to disable the system, I think.

"I was just gonna ask you to check on it for me while you're here. It's on the light pole in the far corner of the lot."

I give a curt nod and spin on my heel, heading back into the cold. Marching across the salted blacktop, I stare up the post where the shiny black half-circle that was once Margot's surveillance camera has been smashed. This isn't just a coincidence. This is someone covering their tracks.

The killer is still in Coyote Cove.

56
MICAH

Micah's come too far, he's too close to give up now. He knows he can do this. So he's going to give it one last try.

This time, he's got to set himself up for success. Plan everything down to the smallest detail. Make sure there's no room for error.

He grabs the notepad from beside the phone on the bedside table, scribbles with the complimentary motel pen until he gets it to write, then he starts making a list. And at the very top is the lady cop.

There's only one way this will work. There's no use even trying unless he can get her out of the way.

He considers phoning in a fake call for her to respond to, but what if she wraps it up too quickly? No, he needs something guaranteed to keep her out of his hair. Something longer lasting. More permanent.

He could always call a friend to come help, but he wants to do this on his own. He doesn't want to share credit or anything else that comes from this. Not a single dime.

Micah pulls at his lip, scowling as he thinks. Becomes distracted by the noises coming through the thin walls from next door. The lady who'd been staying in that room, number eight, crying uncontrollably day and night, must have checked out, because whoever's in there now sounds like they're laughing.

He flicks on the TV to drown out the sound. Stares at the screen, noticing the little red ticker tape trailing along the bottom. Squints at the tiny block letters until he can read them.

A blizzard is coming. Severe conditions are expected. Residents in the viewing area are being advised to seek shelter and stay in place.

Perfect. It makes his part a little riskier, but hasn't the danger always been part of the thrill? The snowstorm is exactly what he needed. The pieces are all starting to fall into place.

He allows himself to get psyched up for what lies ahead. Starts telling himself all the idioms he usually uses. Time to take the bull by the horns. Go big or go home. Do... or die.

57

MAGGIE

I hurry inside the department, closing the door behind me against the cold. Against the prying eyes I can feel but not see. I need that backup from the state police to get here immediately. I need them to send a forensic unit to analyze the Marshes' abandoned car. I need to apply pressure and get the NCIC to give me the records I've requested. And I need to figure what it is that I'm missing, and fast. Because I am missing something.

Which makes me worried. That I've lost my touch. That maybe I shouldn't be doing this anymore.

And there's so much that needs to be done.

I swap the switchboard back from the call forwarding option I use at night and settle behind my desk. Almost immediately, the phone rings.

"Coyote Cove Police Department, this is Chief Maggie Riley speaking."

There's a long pause on the other end, accentuated by a person sniffing.

"Hello?" I try again. "May I help you?"

Another long, drawn-out sniff before a voice cracks through

the line. "My name is Kay. My sister is—" A sob. "Was, Amanda Marsh."

Oh. I guess the Springfield Police Department forgot to call me before they made notification.

"I'm so sorry," I say. "So incredibly sorry for your loss."

"The officer this morning said she and James had been found on a mountain. But that makes no sense. They weren't hikers, but still? Both of them? I asked him what happened, and he said I needed to call and talk with you. Did they have some kind of accident?"

I bite my finger, debating what to tell her. Decide that I need her answers as much as she needs mine.

"We're still investigating what happened, but I'll be honest. It looks suspicious."

"Did James do something to her?"

"I don't believe so."

"Then what?"

"Ma'am. Did your sister and her husband have a baby?"

"What? No. I mean, they'd been trying for a long time. But they weren't seeming to have much luck. And I think they were running out of money to spend on more in vitro treatments. Amanda was pretty torn up about it, actually. She was starting to lose hope. We couldn't even go out to lunch, I mean, if she even saw a baby she'd start crying." Her tone turns wary. "Why do you ask?"

"Do you think it's possible that your sister would adopt a child?"

"I'm sorry, I'm not comfortable answering any more of your questions until I know what's going on."

It's a gamble. If I tell her what she wants to know, she could hang up. Refuse my calls. It's why I'd wanted the notifying officer to coordinate with me, so they'd be there when I called to speak with the next of kin. But what choice do I have other than to show my hand? I need help, and right now Amanda's sister, Kay, is the only one I'm aware of who can give it to me.

"There was an infant found on the mountain with your sister and brother-in-law."

I hear a gasp. A whispered, "Oh, Amanda. What have you done?"

I give her a moment to process before I continue. "The baby is okay. She's alive. But we've been unsure who she belongs to. May I ask the last time you saw your sister?"

"Last weekend. She and James came over to my place for Sunday brunch."

"And they didn't have a baby with them then?"

"No."

"Did they ever mention anything to you about adopting a child?"

"No, but they probably couldn't. Adopt. I mean, I don't think they'd be approved."

I straighten in my seat. "And why's that?"

"James faced child abuse charges when he was younger. I don't think he meant to do it, but he hurt his nephew once. Grabbed him by the arm too roughly. Gave him a spiral fracture."

That kind of break, caused by a twisting force, is often a hallmark of abuse in young children. That would definitely be grounds for an automatic rejection of an adoption application.

With these new pieces of information, a picture is finally starting to emerge. I have a woman who was desperate for a child. Who seemed unable to conceive one of her own. Who wouldn't be approved for adoption. Who was found on a mountain with a baby that wasn't hers. And a young man who'd been charged with kidnapping before. Both of them, along with her husband, dead.

"What about James? How did he seem to feel about Amanda's desire for a baby?"

"He was almost as torn up about it as she was. Blamed himself for making adoption impossible. Honestly, I think he would have given her the world if he could have. They loved each other so much. I just can't believe they're both gone."

The answer erases the last box on my list of doubts. The little box that said maybe. Maybe the husband didn't want the baby. Maybe he panicked. Maybe he killed them all and committed suicide.

"Thank you. I know it can't have been easy to share all this with me."

"Will it help? You figure out what happened to my sister, I mean?"

"Yes, I think it will."

She exhales loudly into the phone. "Then at least there's that."

"May I have your number? In case I have any more questions that I think you can help with?"

As I enter her contact details into my cell, I think about what I've just learned. There's no way the baby from the mountain belonged to the Marshes. So then, where did she come from?

My thoughts immediately veer to Justice Panettiere. Without the details of the kidnapping charges that were brought against him, and later dropped, it's impossible to know what happened for sure. Was it just a misunderstanding? Or had he actually stolen someone's child? If so, why? And perhaps more importantly, had he gone on to do it again?

Then there's the twist of fate that led to three deaths. Is it possible that the two mysteries are completely unrelated? And how does the mountain come into play?

I'd wanted to believe that this was an isolated incident, but now I'm not so sure. In fact, I suspect that I was wrong. And that has me very, very worried. Because if I can't trust my gut, what do I have? This job isn't just dangerous without dependable instincts. It's downright deadly.

58
BRAD

Brad lingers at the base of the steps, working up his nerve. He knows he shouldn't be here. He knows he's being ridiculous. He knows he hasn't been able to get Chief Riley out of his mind.

He wonders if she knows that Officer Miller is still in town. Because Brad doesn't think she does. Which means she's in for a nasty surprise. Or maybe not. Maybe he can save her from that.

He climbs softly up the stairs, opens the door, and slips inside. She's standing right there in front of him, her back to him as she leans over her desk, studying something on its surface. He notices as she stiffens, obviously realizing he's there, but whether she heard him or simply noticed the draft of cold that crept in with him, he doesn't know.

"Don't you ever go home?" he asks.

She turns to face him, then angles her spine to the wall. "On a lovely day like today?" Her tone is light, but her face is weary. She takes a step backward, away from him.

"How's the case going? Make any big breakthroughs, yet?"

"No." Another step. "Not yet."

"Well, it's only a matter of time. I'm sure it'll happen soon."

He stares deep into her eyes, watching her reaction. "I have faith in you."

She laughs nervously. Takes another step backward. "I appreciate it. Unfortunately, I think this storm's going to cause some additional delays."

"I can imagine," he says. "Especially with you being the only law enforcement officer for miles and miles around. It must be tough."

She clears her throat. Moves away, but she's run out of room. Her back is against the wall.

Brad closes the distance between them. Stares down at her, her full lips close enough to kiss. Her pulse throbs at the base of her throat. It reminds him of a bird, delicate and fragile.

"You look cold," he says, and leans a little closer.

59

MAGGIE

This is more than just an invasion of my personal space—Brad's way too close to me. I try to take a step away, to increase the distance between us, but I'm already up against the wall. I've backed myself into a corner. It seemed smart at the time—no way someone can sneak up on you if they can't get behind you—but now it just seems silly. Stupid.

"You look cold," he says, leaning forward.

God, what's this kid going to try and do? Offer to warm me up? I don't have time for this.

I gesture toward the window without looking, not wanting to take my eyes off him. "The snow is starting to come down heavy now. You should probably get home while you still have a chance."

His eyes don't leave my face. "I'm not worried about that."

"Well, I am." I put my hand against his chest to push him away from me, when there's a noise at the door. I freeze as the wind catches it and throws it open wide. Diane stands in the gap, gawking at us. I look from my hand to Brad and back, before continuing the push, shoving him away. This does not look good.

"Am I interrupting?" Her tone drips more ice than the snowstorm outside. Her left eyebrow, that perfectly shaped, judgmental arch I'm starting to know so well, rises on her forehead.

"No." My voice shakes, catching on phlegm and fear. I clear my throat and add, "He was just leaving."

For a second I think Brad's going to argue. I cross my arms and sharpen my glare, praying that he takes the hint. After a pause that seems like an eternity, he takes a step back. "Yeah, sure. If that's what you want."

Diane takes a step aside to let him by. Her body language mirrors my own, except her contempt is directed at me, instead. She doesn't give him a second look, not even when he stops in the doorway and says, "I'll catch you later."

I have a hard time not rolling my eyes, growling, shouting for him to leave, anything to end this excruciatingly awkward moment. And it is excruciating. Especially since "caught" is exactly how I felt. I'm grateful Diane is here, even if I would have preferred that it was anyone other than her.

She crosses the room and holds my gaze as she turns the chair in front of my desk so that she can sit while facing me. The eyebrow is still raised high.

"Did you drive yourself out here in this alone?" I ask, trying to divert her attention to a less uncomfortable subject. And make sure that Steve wasn't with her until he misinterpreted what was going on and took off.

She nods, expression still flinty. "I came to a conclusion that I thought you should know."

Here it is. I feel my shoulders round, my head down as I prepare for the onslaught. She hates me. She doesn't want Steve to marry me. I'll never be a part of her family, not if she has her way about it.

Even though I've imagined her saying the words enough times since we've met, it's still not going to be easy to hear them.

I know that I can't expect pity to soften her blows now, so I prepare myself for her full wrath. And after what she thought she saw, I'm sure she's convinced I deserve it.

Maybe I do.

So when she tells me that the conclusion she's drawn is that she's certain there must have been a fourth person on the mountain who removed the baby's gear, I'm flabbergasted. Totally and completely floored. Because here's this woman who obviously doesn't like me, but you know what? She was going to try. She was working to find some common ground between us besides her son. She wanted to help me. And I totally and completely blew it.

Diane avoids looking at me once she's finished revealing the reason for her visit. Her gaze hovers somewhere in the distance as she stands and says, "So now you know. I believe I'll go now, before the storm gets any worse."

"Diane."

She stops, hand on the doorknob. I struggle to keep the emotion out of my voice. To maintain my dignity. To behave as though she didn't catch me doing anything wrong, because she didn't, not really. Yet there's no denying that the thing I'm feeling the most right now is guilty.

I could tell her what she really walked in on. I could try to defend myself. Instead, I say, simply, "Thank you."

My stomach begins to ache as I watch her leave without her taking so much as a backward glance in my direction. Now I'm left here, alone, wondering if that applies to my entire life, or just my present situation. And afraid that I don't want to know the truth about that.

60
STEVE

I come inside, bringing a gush of cold air and two hyper dogs with me. I hang my snowy jacket on a hook by the door, and brush a hand over the flakes still clinging to my hair, before grabbing a towel and calling the dogs back to me. They may be full of energy, but both love a good rubdown.

When I left, the room was quiet, but now the atmosphere is downright sullen. And my mother is no longer sitting at the table. I'm no scientist, but I suspect I've stumbled onto cause and effect.

"What's going on?"

Sue gives me a grim look. "Maggie texted. She's found the Marshes' vehicle. It was in Margot's lot."

Oh. *Oh*. Now I get it. The change in mood. If the victims' car is in Margot's lot now, and it wasn't before, that means someone moved it.

The killer is still in Coyote Cove.

My mouth is dry, and my stomach feels soggy. I force my hands into fists to keep from reaching for my phone. I want to call Maggie.

It was one thing when she was working a case that was

possibly a homicide, but now that all signs point to definitely, and the culprit is still out there—here, local—I want her home, safe, with me. I know I can't ask her to do that. I know that I need to let her do her job, but still. I need to feel like I'm doing something useful.

"She's also confirmed that the baby didn't belong to the victims."

I shift my focus to the infant sleeping peacefully in the car seat on the table. She's not an orphan after all. Somewhere, there's a family out there missing her. And I know that no matter what happens, Maggie would want us to find them.

The impatient tapping of my boot is the only sound. Then the soft clicks of Sue's typing joins the mix and I swivel to face her. "What are you doing now?"

"I'm working on having the victims' car towed to the state crime lab for analysis, but no one wants to take the job until the storm's over."

I turn to Dr. Ricky. "And you?"

"I'm searching the missing persons database to see if I can find a match for the baby."

I nod. These things are helpful. They're progress. This is what I need to be doing, too. Focusing my attention on something that could assist Maggie instead of letting my thoughts run wild and free. "What can I do to help?"

I pretend not to notice the look they exchange. I get it. I'm not law enforcement. They aren't either, exactly, but there's no denying that they have more experience with this kind of thing than I do.

Sue nibbles on her thumb, eyes raised like she's searching her brain for a task simple enough for me to execute. I vow to myself that whatever she says, I'll do it. Not just that, but I'll do it better than it's ever been done before.

Because I've been spending too much time inside my own head lately. I've been psyching myself out, giving myself doubts, even though I know with every cell of my body that there's only one woman I want to spend the rest of my life with, and her name is Maggie Riley. I didn't even tell her that I loved her before she left. She needs to know. I need to get that chance.

Finally, Sue says, "Why don't you check different social media venues? See what you can find out about the victims? Maybe you can discover how they were connected. Leave no stone unturned, right?"

I force a smile. "Consider it done." But what I'm thinking is that I'm the wrong man for the job. I haven't been on social media since Myspace, and even then my use was infrequent. I'm not even sure that site exists anymore. I'll have to Google what places I should even look at.

Obviously, I'm not ideally suited for the task, but I'm going to do it. I'm going to help catch this creep. Because the killer probably had some moments of doubt, too, and they didn't let that stop them. And if they manage to get Maggie in their crosshairs, well, I don't want to think about that. So, instead, I'm going to focus on helping the woman I love come back to me safely.

61

MAGGIE

I'm trying to concentrate, but my thoughts keep drifting. I know I haven't done anything wrong, but that doesn't stop me from feeling like I have.

How must it have looked to Diane? Coming in here, finding me pinned against the wall by a young and, let's be honest, extremely attractive man? I rub my eyes, conceding to my guilt, and make a bargain with my brain—I'll give myself two minutes to think about it, to face my concerns, but that's it. Then it's back to work.

I search my memory, drawing myself back to the moment with a detective's eyes. His head was lowered toward my face. I thought he was going to kiss me, so I raised a hand to his chest to push him away. And that's when she came in.

Bad. It looked bad, there's no denying it. It must have looked like an intimate gesture instead of a defensive move. She already didn't like me. Now she's probably convinced I'm cheating on her son. She must hate me. Oh, God, what if she tells Steve?

My two minutes are up, but they haven't made me feel better, just much, much worse. But it doesn't matter. I don't have the luxury of stewing in my own feelings right now, not when more lives may be at stake and it's my job to protect them. I need to figure out what's going on here before someone else gets hurt.

Waking my computer, I scroll through my email and find a response from the officer who investigated Justice Panettiere's kidnapping charge. Finally. I click to open the file. There has to be a clue in here. It's just too much of a coincidence for there not to be.

The case file reveals that Justice Panettiere was arrested for taking his cousin's infant seventeen months ago. He said she had asked him to find an adoptive family for the baby. She claimed he'd taken the child without permission, but later recanted, admitting that the discussion had taken place, but that she hadn't made her mind up yet when he took the child. The charges were dropped.

There's nothing about the fate of the baby. Not that there would be. It wasn't the investigating officer's job to follow up and see if Justice's cousin decided to keep her baby or not. But there is a red flag that was missed. If she wanted to give her child up for adoption, why would she have her cousin find a home for the child instead of going through an agency?

If he took the infant, does that mean he had already found a home for the child? And if he had, and his cousin changed her mind, what then? Did he tell the expectant couple they were out of luck? Or did he find them another baby?

He stole a child once and got away with it. What was there to keep him from trying again?

I search my memory for reports of missing babies, but come up blank. I rarely get a chance to watch the news, and an alert wouldn't have crossed my desk unless the child was local, or they or their abductor were believed to have ties to the area. But that doesn't mean it isn't possible.

Opening a browser, I type in *missing baby Maine*. None of

the results are from the last nine months. Our baby Doe is definitely younger than that. But the couple found on the mountain with him were from Massachusetts. Maybe Justice had traveled from somewhere else, too.

His parents had told the officer who notified them of his death that they hadn't heard from him in months—that they had no idea where he'd been, or where he was living. DMV records still showed his last known address as their home in Rhode Island. I type it into the GPS app on my phone—just about seven and a half hours from here. Less than a day's drive, but separated by two other states.

I type in *missing baby Rhode Island*. And discover that four babies have been reported missing in the last year and a half. I try *missing baby Massachusetts*. And find six more babies that have been recently snatched. Next, I search *missing baby New Hampshire*. Two infants have gone missing in the last two months. Both from towns right off the I95 corridor that leads between Coyote Cove and Justice Panettiere's parents' house in Providence.

I need to speak with Justice's cousin and find out why she spoke with Justice about finding an adoptive home for her baby. My guess is it's because he'd done it before. And that he went on to do it again and again.

Is that what they were doing when they died? Exchanging a baby as part of a black-market adoption? On a mountain!

Who in their right mind would do that? But the more I think about it, the more I realize that no one involved was in their right mind. James and Amanda Marsh were desperate to have a baby, so much so that they were willing to do whatever it took. And Justice? It's obvious he was an opportunistic predator. But what about whoever he was working with?

By having the exchange take place on a mountain, they must have known they'd have the couple completely at their mercy. Were they even going to give the Marshes the baby, or just take their money? Was killing the couple part of the plan? If so, how was Justice caught in the crossfire?

I need to find out who Justice was working with. How many times they've done this. And how many missing babies they're to blame for.

Skimming the report, I find the phone number for the plaintiff, Justice's cousin. I pull out my cell and dial, hoping she still has the same number. But nothing happens.

The number isn't even in my call log. I stab it in once more and press the green phone icon. The screen defaults back to the dialer.

I give an exaggerated sigh to vent my frustration and grab the landline. One of the hardest things about adjusting to life in the mountains was the unpredictability of my cell reception. It's a small thing, sure, but once you've come to rely on something, it can be brutally hard to adjust to life without it.

Like warmth and sunshine. I glance outside and notice that the snow is falling thicker and faster. *Ugh.*

I pick up the handle and place the receiver down on my desk. Push the speakerphone key. But there's no dial tone. Pressing the hang-up button, I get a flashback of my first cell.

It was a flip phone. It didn't take pictures. The screen was barely larger than a postage stamp. There was no keyboard for texting, no apps, no streaming movies or TV shows or reading books. There have been so many technological advancements over the years. So why haven't they been able to fix all the issues and create something that reliably works? I jab the button repeatedly, even though I know it's useless, before snatching the receiver and slamming it down on the base.

I grab the computer mouse and roll it roughly across the desk to wake up my screen. There's no connection. The internet's out too. Then the lights flicker.

"Don't you dare," I warn.

Like a brash kid, the universe tries my last nerve. The room falls dark. And stays that way.

"You've got to be kidding me."

My foot taps impatiently as I wait for the backup generator to kick in. I give it a minute, two—check my otherwise useless cellphone to make sure I'm judging time accurately—three. It doesn't come on.

Without the heat blasting away, the chill finds me almost immediately. I push away from my desk and stand. Shivering, I grab my jacket off the back of the chair, pull it on, zip it closed. Cross my office into the lobby, part the blinds so I can peer out, see if everyone else has lost power too.

Oh, wow.

I hadn't realized how heavily it was snowing. At least six inches of fresh powder have accumulated since I came inside. My Jeep is a snow-covered lump in a sea of white.

I'm torn. I can't receive calls. The only way people have of reaching me right now if they need help is to come here. But I can't stay here without heat—there's not even a spare blanket lying around. I consider running to the shed out back, taking a look at the generator, but even if I did, I wouldn't know where to start troubleshooting.

I eye my Jeep. I don't know how far it'll take me if the snow keeps getting deeper, but at least I'll have heat. My arm hair struggles to rise under the weight of my jacket as I shiver again. I can already see my breath.

Screw it. The difference between being a chief of police versus being a boat captain is that there's no rule about having to go down with the ship. Besides—you'd have to be crazy to go out in this. The irony—that this is what I think as I run out into the storm—is not lost on me.

62

STEVE

The wind whistles outside, whipping up a maelstrom of white and flinging it at the windows so thickly that it's impossible to see beyond the foggy panes. I'm trying not to think about Maggie being out in all this. I'm trying to imagine her warm and safe, enjoying the peace and solitude of her office while making great strides in solving this case. Preferably by discovering that the killer is halfway across the country already, or, better yet, on an entirely different continent. But as the storm howls and the roof creaks, I feel my positivity wane.

Tempest whines, as if sensing my distress, which she probably does. I reach down and give her head a pat, get rewarded with a lick. Then she settles on the pillow in front of the fire beside Sullivan, where they both lie staring at me with worried eyes. I wish I could alleviate their anxiety, but I can't even control my own.

I return my focus to the webpage in front of me, continue skimming an article about the different ways to search for a person on Facebook. Then I click to the open tab with my newly created profile and give it a try.

I don't expect to find anything. I've already exhausted my

search efforts on WhatsApp, WeChat, TikTok, Instagram, and Twitter. But my sense of helplessness is mounting with the strength of the blizzard outside. At this point, any distraction, no matter how senseless, is welcome.

I type Justice Panettiere's name into the search bar and hit enter. Narrow the search by people. Scroll down what seems like an endless list of individuals who share a name with the deceased young man, none of whom look the right age in their tiny thumbnail profile pictures. It's hopeless. The kid was too busy being a criminal to use social media. Although, from the pictures I've seen posted, that assumption really doesn't hold true...

So I continue. I switch the search to posts containing the name. The screen blurs as I work my way down an impressive page of hits.

On the chair beside me, Laurel twitches in her sleep. It's so quiet in here that I find myself fighting not to join her. And maybe I do, if only for a second, because when Dr. Ricky cries out I startle so hard that I almost knock my laptop off the table.

All three dogs raise their heads, watching with concern as she soothes the baby. "There, there. Don't cry, little Nina."

The baby's sobs soften.

"Is that your name? Are you little Nina Keaton?"

"You IDed the baby?" Sue jumps to her feet and rounds the table, inspecting Dr. Ricky's screen from over her shoulder. "This says that she has a birthmark on her upper back."

Sue deftly unsnaps the top of the onesie. She takes the baby in her arms and props the infant against her shoulder like she's trying to burp her. Rocks from side to side as she draws the fabric down. And there it is. A coffee-colored spot darker than the surrounding skin.

"We've got to tell Maggie," I say, righting my screen. I squint at the display. Lean forward, rub my eyes, and look again.

"She was kidnapped! Reported missing five days ago by her

mom in Portsmouth, New Hampshire. There's a number here."
Dr. Ricky tucks a strand of hair behind her ear. "Looks like it's
for one of the FBI agents working the kidnapping. Who should
I dial first?"

"Maggie," Sue and I say simultaneously.

"Great. Now that that's decided, can either of you get a
signal?"

"You can't?" Sue settles the baby onto her hip and tries her
own cell. "Me neither. Steve?"

There's a marketplace ad that's caught my attention. I click
on the post to get a closer look.

"Uh. Steve?"

The listing is for a used snowmobile. It's been edited to
include a message to the buyer.

Sold! New owner is Justice Panettiere. Hope you enjoy it, man!

The name isn't hyperlinked, so there's no profile connected
to it, but there is a picture in the comments. I tap to enlarge it.

"Steve? Everything all right?"

I turn the computer around and give it a push across the
table. "Do me a favor, will you? Tell me if you recognize
anything in this picture?"

"That's the moose statue outside Em's Diner," Sue says, at
the same time Dr. Ricky gasps, "That's Justice!"

"Wait." Sue carefully sets the baby back in the car seat.
"That's him? Your dead guy from the mountain?"

"One of them, yes," Dr. Ricky confirms.

"But that picture was taken here. In Coyote Cove."

"He would have had to pass through, wouldn't he have, to
get to the—"

"No!" Sue says, a note of hysteria edging into her voice. She
jabs at the screen. "Look. That picture was posted over a month
ago. He didn't just pass through," she says.

"He was living here," I finish for her.

"Well," Dr. Ricky says. "I suppose this changes everything, then, doesn't it?"

She doesn't need us to confirm that it does. Because if one of the victims lived here, chances are, his killer might have, too. And if that's true, it stands to reason that they still do.

If the killer is local, Maggie might know them. And it could be someone she'd trust.

I grab my phone, desperate to hear her voice. But I don't have a signal either.

63
ERIKA

I flinch as Steve curses and slaps his cellphone onto the table. The baby squawks in protest. As Sue tucks a blanket tight around her, I can't help but notice that her hands are shaking.

We both watch Steve get up and check the landline. He turns toward us, shaking his head, a deep trench formed between his eyebrows. "No dial tone. The phone lines must be down."

"Maggie will be fine," Sue says, but it seems to me that she's saying it as much as for her own comfort as Steve's.

I follow her gaze to the small handgun that Chief Riley left behind, now sitting on the credenza. What had seemed like an overly cautious measure before now seems like an incredible stroke of foresight—if we were the ones facing off with a killer instead of her. But we don't know that she is. Chances are that she's at her office, looking for the detail that will crack the case, same as we were just moments ago, or even on her way back this very minute.

"We should send her an email," I suggest, just as the lights flicker. We're cast in darkness for a very long second where we're left to wonder if they'll come back on or not. Then they do, and it's almost worse, because now we can see the fear etched across each other's faces.

Steve taps at his computer, then curses again and pinches his eyes shut. "Internet's down now, too. We don't have any way to reach her."

Warn her is what I hear.

"And it doesn't look like this storm's going to let up any time soon. I'm going to hike on over to Maggie's while there's still the chance. I've got several containers of gas for the generator, but if we lose power we're going to want her backup fuel as well, especially with the baby here."

"Wait, you're not just going to leave us here, are you?" The whites of Sue's eyes flash. I suspect mine are doing the same. "What if something happens and you can't make it back?"

"It's not that bad yet."

"But what if?" she asks.

What I hear is, *what if the killer comes while you're gone? For the baby? To finish what they started?*

"Would you rather come with me?"

Sue looks at me. I can tell we're thinking the same thing. I give a tiny dip of my head.

"Yes, we would."

"You sure?"

We both nod.

"Okay, then." He pushes back his chair and stands. "Everybody bundle up and we'll meet back here in five. There're plenty of spare jackets and such in the hall closet. Help yourself to anything you find and let me know if you need anything else."

He gets halfway down the hall, then spins and returns. "Does anybody know where my mother went?"

Sue and I exchange frowns before shaking our heads.

"Mother?" he yells. He rushes by us, heading to the front of the house. "Mother?" The dogs follow close at his heels, escorting him from the room as he calls for Diane. They're still shadowing him a moment later when he returns. "Her car's not here."

He stumbles like his legs have gone weak, his back smacking against the wall, hard. The thud sounds like it hurts. The framed photo of a field of lupines on a mountain tilts precariously, threatening to fall. "Why would she leave? Where would she have gone?"

"Oh, God," Sue mutters. "I think I might know." She gives Steve a desperate look. "I had no idea she'd, I mean, if I had known she was going to... You have to believe that—"

"Sue." Steve rights himself off the wall, reaches forward and gives her arm a gentle squeeze. He somehow manages to pin a believable smile on his face. "It's okay. My mother's not the kind of woman to let anyone talk her into doing anything she doesn't want to do. And this isn't her first blizzard. I'm sure she'll be fine." He glances at me, and I can see the lie in his eyes. "Now. Where do you think she went?"

Sue raises a hand to her temple like she has a headache. "She was asking me about Maggie."

"It was probably more like an interrogation," Steve says gently.

Sue gives a single, "Ha," covers his hand with her own and gives him a grateful look. "You do know your mother, don't you?"

He nods.

"We were discussing Maggie, and the baby, the case, and suddenly she says to me, 'You really like her, don't you?' And I said, 'Of course. Maggie isn't just my boss, she's my friend. And a pretty all-around remarkable woman.' And then I told her some of the things about Maggie that she should know. Then she asked me, 'If I wanted to get to know her better, what should I do? Where can I find some common ground?'"

Sue bites her bottom lip and draws a deep breath before

saying, "I told her Maggie loves her dogs, her job, and you. And Diane said, 'So, helping her with this case might bring us closer together.' And I said that I imagined it would."

Steve stares out the window at the falling snow. "How long ago was this?"

"I'm not quite sure, but it's been a while. At least an hour." Her voice wavers as she adds, "Right before your mother found out that none of the baby's gear was discovered on the mountain with her."

He blinks long and slow. "Then I'm sure she made it there just fine. They're probably doing the smart thing and sheltering in place right now. I'm sure we'll hear from them once they're able to get word out." A vein protrudes on his forehead as he forces a bad imitation of a smile. "Well, then. Same plan as before. Let's get moving."

Sue looks relieved, but I'm not buying it. Steve was sure Chief Riley would try to make it back here once she saw how bad the weather had turned. And though I'm reluctant to say it, because I don't see the point in causing any additional stress or worry, it's been *well* over an hour since the last time I saw Diane —probably more like two—which should have given her ample time to have made it back already.

I'm fairly certain that the leaden hollowness in my stomach is trying to tell me that something bad is happening. But it's too late to run back to my lab to hide. I'm the one who chose to draw myself into this dark web—there's no one else to blame. I wonder how my cats are doing. And if they'll miss me if I never return.

64

MAGGIE

My hands are cramped, fingers begging for relief, but I don't dare release my stranglehold on the steering wheel for even a second. I squirm in my seat, leaning closer to the windshield as I struggle to see through the vortex of swirling white, and toe the gas pedal. The car fishtails. I correct. Then push the gas again.

It's a tedious tightrope, but it's working. Sure, I might be able to walk faster, but then I wouldn't have the heat. And considering that the stiff, painful chill that's affecting my half-frozen toes has started creeping up my calves, despite having the thermostat cranked to the highest setting, I'm not about to give up what little I have going in my favor. I wait until there's enough of a break in the blinding flurries to make sure a moose isn't standing right in front of me, then press the gas again.

I wish I could see a house. A street sign. Anything that would let me know that I'm actually on a road right now, but there's nothing but white, a thick layer of snow clinging to every surface. I could kick myself for not staying in the parking lot and waiting until a plow truck came by to flag down, but it's too late now.

As if conjured by the very thought, I hear the rumble of an

engine. But it's not for the first time. Even so, I stop and wait, holding my breath, trying to locate which direction it's coming from. And like that, it's gone again. Probably just my ears acting up from clenching my jaw so hard. Or maybe I'm getting sick. Wouldn't that be perfect?

"I hate you!" I yell it at the top of my lungs. Lifting my hands since I've stopped moving anyways, I decide the most mature way to stretch them out is to give the snow around me the finger. Then I curl them back around the wheel, wait for a glimpse of the road in front of me, and give the Jeep gas.

We could go somewhere warm for our honeymoon. If Steve still wants to marry me after whatever his mother is probably telling him at this very moment, that is. And if I can find a decent lieutenant to keep watch over the town. Both seem like impossible feats right now.

Maybe I should quit. Go back home. Try to make amends. I haven't seen my parents in years, and they aren't getting any younger.

I thought I'd gotten over it, that I'd come to terms with my orphaned-by-proxy status, but now I know that's not true. Because this morning, when I overheard Steve's mom asking Sue if she knew how my parents felt about our impending nuptials, it hurt. Scratch that. You could eviscerate me, flay my skin off, remove my teeth and nails one by one and it wouldn't even start to compare with the overwhelming pain I felt.

Rejection is never an easy pill to swallow, but when it's from someone who's supposed to love you unconditionally, it burns even deeper. And yet, despite being abandoned, despite the years I've spent struggling to keep my self-worth out of the toilet, I suspect I'd forgive them in an instant if given a chance.

I'm cold, and I'm scared, and I want my mommy. But I'm fairly certain that she doesn't want me.

I blink back the tears threatening to invade my eyes.

Wallowing in my past is a bad idea. Especially when I have enough to worry about in my present.

I peer out the window. Check to make sure the road is clear. Then push the gas.

My thoughts stray to Justice Panettiere. He had a history of bad ideas. Battery. Burglary. Being forcibly removed from a hospital emergency room after becoming disruptive and violent while accompanying a friend. Taking his cousin's baby, possibly as a misunderstanding, but still—taking a baby. Most likely more than one. And whatever it was that caused him to be on that mountain, where he met his untimely death.

A death caused by a surgical paralytic. A baby who had been sedated. There's one place where both of those substances could have come from.

He was at the hospital to cause a diversion while whoever he was working with grabbed the drugs. Suddenly, it all makes sense.

The Jeep lurches forward. Sideways. I bite my tongue, drawing blood as I struggle to bring the car back under control, but the tires aren't responding to the movements of the steering wheel. I'm at the mercy of my own foolishness. I fight the urge to slam on the brakes and pump them instead. And am rewarded as I draw to a stop less than a foot from the trunk of a tree.

My skin feels sticky. My palms are damp inside my gloves. I struggle to draw a steady breath, racking my brain for how the hell I'm going to right my vehicle and continue on my way. Or maybe I shouldn't. Maybe it's safer to stay here. I wouldn't want to end up like that car over there, disappearing under a thick sheet of white, quickly becoming part of a giant snowdrift.

I swallow the taste of copper assaulting my mouth as I register what I'm looking at. What I would have missed if my Jeep hadn't spun out. The smell of my sweat becomes over-whelming as it turns sour with fear. This isn't just about me anymore. It's not just my own life in my hands. Someone could be in that vehicle. I have to find out.

Even though I doubt my car's going to move on its own, I put it in park. Debate leaving the engine running and wasting fuel, decide it's best to keep what heat it's managed to acquire. Besides, this won't take long. I hope.

65
STEVE

A gust of wind practically blows me into the house as I bring up the rear of our foraging expedition. The door slams shut behind me, leaving us in darkness. I try the lights, but they don't come on. I wonder if the power's out at my place, too, if the outage happened during our walk over, as I pull my glove off with my teeth, dig my cell out of my pocket, and thumb the flashlight app on.

"There should be extra blankets in the bedroom closets." I drop to my knees and call the dogs over, running a finger around their paw pads and between their toes, removing the ice balls that have formed. They frisk about when I'm done, largely unfazed by the snowy hike. I wish I could say the same for myself, but... I just wish I knew where Maggie was right now. And my mother.

I glance up, catch Sue and Erika staring at me, both with concerned looks on their faces. The shadows cast by my light gives them haggard expressions. Or maybe they really are haggard. I know I am.

The baby gurgles from under Sue's coat. Actually, it's mine. There wasn't much that would fit around both her and the child. I wonder for the hundredth time if we're crazy, bringing an infant and two small dogs out in this weather. I think about Laurel, still sleeping off her latest dose of sedative, and hope she won't get scared back at the house by herself if she wakes up.

This was really the best move. It had to be done. Maybe if I keep telling myself that, I'll believe it.

"I'll grab the gas out of the garage." I wait until they start moving to stand. Wait until they've disappeared down the hall to creep into the kitchen.

If this storm lasts, we'll definitely be glad for the extra gasoline. And the extra blankets. But that's not why we're here, not really. The truth is, I dragged us all out into the storm and over to Maggie's purely for my own selfishness.

I check over my shoulder, then lift the receiver of Maggie's landline from the cradle, holding my breath as I raise it to my ear. Nothing. I knew in my gut that it was a long shot, but I had to try.

Crossing to the garage door, I open it as silently as I can. Close it behind me, keeping my hand on the knob as I lean my back against it. Take several deep breaths before blinking away the tears stinging my eyes. I tell myself they're from the cold, but that's a lie.

Another one. I'm just full of them tonight.

My hand shakes as I raise my phone and shine my light around the room. The lurking shadow in the corner is revealed to be a collection of rarely used gardening tools—a shovel, a hoe, a rake. More tools hang from a stretch of pegboard attached to the wall. Underneath is Maggie's push mower, and beside that, neatly lined in a row, are three red containers of gasoline.

Hopefully the power's still on at my place, but I do some quick math, calculating how long we can keep the generator running if we run just the space heaters, and decide to lie about that, too. It's easier to lie. Easier than facing the truth. Easier than voicing my fears.

A crash loud enough that I feel it in my bones makes me jump. I hear the dogs barking excitedly, the baby wailing. Forgetting the gas cans, the phone I drop, and the images of Maggie and my mother, slowly freezing to death somewhere out in the blizzard, I run to see what's happened.

66

MAGGIE

I approach the car carefully. Each step is a hazard, the soles of my boots slipping on the film of ice that's formed under the thickening layer of snow. My heart beats against the walls of my chest, reminding me to be careful. There's a killer on the loose. I have no backup. I can't even send a text to let another human know where I am. And I have no idea who could be in this car.

The wind slings stinging sheets of sleet against my face. It rips at my jacket and hair, pushes against my back, keeping me off balance. I try to think warm thoughts—a roaring blaze in the fireplace, two toasty pups on my blanketed lap, Steve's arms tight around me—but it does little to ward off the freezing cold that's managed to burrow its way under my skin, settling deep inside my bones.

It takes me multiple tries to undo the strap on my holster with my half-frozen thumb. I have no idea how I'll manage to not only draw my weapon, but also shove a gloved finger through the trigger guard and fire should the need arise. I consider taking the glove off, but that'll only make my coordination even worse.

I flex my hands, trying to work some of the stiffness out, and a hot, fiery pain replaces the numbness. I use it to center me, to keep my senses sharp. My right palm hovers over the butt of my firearm as I use my left fist to clear a peephole on the driver's window. I look inside.

A face peers back at me and I stumble away from the vehicle, almost losing my footing. My arms wheel frantically in the air, fighting to maintain my balance. The door opens.

Diane's skin is a pale shade of blue and her lips are trembling. She manages to swing one leg free from the car, almost collapses to the snow-covered road as she tries to pull herself free. I rush forward to catch her, then I'm struggling to keep us both upright as I lead her toward my Jeep.

We move frustratingly slow. Her movements are awkward and leaden. It feels like I've wrapped my arm around an ice cube. She shakes violently against me, and I can hear her teeth chattering. I wonder if she's hypothermic.

When I open the Jeep's door and she feels the heat flowing against her, trying to escape, she sobs, collapsing into the seat. I get her settled then hurry around the front of the vehicle, eager to join her. The bitter cold, the white landscape, the eerie silence—it's like being on a foreign planet. Even the clumsy, laborious steps I'm forced to take must be what it's like to walk on the moon. I'm ready to get out of here.

But as I draw near the driver's door, I hear the same low-pitched rumble of an engine that I thought I'd heard before. I look around, searching the desolate white mess around me. I see nothing. The noise is gone again, but I can't deny the distinct feeling that I'm being watched. The same feeling I've had since responding to the call on the mountain.

As I pull the door open and duck inside, I shiver. This time it's not from the cold.

I lock the doors, panting to catch my breath. Watch for a moment as Diane's car continues to be buried by the snow. If I'd come along even a half-hour later, it would have been completely concealed. I would have missed it.

She shifts in the seat to look at me. Her hands are clutched in fists, pressed together beneath her chin. Her voice wavers as she says, "I spun out, couldn't get my car free. Couldn't even get my tailpipe unburied so I could run the heat. Couldn't make a call for help."

She glares at me like all these things are my fault. It's possible that's true. She drove into town to see me. What she saw when she got there upset her and probably affected her driving. Take me out of the equation, and she most likely wouldn't even have come up this weekend in the first place.

She could have died.

Her face crumples. Tears spill down her cheeks. She flings herself—not at me, but into my arms, leaving me breathless with surprise.

"Thank you, Maggie."

The words are spoken in a tone so high-pitched that I can barely understand them, but I'm pretty sure she got my name right. There's a first. I wrap my arms around her, rubbing her back, trying to provide some comfort—for us both. Because as I stare over her shoulder, out the window swiftly disappearing beneath a blanket of sleet and snow, I have the sickening feeling that this ordeal isn't over yet. Not by a long shot.

67

CHERYL

This wasn't part of her plan. It wasn't what she came here to do. But none of that matters now. Sometimes, you have to adapt.

And isn't that what life is all about? Adapting? Survival of the fittest? Finding where you stand in the tier of the animal kingdom, that gap between predator and prey? There's no denying that she feels like she's climbed a couple of rungs on that ladder.

It makes sense, if you think about it. Because she's not the same person she was. What happened up on that mountain changed her.

She feels better now. Stronger. Smarter.

And if there's one thing that she's come to realize she values, it's her freedom. She's not going to risk letting anything take that from her. It's one of the few things left in her life worth fighting for.

And she will.

She came here to do one thing. But now she realizes she must do another, something entirely different than what she'd imagined. Something that will change everything from here on out. She can never go back to the way she was before. And if it feels like a final reckoning, that's because it is.

68

MICAH

Micah can hardly hold still. Adrenaline thrums under his skin like electricity, every beat of his heart carrying a surge of energy, boosting his courage. And he's going to need it. A lot of it.

He's pulled a lot of insane stunts in his life, but this? This is definitely the craziest.

He should probably be scared. He knows that most people would be, if they were planning to attempt what he is. But all fear does is slow you down. Make you think twice. And if he stops to think, really think, about what it is he's going to do, he'll lose his nerve.

Because there's a lot that could go wrong. And he's already injured.

But there's no time for that. He's been watching, waiting for the right opportunity to strike and he knows—it's almost here.

He's only going to get one chance.

This is it. It's now, or never.

69

GLEN

He doesn't want to do it. But he doesn't think he has a choice.

He doesn't want to dig himself in deeper, get himself in more trouble than he possibly already is, but the game has changed.

Officer Miller obviously hadn't actually known anything. And Glen doubted he was smart enough to figure it out. But the chief... she's different. He's had too much time on his hands to think about how different. The shrewdness in her gaze. The confidence she exudes. She's not playing around.

She already knows that his fly-fishing story was a lie. It's obvious she's not the type who's going to rest until she gets the answers she wants. It's only a matter of time before she finds out the truth about why he's really here.

Chief Maggie Riley is out for blood. He really doesn't want to give her any of his. And the only way to keep that from happening is to make the first move.

"Dr. Ricky. Dr. Ricky, can you hear me?"

I groan and lift a hand to my head. Dogs bark frantically. A baby cries. The sound of my own pulse keeps time with the throbbing in my occipital lobe. It's way too loud inside my skull.

I struggle to sit up, discover I'm already in a sitting position, propped against a wall. Wincing, I force my eyes open. And see the top of a tree right in front of me, the uppermost branches hiding my feet.

"That's not supposed to be here." I raise a hand to point, but my movements feel as sluggish as my brain. I tear my gaze from the pine and search the room. Sue stands in the corner, jiggling the baby, trying to calm her down. Steve crouches beside me. Both wear worried expressions.

I glance down, see my left hand, the one I haven't used yet, folded between both of his. I feel like I should be more scared than I actually am. I just met these people today. I don't know them. But in this moment, I find that I trust them.

"What happened?" My voice sounds better to my own ears, a little stronger, a little less slurred.

"A tree fell through the roof," Steve says.

"On me?" I stare at my hidden feet.

"Almost."

I wiggle my toes. Roll my ankles. Bring my knees to my chest, revealing my boots, and breathe a sigh of relief. Besides a killer headache, I'm fine.

"How do you feel?" Sue asks. Even though she's done talking, her mouth remains open. Her wide eyes give her a haunted look. I wonder if she saw it happen.

"Like I almost got squashed by a giant tree. Why's my head hurt so bad?"

"My guess would be that you knocked it pretty hard against the wall. You were like this when I found you." Steve chews on his lower lip. There's already a raw spot forming. "We should get out of here. Do you want to try standing up?"

I think about his house across the street, much warmer and with a second story to keep trees from trying to fall on my head. I nod.

He grips me by the elbow, looping his other arm around my back. It should feel awkward, but it doesn't. It's comforting.

He tells the dogs to stay back as he helps me to my feet. A rush of black fog envelopes me.

"Dr. Ricky?" He half drags me across the floor, then I'm sitting in a chair. "Dr. Ricky?"

He's wrapping a blanket around my shoulder when the fog clears. I look up at him and try to smile. "Given the circumstances, call me Erika."

Steve chuckles and squats down beside me. Good. I made him laugh. Hopefully he likes me. Hopefully they both do. Because I have some bad news.

The air is so cold it's burning my cheeks, and it's only getting colder. A swirl of snow blows across what used to be a bedroom floor. This house can no longer be considered shelter. He was right—we need to get out of here.

But the way my head felt when I tried to stand? The way

my consciousness was quickly swaddled by a blanket of darkness? The jittery, weak feeling in my limbs? I don't think I'm going anywhere anytime soon.

Erika doesn't look good. She's abandoned the chair, lying on the floor beside the puddle of vomit she just made. Sue gives me a worried look as she dabs at the yellow bile collected in the corners of Erika's mouth. The doctor's ashen features turn a lighter shade of pale as she rolls onto her back, raising both hands to her head and groaning.

"Don't worry, it's just a concussion," she says. I almost miss the, "I think."

I've tried to tarp off the hole in the house, but it hasn't stopped the cold from seeping in. The air in front of my face fogs with each breath. My exposed skin feels hard and frozen. We can't stay here. But we can't go out there, now, either.

I rack my brain as I go to the kitchen, grabbing a roll of paper towels and a bucket from under the sink to clean up the mess. We can't even run the water right now—without electricity, the well pump won't work. Maybe we should just hole up here. I could start the generator, try to warm it up, make it more comfortable.

Then I think of Maggie and my mother, who might be back already. Of Laurel, at the house by herself. I didn't even leave a note. I didn't even think to wrap a blanket around the poor injured dog.

Sue comes up behind me. The baby she holds is asleep.

"What are you thinking?" she asks.

"I could start Maggie's generator. I know she has some canned food over here. I think there's a camping stove in the garage that we can use to melt snow and make some water."

"Do you really think that's for the best?"

I look at her, startled. "Don't you?"

Her lips press into a hard thin line as she shakes her head. "I don't know. Even once this storm lets up, it's going to take some time for the plows to make their way out here to dig us out."

She glances over her shoulder, then places a hand on the baby's head as if to cover her ears from Sue's next thought. "With that hole in the house, we're not going to be able to keep it warm enough."

"Maybe if we seal off the rest of the house, only heat one room..."

"We can try it." Sue gives me a hopeful smile. "How long do you think we can keep the generator going?"

With the fuel we have here? Not nearly long enough.

I look out the window over the sink, but I can't see a thing through the white maelstrom churned up by the storm. Ignoring her question, I say, "I think the front bedroom would be the best choice. It's the smallest and has its own bathroom. I'll tape off the window, move the supplies you'll need in there, the food and space heaters, and get the generator going."

Sue gives me a suspicious look. "You're talking like you're not joining us."

"We need a backup plan."

"You're not joining us?" There's a note of fear in her voice. It makes what I have to say that much harder.

"Once I get you guys settled, I'm going to hike back over to my place."

"What? Steve, why? Look at it out there. It's crazy to go out in that mess if you don't have to."

She's right. It is crazy. I feel like a coward, avoiding her eyes. "Most of the fuel is over there. We're going to need it."

Eventually—though I only think the word and don't say it. We have plenty for now. Enough to keep the generator going for the night, especially if we're only trying to heat one small room. There's no reason why I couldn't wait a while, see if the snow stops. Except that for some reason I can't explain, I have to get over there. Soon.

"Are you sure?" she asks. "We might not need it."

"I'd rather go sooner than later in case we do. The snow's only getting deeper." And the almost desperate need to go is only growing greater.

"But what if..." Sue uses a hand to cover her mouth like she's trying to stop herself from speaking. She pulls at her lower lip, her eyes moving furtively around the room, looking everywhere except at me. "What if something happens to you?"

I clap my hand on her shoulder. Smile as I give it a gentle squeeze. "Trust me," I say. "That's not going to happen."

I regret it the instant I say it, but the words are already out of my mouth, it's too late to take them back. I keep the smile frozen on my face, hoping it conceals my true feelings. Wondering if Maggie ever told Sue what she'd once told me.

I still remember the moment, sitting on the couch together, snuggling, watching a news commentary on TV. She'd pointed to the pundit, and said, "People only say trust me when they're lying."

At the time I thought she was just being hypercritical. I knew she didn't like the commentator and she hadn't been shy about her disbelief that I did. We had some different political views and didn't always see eye to eye on how we interpreted certain events, but less than two weeks later a scandal broke, and guess who was at the middle of it, facing charges for theft by deception for the very thing they'd said that night?

There was no way to misinterpret that, just like there's no way to mistake the reason for the uneasiness that's settled deep in the pit of my stomach. I had only wanted to reassure Sue. I hadn't meant to lie. I hadn't even realized I was doing it until the dark little voice at the back of my head whispered the truth —that I'm not sure I'll be all right. That I fully expect something bad to happen.

72

MAGGIE

Sleet crunches under the tires as we crawl along the road in what's become full-on whiteout conditions. I'm down below an eighth of a tank of gas, and while I'd like to turn the heat down a little to help conserve fuel, just one glance at Diane's still trembling body stops me. I need to get her as warm as I can before... well, in case we have to brave the cold again.

And if that happens, I'm afraid I might have made a very bad decision.

Before I got back in the car, I heard the buzz of a snowmobile motor. That in itself isn't odd. Plenty of the locals have them. There's even a shop in town that rents them to tourists.

What is odd is that as much as I wanted to yell out for help, I couldn't bring myself to do it. Because in that moment, I'd felt eyes on me. Like whoever it was knew we were there. Knew we were in need of assistance. And watched us as we struggled. Almost like that was what they were there for.

I can't deny that a snowmobile would have solved our problems. It will be a miracle if we make it to shelter before the snow makes our way completely impassable. If that happens, we can't stay in the car. We have to keep moving. But we also have to stick together. That whole safety in numbers thing again. Because who knows who it is that's out there? And what their intentions are.

The perilousness of our situation isn't lost on me—there's a chance we'll freeze to death if we have to strike out on foot. Then again, there's a chance we'll freeze if we stay in the car, too. If that's the choice we face, I'd rather die trying. Of course, I'm not alone anymore. I don't get the only vote. I wonder what Diane would choose to do.

Like she can feel me thinking about her, she says, "I've always tried to keep my kids from making painful mistakes."

So that's what I am. A painful mistake.

"I think that it's only second nature, as a parent. When your child aches, you hurt right along with them."

I'm so busy wondering if this is true that I almost don't see the break in the trees to my left. Afraid to halt what little momentum the Jeep has, I turn the wheel as far as it will go, practically standing in my seat. The turn is neither smooth nor easy. Diane grabs the dash with one hand, braces against her door with the other. I think we both hold our breath and our bladders while we see if we'll make it.

The vehicle is almost at a stop. A thick layer of snow impedes our progress, fighting against us. But we're so close. This is the street home. If we can just make it a little further, we might survive this.

I give the car as much gas as I dare, then more. It's a split-second decision. One that could end in disaster or... Tears fill my eyes as we round the bend, facing the right direction. Still moving, if only barely. Beside me, Diane releases her grip and relaxes back into her seat.

"But something that I'm just starting to realize is, you can't protect them from everything. You have to trust your kids. Let them make their own mistakes. Some things they have to learn on their own."

I wonder about my own parents, if they forgive me for my mistakes. If they ever wonder if I'm safe. If they regret what happened between us.

"And some things they teach you."

Diane turns in her seat, facing me. Even though I can barely see a thing, I maintain a steady gaze straight ahead, hands clenched in a death grip on the steering wheel. I've got the gas floored but we're barely moving.

Her voice is low as she says, "I've always had this idea about the type of woman that I thought Steven would be happiest with. But I was wrong."

I glance at her. She's looking right at me.

"I didn't raise my boy to be weak."

We come to an abrupt stop. I pump the gas pedal. The engine revs but the car doesn't move. It's the end of the road for the Jeep.

"So why would I want him to be with a weak woman?"

Anger flares beneath my skin, giving me a boost of much needed warmth. I might be many things, but I'm not weak. I can't tell you what my parents raised me to be, the kind of person they wanted me to end up with, or why they found it so easy to turn their backs and walk away, but I am not weak.

"I guess what I'm saying is, I was wrong about you."

I turn toward Diane warily.

"I won't lie and say I was happy when Steven's sister told me he was getting married to a woman I'd never met. Or that I didn't come here with every intention of stopping the wedding. Or," her gaze drops to her hands in her lap, "that I didn't know what I walked in on earlier."

I start to speak, but she raises her hand for me to hear her out.

"I could see how uncomfortable you were. I've been in that position a time or two myself, and it made me feel dirty, guilty, like I'd done something to ask for the unwanted attention, even

though I hadn't. And I'm very, sincerely sorry that I did my best
to make you feel that way even more so instead of doing what I
should have done, which was to comfort and protect you the
way a parent should comfort and protect their soon-to-be
daughter."

Diane cuts her eyes at me, a smirk playing about her lips.
"Even if you are the one with the gun." She reaches over and
squeezes my fingers. "My Steven found a strong, beautiful
woman to share his life with, and I couldn't be prouder. I'm
honored that I'm going to get to call you family. So we both
better survive this."

She pats my hand before she releases it. "You ready?"

I stare through the windshield at the blinding white
swirling beyond. The hole made by the wiper blades closes up
in an instant. We're so close, yet so far. It'll be insanely easy to
get turned around once we're out there in the storm. The tiniest
mistake could be deadly.

I wait for a gap to appear on the glass again, hoping to recognize anything outside the window, and catch a glimpse of one of
the orange reflective poles Steve uses to mark the edge of the
low stone wall that runs along the front of his property for the
plow trucks. At most, we're five hundred feet from the front
door. Still, it isn't going to be easy. It's not just myself that I have
to get through this, yet the worry I felt only moments ago has
receded.

Because I'm starting to suspect that under her carefully
coifed hair, perfect makeup, and stylish clothes, Diane and I are
a lot more alike than I thought. And if that's true, then I'm sure
that we can do this.

73
STEVE

I hear the dogs howl as I slip out the door into the icy grasp of the storm. Or is it the wind? As the cold takes my breath away and swaddles my brain, I realize that I can't rightly say.

They weren't happy when I left them behind. I could hear their high-pitched whimpers as I tucked a towel under the door and taped a tarp I'd found in Maggie's basement over the opening to help keep the cold out. But now that my journey's underway, and a mournful cry is still loud in my ears, I'm starting to suspect the noise is not one made by a living creature. But that makes it no less deadly.

The sound makes me think of a book of ghost stories set on the moors of Ireland that I read as a child. How I could feel the very atmosphere of those tales leap off the pages and wrap themselves around me, leaving me breathless and lightheaded and spooked. I spent months sleeping with the lights on, unable to shake the uneasy feeling that something bad was out there waiting for me—around every corner, in every shadow, down every path that I couldn't force myself to take.

I have a similar feeling now.

It's not just the storm, or not knowing where my mother has

gone to, or where Maggie is. No. Something is wrong. Very, very wrong.

The flesh on the back of my neck ripples, rising into goosebumps. But not from the weather. I barely feel the cold, kept warm by the engine of my thoughts.

Like how it would be so easy to get lost out here. To die. One wrong step, an accidental change in direction, an injury.

I force myself to think of something else. Maggie and I should set a date for the wedding. And go somewhere tropical for our honeymoon. Costa Rica, maybe. What I wouldn't give to be on a nice, warm beach right now, the woman I love beside me, a strong margarita in hand.

Or maybe Africa. We could go on one of those tourist safaris. See some of the world's most impressive animals before they go extinct. I could get a camera, a good one with a zoom lens, learn how to take a proper picture. I wonder what drinks they serve on the Serengeti. I could probably still get that margarita.

Out of nowhere, a wave of anxiety crashes against me so hard it almost bowls me over. But it doesn't belong to me. It's not mine. I'm picking up on emotion felt by someone else, a frequency I'm tuned into but don't control.

Maggie.

I hurry forward, staggering down the drive as fast as I can, the wind at my back driving me forward, that howl rising, letting me know that the storm is the beast that I hear. But I suspect it's not the only monster on the prowl tonight. Or even the one from which there's the most to fear.

I keep a tight hold on Diane's hand as I create a path for her to follow me. I'm in a full sweat from breaking through the icy crust that's formed over the snow, lowering my weight carefully and deliberately as I crush the powder underfoot. Our progress is agonizingly slow. Each step is a struggle. My face feels chapped and raw, my eyes sting from the sleet and the wind, my leg muscles burn.

By the time we reach the end of the stone wall and turn down the driveway, I'm breathless. I pause a moment, trying to draw enough air to fill my lungs, but it's useless. The wind is too strong and alternates between forcing too much oxygen at me and snatching it away.

A sudden, violent gust almost knocks me over. A loud pop sounds, no doubt the limb of some unfortunate tree breaking, but in the split second afterwards, there's just enough of a lull in the gale for me to see more than three feet beyond my face, and what I see is the front porch of Steve's cabin. And it's close.

I tighten my grip on Diane and surge forward with renewed vigor. I think of hot showers, dry clothes, and food. Dog kisses and hugs from the man I love. How wonderfully quiet it will be without the constant shriek of the storm in my ears.

The toe of my boot kicks against the bottom stair. I half pull, half push Diane in front of me and up the steps. She tries to sink down to the wooden deck, but I won't let her, afraid that if we stop moving now, we'll never start again. Looping an arm around her back, I mostly drag her over to the front door.

The knob turns freely under my palm. As soon as I get Diane over the threshold, I let her go, needing both hands in the fight to shut the door against the wind. Then I collapse beside her, wincing against the brightly burning lights overhead.

There's a puddle growing around us as the snow coating our clothes melts off. The glorious warmth quickly turns uncomfortable. My flesh feels like it's on fire as it defrosts. I yank my gloves off and toss them on the floor, claw at myself in my desperation to remove my scarf and jacket, then help Diane to free herself from her coat.

"Steve?"

It sounds like I'm using someone else's voice to speak, his name cracking as I say it. My throat feels dry and chapped. I need water.

I push to my knees, use the wall to pull myself the rest of the way up. Where is everyone?

"Sue?"

The house feels empty, but more than that, there's something missing. The greeting I receive every time I come home. The tiny ears that hear every sound no matter how quiet I try to be, who know when I wake every morning even when I'm lying still. My panic is mounting, fast.

"Pups? Tempe? Sully?"

I stagger into the living room. Nothing. Trip my way to the kitchen. No one. The silence is overwhelming, not just after being out in the blizzard, but because of what it means—my family isn't here. They're gone.

My pulse is so loud in my ears it sounds like I'm standing under a waterfall. My vision narrows to two pinpoints of light. I find the wall with my back, use it to keep myself upright as I fight against a panic attack.

There's a crash in the other room, the sound of glass breaking. "Diane? Was that you?"

An icy draft finds me, shocking me back to my senses. I take several deep breaths and the kitchen comes back into focus as I regain my sight. "Diane?"

Something's wrong. The hair on the back of my neck prickles and the vestigial part of my primitive brain screams for me to run. I reach for my gun, but it's gone. The vague memory of undoing the thumb strap of my holster but never re-latching it surfaces, but it's useless. It doesn't matter what happened. All that matters is that I'm here, now, without my firearm. And in possible need of defending myself.

I grab a knife out of the butcher block—not the big long one like the serial killers in movies use, that's for amateurs—but the meat cleaver. Make no mistakes about it. I don't intend to stab anyone. If I'm stuck defending myself with a blade, I want one that can hack through bone.

All my senses tingle with the threat of imminent danger as I backtrack through the house. Every few steps I call for Diane and pause, listening for an answer, but none comes. It's no surprise when I reach the spot where I left her and she's not there. What is a surprise, though, is that the front door is wide open.

I glance around, on high alert as I bypass shards of broken ceramic—a fallen bowl that had been on the entry table—and stick my head around the threshold to peer outside. "Diane?" I yell her name as loud as I can, but the wind steals the word from my lips and tosses it away.

This is my fault. I shouldn't have left her alone. I've heard about people suffering from hypothermia believing they're hot and stripping off their clothes as they freeze to death. Something similar must have happened to Diane. She must have run out into the snow thinking she needed to cool off.

I should go after her, try to find her, but I can't. It's useless, a death sentence, a sacrifice that I'm not willing to make. And yet my feet carry me through the doorway and onto the porch. I shiver violently against the cold, my discarded jacket still inside, promising myself that I'm just going to check to see if her tracks have been wiped away already or if I can tell which way she went.

But I don't even get to the stairs when I stop, frozen in place. The snow blowing onto the deck has already covered our footprints, but there's another, larger set that's still fresh and clearly visible. The good news is that Diane appears to still be in the house. The bad news is that someone else is, too.

75

MAGGIE

I stare at the melted snow on the floor, searching for answers—where Diane went. Who might be with her. Why they're here. But all I see is a mess that needs to be mopped up, the trail of wet footprints fading before they can tell me anything useful, other than, whoever the newcomer is, their feet are big. And that they came here in the middle of a blizzard.

In these conditions, they couldn't have traveled far on foot. There aren't many houses on this street. Most are second homes and vacation rentals, inhabited only during peak season. This is not that time. Winter this far north is not kind. Nobody wants to get stuck extending their vacation because they're snowed in.

There aren't any hiking trails near here. No stores. No reason anyone would come this way without the specific intention to do so. You can barely even see the turn off the main road unless you know to look for it.

Whoever this is, they came here on purpose. I think of the snowmobile engine I'd heard, the eerie feeling I'd had. The one I've *been* having. My throat tightens. I wish more than ever for the comfort of my gun.

I long to wipe my sweaty palm dry, worried the dampness

will loosen my grip on the knife clenched in my fist, but I don't dare. I can't let my guard down for a second. For all I know, the intruder is watching me right now.

The thought forces me into action. I stand up straighter, take a step away from the door. I can't show any symptoms of fear, no signs of weakness. This is my turf.

I think of the drug used to kill the victims on the mountain. What a horrible way that must have been to die, paralyzed, aware, and yet unable to even draw the breath that would keep you alive. I draw in a big gulp of air and hold it. Close my eyes and listen, tuning my senses to my surroundings.

I hear the tick of the baseboard heater clicking on, the soft whir as hot air pumps into the room. The muffled howl of the wind. The tap of sleet hitting against the windows at the side of the house. I smell the wet wool of my uniform, the lingering aroma of coffee, and something else, faint, but just barely perceptible—the stench of sweat, and not my own.

I turn my head to one side, then the other. I'm unable to tell which direction the smell is coming from, but when I turn my head to the left, away from the downstairs bedroom, the skin on the back of my neck crawls and the fine hairs on my arms rise. Bingo.

It's a battle to keep my expression blank, my body language neutral, to not betray that I know my opponent's position. Opening my eyes, I tighten my grip on the knife and stride down the hallway, pretending like I have nothing to fear. I quickly pass by the bedroom, forcing myself not to glance at the half-inch gap left by the open door, and duck around the corner, pressing myself against the living room wall while I wait for my prey to show itself.

The person I'm dealing with is dangerous. They've already killed at least three people.

Maybe they thought that taking me out would be the easiest way to solve their problems, but that was a mistake. Chances are, only one of us is making it out of this alive, and it's going to be me. I am the apex predator here.

I take shallow, silent breaths, my muscles tense, ready to pounce. Keep watch on the shadows on the opposite wall while I listen for the soft, telltale creak the bedroom door makes when it opens, hoping to keep the element of surprise in my favor. Do my best not to think about what's happened to Diane just yet.

I'm so confident that I'm right, that I know my adversary's position, I'm wound so tightly, that when I hear a noise coming from the dining room, I jump, knocking into the console table beside me and cursing. I must have been mistaken, and now I've given myself away. But so have they.

I stalk into the dining room, my right arm crossed over my chest, fist at my left shoulder, ready to swing the meat cleaver with all my might, but no one's there. And there's no way out of the room except past me.

That's when I see her.

Laurel stands on a chair, feet pitter patting in place as she tries to find a way down. I spin around, but it's too late. I've lost my advantage. I'm no longer alone. But at least I've found Diane.

"You." I lower the knife, trying to hold it flat against my leg, but I was a second too late. Backing farther into the room, I round the table, trying to put as much space between us as possible.

"That's right. Me. Now let's hurry up and get this over with. Drop the knife."

76
BRAD

"That's right. Me. Now let's hurry up and get this over with. Drop the knife."

Diane yelps as he tugs her farther into the room by the roots of her hair. He keeps her off balance on purpose, using it to elicit another cry of pain to emphasize how serious he is. He can't help but grin as the chief lays her weapon down on the table between them.

"Now slide it across."

It's almost too easy. Not that he's complaining.

The way he sees it, after what happened up on the mountain, the universe owes him a solid. That was one plan that blew up in his face and completely spiraled out of control. But this time, everything is going to go in his favor, he's sure of it.

Not that this is actually a plan—just cleaning up loose ends, really. Nobody was supposed to get hurt. He hadn't intended on killing anyone. But accidents happen.

Justice had said he was getting out, that this would be the last job they pulled together. The thing was, the only way Brad could afford to quit so soon was if he was the only one taking a cut, and since he didn't think Justice would agree to that, Brad decided to temporarily remove him from the decision-making process.

That was all it was supposed to be—temporary. And it would have been if Justice wasn't such a screwup. This was all his fault. He was the one who was supposed to grab the drugs. Brad was supposed to provide the diversion.

But no. Justice had been too obvious, practically salivating when the nurse unlocked the drawer in her cart as she prepared to give Brad a shot of local anesthetic before giving him stitches. Noticing his interest, she'd asked Justice to leave. He'd refused.

It wasn't until then that Brad had noticed the glassy look in Justice's unfocused eyes, the way he shifted his weight from foot to foot, pinching at his nose and scratching at phantom itches like a junkie. No wonder they were almost out of sedatives so soon. They were only drugging babies, and only enough to keep them sleepy and easier to handle while Justice arranged the handoff to their new adoptive parents.

Brad had been preoccupied by the bleeding gash on his palm, the one Justice had made too deep, but once he saw Justice the way the nurse must have, he couldn't blame her for calling security. But he was nothing if not resourceful.

The moment he realized that the roles had changed, and Justice was now the diversion, intentional or not, he'd backed out of the curtained cubicle. Spotting an angry looking ogre in a blue security uniform stalking down the hall, aimed toward the room he'd vacated just moments before, Brad headed in the opposite direction, trying to look nonchalant as raised voices filled the corridor behind him. He made it to a set of swipe-card protected doors just as another two guards burst through them.

Pressing himself against the wall, he waited as long as he dared to make his move, slipping into this new section of the emergency room unnoticed, the entry locking behind him with a soft click. To his relief, he found himself alone. Wanting to grab what he came for and leave before he was discovered, he peeked through the window in the first door he came to.

At first glance, the room appeared empty, so he snuck inside. A tray of instruments sat beside a lumpy, sheet covered table. He watched his step, tiptoeing past rust-stained rags littering the floor between congealing puddles of red. It made his own bloody wound ache as he sought to get a better look at a vial left on the tray.

It was only once he had reached his destination that he realized the shape on the table was a shrouded corpse. Thoroughly disgusted and more than a little nauseous, he grabbed the half-empty container and shoved it in his pocket as he made a hasty retreat. How was he supposed to know he was grabbing the wrong drug? Justice was the one who knew about that kind of thing.

But now Justice was dead and the mess he'd left behind was bigger than any he'd made while alive. Brad regretted the day the scrawny felon had wandered into the shop, pretending to browse until all the other customers had made their purchases and left. Sidling up to the counter with a lazy grin on his face like he knew all the answers to life's juiciest secrets.

"You own this place?" Justice had asked.

Brad snorted in reply.

"Boss pay you well?"

"Yeah, if I was a six-year-old working in some third-world sweat shop."

"I hear ya. So you might be open to making a little extra on the side then?"

Brad had heard rumors about the bevy of illegal activities that took place in the local mountains. Crime wasn't his forte, but he'd been stuck in the same backward town for the last six months, abandoned by the old hippie he'd hitched a ride with. Days of being forced to breathe in patchouli and BO only to be ditched as soon as he couldn't cover his share of the gas.

The plan had been to travel, see the country. Now his goal was to be anywhere besides Coyote Cove. In his desperation to earn enough money to move on, he'd placed a couple of bad bets at one of the local logging camps, leaving him in debt up to his eyeballs with no hope of escape. He would have done anything short of murder to bankroll a new start someplace fresh. So he'd said, "Sure."

And that's how he'd gotten a roommate. And his start in black-market adoptions.

Justice had gotten his start back in high school, when his sister had gotten knocked-up and he'd convinced her he could find someone to buy the baby, make them both a little cash. He'd had himself a lucrative little business as a baby broker until one of his cousins changed her mind and charged him with kidnapping. That's when he decided to move on and came up with a new plan. One that involved his new friend, Brad.

In the past, Justice had had issues with his clients deciding to change the price on him, showing up with less than the amount they had agreed upon. And after the bit with his cousin, he'd become paranoid about cops. So he'd decided the only way to protect himself was to arrange for the exchange to take place in a location where the buyers were so vulnerable that they wouldn't dare try to pull anything.

Which is where Brad came in. He'd drop Justice off to hike up the mountain with the baby, and the punters were told to hire Brad as their guide to bring them to the exchange location under the cover of darkness. It was foolproof. Until it wasn't.

All he'd wanted was a fresh start somewhere new. But he needed Justice's payday, which was much larger than his own, to make it happen. He hadn't meant to kill anyone. He'd only intended to sedate them long enough to get down the mountain with the money—that's all he needed. Once he reached the parking lot, he'd be a free man. What were they going to do? Call the cops?

Justice had an arrest record, and the couple? He doubted they'd report the theft of the money they intended to use to purchase a black-market baby. Besides, they were still getting what they wanted. He had no use for the infant once he had the cash.

But that's not how it had gone down.

After he'd given them the dosed water, Brad watched and waited, biding his time. Justice, being so small, succumbed to the effects of the drug first. The woman had screamed, grabbing Justice as his knees buckled, somehow managing to hold him up until her husband helped her guide him gently to the ground, the baby still strapped in the carrier on Justice's chest. She released the child, cradling it to her as she scooted away a safe distance, watching warily as her husband checked Justice's pulse.

By the time the man noticed that his wife was also flat on her back on the trail, his own legs were faltering. Brad hadn't expected the drug to work so fast. Or so well. Even though they were still conscious, it didn't appear as if they could move.

Once the husband was down, too, Brad approached. The man's terrified eyes watched as he knelt beside him, rolling him onto his side to access his pack.

The money was bundled in a paper bag at the top—they hadn't even tried to hide it. And why would they? That's why the plan was so perfect. There's no way they'd dare try to pull something over and risk being left to the mercy of the mountain in the dark with a baby.

With the money stashed safely in his own bag, Brad stood over Justice. "Sorry about this, man. Nothing personal."

He'd expected some kind of reaction, but there was none. Justice didn't even glance at him. His eyes had taken on a cloudy, glazed look.

"Hey. Are you okay?"

Worried that it was a trick, Brad nudged Justice with the toe of his boot. He glanced over at the woman, then her husband. None of them were looking too good.

"Dude?"

He squatted beside Justice. Took in the waxen pallor of his skin, the utter stillness of his body. It didn't even look like he was breathing.

Brad's mouth had gone dry, his heart hammering in his chest as he reached out to put his hand under Justice's nose, but a low growling made him freeze. He looked at Justice's dog, the mutt he insisted on taking with him everywhere.

"Fine. Have it your way."

Grabbing a pebble, he threw it at Justice's face, confirming what he suspected. Justice was dead. They all were.

"Shit."

He said it louder than he intended. The noise startled the baby, who started to cry.

Brad stared at the infant with growing horror. He'd intended to leave the child behind, but that was before, when he thought everyone was going to eventually wake up and go on their merry ways, poorer, but alive. What the hell was he supposed to do now?

He stared at the scene, imagining how it would appear to someone who didn't know what had happened. Three dead people with no obvious injuries. Three people who could have easily died from coming into contact with something mysterious, possibly in the air or water. If the drug was found in their systems, who's to say group suicide hadn't taken place?

But none of that would be believable if the baby was there, alive and well, when the bodies were found. As far as he could see, she was the only evidence of a crime. He'd have to take her with him, get rid of her somewhere else.

The dog watched as Brad went through the strangers' packs, removing their identification and everything infant-related and shoving the items into his own bag. She circled warily as he unhooked the baby carrier and tugged it off Justice's body, strapping it onto his own. But when he went to pick up the still mewling child, she went crazy barking, guarding the infant.

He kicked her away, hard, taking satisfaction as she yelped.. Bending to snatch the kid up, the dog lunged, sinking her teeth deep into him.

"Ow!"

He scrambled back, yelling obscenities, clutching his bitten arm. Peeked under his shirt at the holes torn into his flesh. "Stupid mutt." He kicked at her again, but she evaded his foot this time, still refusing to let him closer to the child.

Time was ticking. The day was growing older, and so was the chance that he'd be discovered, alone on the trail with three dead bodies, a bundle of cash in his backpack, and a stolen baby. He was desperate to get out of there. He had to be gone before daybreak.

How long would the infant survive exposed to the elements of the mountain on her own? Probably not long. He tried one last halfhearted attempt at reaching her, but the dog again lunged forward, snarling.

"Screw this. Eat her for all I care. I hope you choke and die."

So Brad turned his back and descended the mountain. He'd taken the carrier, the baby bag, everything but the damn infant herself, which was the dog's fault. Justice's dog. He hadn't wanted to leave the baby behind, but if the dog had other plans for it, who was he to interfere?

The trailhead parking lot was still empty when he got there. He jumped into the expedition van and hurried back to the shop in the dark, before the town started waking up and someone noticed it was missing. Next, he drove the couple's sedan to the town's salt shed, ditching it behind the hulking warehouse.

Brad thought he had gotten away with what he'd done, that he just had to lay low for a week or two so it wouldn't look suspicious when he took off, until he'd seen the chief with that damn dog and baby. Then, when he saw the blizzard on the forecast, he knew the couple's car would be discovered earlier than he'd anticipated, so he moved it to the motel parking lot, hoping to cast further suspicion on the woman who'd found the bodies.

It's true, he hadn't meant to kill anyone. But he can't deny that there's a part of him that liked it. Perhaps that's why he's here. Not because it's necessary to kill Chief Riley, but because he wants to.

77

MAGGIE

The eerie grin on Brad's face makes him practically unrecognizable. The nice kid who'd helped guide me up the mountain is gone. In his place is a soulless man with empty eyes and the bloodthirsty smile of a killer.

At his order, I slide the knife across the table, watching helplessly as it falls to the floor by his feet. I look around the room, searching desperately for another weapon, and then I see it. My backup firearm, the one I had given Sue earlier, lying on the sideboard.

"Where's Steven? Where's my son?"

The anguish in Diane's voice matches what I feel. I've been wondering the same thing. How long has Brad been here? Where are the others?

"Who?"

"My son, Ste—"

Diane cries out as he viciously jerks her head back with a fistful of hair.

"Listen, lady. Whatever you're trying to pull, it isn't going to work. Nobody's coming to your rescue, so you might as well get used to it."

It's clear that Brad doesn't know who Diane is talking about. I have no idea where Steve has gone, but I need to end this before he comes back. But before I can do that, I need to get Diane somewhere safe.

"Let her go." I use all the authority I can muster.

Brad laughs. I stare hard into his eyes, refusing to show fear.

"Why the hell would I do that?"

"She doesn't know who you are. She won't be able to name you. Let her go, and I won't fight. I promise."

The look he gives me makes me feel sick. It's obvious—there's no bargaining with him.

He laughs, cruelly. "Say I do turn her loose. Where's she gonna run to?"

He's right. Even if he did release her, she can't get away, not in the storm. I consider the options, right down to having her barricade herself in a room, but there's no guarantee that he wouldn't simply burn the house down.

I shift a hand to my hip, to the hilt of the knife I keep strapped to my belt. It's not much, intended more for cutting rope than flesh, but it's better than nothing. I slip it free as Brad's gaze darts around the room, calculating.

There's a moment of utter stillness, then he springs like a striking snake, tossing Diane to the ground as he lurches toward me. Even though it's too far away and I know I won't make it, I lunge for the gun.

Seeing what I'm after, Brad grabs the table and shoves it into me, slamming me into the wall. The side of my head hits with enough force that I see bursts of light. The knife drops from my hand as I feel myself sliding toward the floor, then my momentum is stopped as an iron fist locks around my throat, pinning me in place.

I struggle to get my legs under me, but I'm too low, the angle too awkward. My feet scramble uselessly, unable to gain traction. I claw at his hand, trying to loosen his grip, but I'm too weak and dizzy, my brain still spinning from the impact.

His grip tightens, trapping out the air my lungs so desperately need. I hear myself choking, can feel what little strength I have fading. My coordination is gone, limbs leaden and uncooperative. My time is running out, fast.

He leans his face close to mine—I can't see him through the gray haze clouding my vision, but I can feel his breath against my skin. Using the last burst of energy I have, I throw my arms up, aiming my thumbs for where I think his eyes are. He swats away one hand, but the other brushes against the side of his head.

My fingers manage to clasp his ear and I latch on, digging my nails deep into the tender flesh, twisting with all my might. The back of my skull strikes the wall as he hits me, once, twice, the ringing in my ears so loud that I can't even hear the thwack of his fist meeting my face, but I refuse to let go.

Then the sound of a scream breaks through it all.

I gasp in air as quick as I can as Brad's grip loosens. Splotches of my eyesight returns as he releases me completely, trying to fend off the dog attached to his bicep. Laurel. She must have hopped onto the table to launch an attack. Blood stains the parka surrounding her mouth. Brad shakes his arm, but the dog maintains her hold.

I stumble, grabbing onto the wall, needing to reach the gun. Needing to help the dog before it's too late. But my legs are rubbery, the room spinning, everything fading in and out of focus.

"No!"

It's Diane's voice. Steve's mother. I'd forgotten about her. I need to fight. I need to keep her safe. But oblivion is calling to me with a siren's song, promising relief from the pain that's permeated every cell of my body, if only I cede to it.

"Don't you touch her."

Digging deep, I fight with everything I have left, commanding my eyes to work. Diane brandishes the fireplace poker, swinging it against Brad's hands every time he tries to grab at the dog. I need to do my part to help.

I keep my shoulder against the wall for balance as I stagger forward. Grab the cold steel of the five-round mini-revolver I'd removed from my ankle holster this morning, never suspecting that the day would end like this. I slide down onto the floor and raise my knees, using them to brace my elbows and steady my aim.

My voice is hoarse, throat painfully raw as I shout, "Brad Peterson. Stop what you're doing, interlace your fingers and place your hands on your head, or I'll shoot."

I stop to catch my breath. Again. It's taking me too long, but I don't have a choice. As soon as the lightheadedness fades, I move on. Slog another dozen steps through the knee-deep powder. Pause for breath.

Although the snowfall has almost ceased, the wind is still fierce, whipping up what's already on the ground into an angry maelstrom of white, and freezing the top layer into a hard crust that I have to stomp through with each step.

I glance over my shoulder, but I can no longer see Maggie's house where I left Sue and Erika, the baby and the dogs. I can't see my cabin in front of me, either. But judging from the long, erratic path of broken snow behind me, I have to be getting close.

I take another unsteady step, lose my balance and tip over. Ice shoves up the sleeve of my jacket, scraping my arm as I catch myself. The abrasion stings. The cold stings. My pride—as I struggle to right myself, with ab muscles I apparently only imagined having—stings.

When this is all over, I'm joining a gym. Getting some

snowshoes. And buying a snowmobile. Seems ridiculous to live this far north without one.

I imagine how differently things would be playing out right now. I could have zipped on over to Maggie's, checked the phone, grabbed the extra gasoline, and been back in mere minutes. Then I could have headed into town, tracked down Maggie and my mom. Even gone back and forth a couple of times to bring them both home, if necessary.

Instead, I'm practically killing myself to cross two driveways and a street. I pause again to ease the gray splotches encroaching on the edges of my vision, because I think I'm seeing things. Or maybe it's a trick of the light struggling to shine through the storm clouds shrouding the sky that makes me think I'm seeing the metal glint of a pair of snowmobiles.

I wrap my arms tight around myself as I wait for my breath to return, trying to ignore the burning pain of my ice-encased calves. Stare down at my legs like I'm making sure they're still there. Funny how it's hot, not cold, like my nerves are too fried to tell the difference.

Looking up, I see they're still there, only several yards away. As I continue to break through the ice, I half expect the image to maintain its distance from me, like the mirage of an oasis in the desert, but it doesn't. If anything, it grows closer too soon.

With a final burst of speed, pushing myself despite lungs that feel like they're going to burst, I reach out and touch it. The metal is cold beneath my glove. Hard. Very definitely there and not the hallucination I thought it was. As if I conjured it up with my thoughts, I'm touching a Ski-Doo. And parked right beside it is a second one.

I'm amazed for one brief second, and then I'm terrified. Because on the far side of the vehicle, I can see four distinct trails carving through the snow that leads to my cabin. Suddenly, the feeling of dread that's been growing inside my gut makes sense.

Leaping over the machine, I break into a run, using the paths already forged to gain speed. The front porch comes into view as I hurry up the driveway. For a second, I think I'm going to make it in time. Then the unmistakable crack of a gun echoes through the gloom, dislodging loose powder from the trees and bringing my momentum to a dead halt.

MAGGIE

The shot rings out, deafening in the confined quarters. Pain lances through my shoulder. My vision wavers.

Fighting against the numbness wrapped tight around me, I crawl forward. Diane meets me halfway, Laurel clutched to her chest with one arm, the other still brandishing the fireplace poker. She kneels before me. Drops her weapon and raises a palm to my cheek. Tips her forehead to meet mine, tears streaming down both our faces.

It takes me a moment to realize the trembling I'm feeling is me, not her, my body still vibrating with adrenaline. I look down between us, notice that the front of her sweater is now smeared with red.

"Oh. I've gotten you dirty," I say.

"Don't you worry about that, dear."

Laurel licks my cheek.

Diane takes my hand and gives it a squeeze. "We need to call the police."

I do my best to sit up straighter, hold my head high. "But I am the police."

"I think you're going to need some backup."

I snort. Pain shoots through the front of my skull in a way that makes me think my nose is broken. "Want a job?"

We both jump, startling as footsteps thud down the hall toward us. I clamber forward to get her behind me, raise the gun in the air, the barrel wavering as I gather the strength to aim. Thumb back the hammer to make the trigger easier to pull.

I only have to wait a moment before the newcomer appears. Eddie Diaz clings to the doorway across the room as he takes in the scene before him. His gaze shifts to his feet, his voice barely a mumble as he says, "I knew he was dangerous. He's been watching you. I would have been here sooner, but I wasn't sure where to go."

I let that sink in for a moment. This kid hasn't been skulking around for no reason. He's been trying to protect me.

He crouches beside Brad, reaches tentative fingers toward his neck. "He's still alive. Maybe you should shoot him again?"

I shake my head as I unclip a pair of handcuffs from my belt. "How about these? Think you can do the honors?"

He nods and crosses the room, hovers over me, his perma-scowl for once replaced with something else. I think it's concern.

"Behind his back," I instruct as I pass him the cuffs with a shaky hand.

He nods his understanding. I watch him flip Brad onto his stomach not so gently, wait until I hear the telltale click that the bonds are in place before I slip the tiny revolver into my pocket. I imagine that I see Steve burst into the room just as the grapples of unconsciousness finally pull me under. It's over.

80
MAGGIE

Two days later

I dry my hands on the sides of my slacks. Take my hair down from my ponytail and put it back up. Ignore the pain in my battered face as I pull a small piece of lint off my uniform shirt, trying to be discreet as I let it fall to the ground.

"Stop fidgeting," Sue whispers at me from the side of her mouth. "Here."

The baby feels heavier than she had only a few days ago. I shoot a frantic look at Sue, but she steps aside, pretending not to notice. As the baby curls one tiny hand around my fingers and shoves them in her mouth, it becomes clear that it's two against one.

Nina's grip is so much stronger than I would have imagined. She smells like strawberries. And her hair, as I smooth the curls tufting on the top of her head like a baby chick's, is velvety soft.

I shift her onto my hip and rock from side to side—I'm not sure why, it just feels like what I should be doing right now, with the infant in my arms. And as I hold her, I realize it's not nearly as scary as I'd imagined. It's not so bad at all. It's almost nice, even.

The door swings open, and the room descends into chaos as a teary-eyed woman enters, followed by a blubbering man who must be her husband, a pair of FBI agents in suits, and Glen Coffrey. She races toward me and Nina, sweeps the baby from my arms and immediately starts cooing to her. The man wraps them both in his embrace, his sobs growing louder.

I step away, into the background, not wanting to disturb their moment, my throat tight as I watch. The back of my nose stings and my eyes burn and water. I look away, dropping my gaze to my boots. Draw a deep breath in and hold it, hoping that my inflated lungs will help hold together the shards of my broken heart.

Don't get me wrong—I am so very, incredibly happy that Nina has been reunited with her parents. It's the kind of thing that makes all the negatives of being a law enforcement officer worthwhile. But a part of me can't help feeling bitter.

Because my parents and I never got this moment with Brandon.

Should I have done more to try and bring him home? *Could* I have done more?

Is that why my parents abandoned me? Do they hold me as responsible as I do?

A soft hand gives my shoulder a gentle squeeze. Giving Sue a grateful smile, I cast one last glance at the elated family before striding across the room toward the suits. Maybe the Rileys will never have a reunion of this nature, but that doesn't mean that others can't, and I intend to help as many as I can.

But for half of the families involved, it means heartbreak rather than a happily ever after. It was gut-wrenching, explaining to Amanda Marsh's sister, Kay, about the real reason why James and Amanda were up on that mountain. No one wants to hear that their loved one was so desperate, in so much pain, that they'd seek their solace at the anguish of another. It wasn't an easy phone call to make. But I hope I was able to provide her with the closure she needs to grieve.

Baby Nina wasn't the first black-market adoption that Brad and Justice arranged. In fact, it was another baby that Justice had taken that brought Glen Coffrey to Coyote Cove. His niece's infant had been snatched from a grocery store while the young mother's back was turned.

Hanging out on a couple of baby broker websites on the dark web, Glen came in contact with a kid named Justice. Though he had come to Coyote Cove to meet with him, that's not what had brought Glen to the mountain that day. He really was just going for a hike, wanting to clear his head and get his thoughts straight before confronting the kidnapper.

But when saw he saw the bodies, and recognized that Justice was one of them, he panicked. Not only did he have a motive to kill the man, but, not knowing about Brad's involvement, he also felt sure that any hope of finding his niece's infant had died with him.

The FBI has already located his niece's baby and another stolen child with the information Glen gave them. My hope is that we can find them all and bring them home.

Because that not knowing? Being forced to live with an empty hole in the shape of a question mark inside you? That's its own special brand of hell.

81
STEVE

I wave goodbye to the two roofers, thanking them one last time for helping me board up the hole in Maggie's house, and watch as they drive away. Hopefully the patch will hold until the snow melts and mud season arrives, when they'll be able to put a crew together to get the place fixed. It would be great if they could make the repairs sooner, but I'm not holding my breath. With the snow we got from the blizzard and what's ahead on the forecast, most of the laborers in Coyote Cove are going to have their hands full.

Snow maintenance is a full-time job for half the year up here. Plowing, shoveling. Moving the gigantic, towering mounds of the stuff, scraped to the ends of parking lots and driveways, into dump trucks to cart away, so there's room to clear them after the next big snowfall. It's a way of life up here, and I don't expect that to change anytime soon. The patch will just have to do.

I take one last look at Maggie's house, lost in thought about how many lives were lost this past month, and how many more came close. I've learned a lot about myself. About pride and humility and trusting my instincts. About compromise and sacrifice and even love.

I clap my hands and Tempest and Sullivan jump off the porch, racing to see who can get to me first. They jump up when they reach me, each vying for my attention, and I'm so overwhelmed with affection that I drop to my knees in the dirty slush that litters the driveway to give them scratches.

I bury my nose in the damp fur on top of Tempe's head and breathe deep while I give Sully a tight squeeze. Close my eyes and remember the way Laurel would look at me the short time we were together, like I was the center of her world. We could all learn something about love from dogs.

And as I stood there the night of the blizzard with Maggie limp in my arms, all it took was one look at my mother holding Laurel, refusing to let her go, and I knew she knew it too. The dog helped save her life. That's not an easy thing to forget.

I never in a million years would have believed that my mother would ever forego her furless furniture and clean floors for a canine companion. Growing up, she had told me that we weren't pet people. Turns out we were both wrong.

I give the pups a final pat, then stand with a groan. They stay close to my side as I trudge down Maggie's driveway toward the road, watching me with bright eyes. I maintain a steady stream of chatter as we cross the street, something I keep catching myself doing in a desperate attempt to keep all the *what ifs* at bay.

What if we had taken Maggie's backup revolver with us? What if Laurel hadn't been there? What if Brad Peterson had maintained the upper hand? It's a vicious cycle, and there's only one way to stop it. Or two, apparently, because as the dogs take off running ahead, all thoughts other than keeping them safe vanish. Cursing, I push into an awkward sprint, struggling to keep my balance as I chase after them.

My mother once told me that having a child was like taking

your heart out of your chest and giving it legs. I imagine that's very much true. I also imagine that infants crawl before they walk to give their parents time to prepare for the day their children outpace them.

The desperation and fear are clear in my voice as I gasp out the dogs' names as loud as I can. Black bears are generally skittish around canines, but if they wake from hibernation, all bets are off. And there've been recent reports about coyotes scavenging close to some of my neighbors' houses. Not to mention that I've finally come to realize how many evil people there are in this world.

There are too many potential dangers out there for a couple of tiny pups. Especially when, like teenagers, they think they're invincible. I add another apology to the list I owe my mother as, clutching at a stitch in my side, I push myself forward at full speed.

Rounding the curve in the drive, I spot the SUV parked in front of the house and come to a halt. Draw several deep breaths. And finally feel myself relax.

Backhanding sweat from my brow, I aim for a leisurely pace as I approach. Then I realize I can't wait another second and break into an easy jog. My grin splits my face wide and my heart gives a somersault for a reason other than the crime of running while out of shape.

"You're back early," I say, scooping up a dog under each arm so I don't have to wait any longer for my turn. As I press my lips to Maggie's, hot terrier tongues lapping at both of our cheeks, I can't help laughing. Because this right here? It's everything.

82

ERIKA

I scan my key badge and walk briskly down the corridor leading to the autopsy suite. It feels weird being back. The halls seem too narrow, the fluorescent lights overhead too dim after the brightness of the real world.

Sure, I got a hell of a concussion and was stranded in the middle of a blizzard. Didn't know if I'd freeze to death or get murdered by a ruthless killer. I've never been so cold or scared or helpless ever before. But I wouldn't trade the experience for anything.

I feel like I've grown taller and stronger. Braver. More brazen. I've got a new sense of self-confidence that's been a real game changer. My phone buzzes in my pocket, signaling an incoming text. That's new, too.

Pulling my cell out, I read the message, smiling to myself. It's from Sue. I type a reply, search for an applicable GIF, and hit send. She's driving down to stay with me next weekend. I've promised her plenty of drinks and trouble. It's practice for the cruise to Jamaica we've already booked for this coming summer. I'm pretty sure I've found a friend for life in Sue. In Maggie and Steve, too.

Returning to work was bittersweet, but it's different now. It's just a job, not my life. Not the means by which I define my worth. And once something better comes along, I'll be leaving it in a heartbeat. I've outgrown this place. I need room to spread the wings I've only recently realized I have.

I push through the double doors, entering what was once my sanctuary. Now it's just the place where I perform post-mortems. Clock in, clock out, get on with my day—which is more than just playing butler to my cats now.

Devon from the print lab is leaning on the counter in the corner, talking to Tony. He glances in my direction, does a double take that turns into a lingering stare. "Erika?"

"Hey, Devon." It's the first time we've seen each other since I got back. Any awkwardness I felt toward him after our lack-luster date has vanished—on my end, at least. I give Tony a smile and a nod, then angle my body so my back is to them, eager to finish my work so I can get out of here for the day.

"Okay if I dip out early?" Tony asks.

How many times have I covered for him in the past, doing his job after I finished mine, even if it meant staying late? "As long as you don't need me to cover," I say. I skim the transcription of my dictated notes, scrawl my signature on the bottom, and hold the papers up for him to see. "I'm heading out as soon as I drop this off."

"Oh, come on. I've got plans."

I don't bother turning to face him. "So do I," I call over my shoulder as I head for the door.

"It's not like your cats can tell time."

"No, but my date can."

I let the doors close after me, cutting off his reply. A moment later I hear them opening again. I sigh, not in the mood to defend my decision, but it's not Tony who rushes down the hall to catch up with me. It's Devon.

"Hey, Erika." He falls into step beside me, darting glances in my direction.

I raise my eyebrows, give him a tightlipped smile. He jogs forward a few steps to reach the next set of doors before me and holds one open.

I step through. "Thanks."

"Um, listen. I was just wondering."

I pause, giving him my attention. "Yes?"

"Well, uh. Would you be interested in going out again? With me." A goofy grin settles on his face.

Drawing a deep breath, I let it out slowly. There was a time when I would have jumped at the opportunity. What a difference a few weeks can make. "Actually, I don't think so."

The grin vanishes, replaced by a frown. "What?"

"It's not that I didn't enjoy the time we spent together, it's just, well, I don't think we're a good match. I don't really think of you in that way." I reach out and put my hand on his arm and add, "But I hope we can still be friends." Catching sight of my watch, I say, "Wow, look at the time. I've got to get moving or I'll be late. Have a great weekend."

I leave him standing there in the middle of the hallway, his mouth hanging open like he's shocked I didn't jump at the chance for a second date with a guy who went radio silent after the first. Guess he thought I was desperate or something. I suppose I was, once.

But things change. I have changed. And as I hurry off with the heat of his gaze still on me, I know that, for once, it's for the better. It might have taken me almost fifty years, but I've finally come into my own.

83

MAGGIE

I had to cancel all my interviews for the Monday after the blizzard because of the storm—the roads were still impassable into the valley. And when the job candidates found out how much snow we'd received? They'd declined to reschedule. I can't say I really blame them.

Had someone clued me in to what winters were like this far north, I probably never would have come here myself. But then I'd never have met Steve, the man who stole my heart. And I'd probably be working some job I was ill-suited for, like crash test dummy. I rub at the tender lump still on the back of my skull, praying for a miracle. Surely a new lieutenant isn't too much to hope for.

It's hard enough trying to run a police department by myself, but when you factor in the forty-minute drive I've been having to make to the county seat, where the jail is, and the forty minutes back, not to mention the time spent in meetings with doctors and lawyers and jailors and even the occasional judge, well, it's enough to make me regret that Brad survived the shot.

But none of that matters right now because it's Friday, I'm

home, and though the weekend is going to cost the taxpayers of Coyote Cove another forty dollars per diem for Brad's room and board, I've been assured that he'll be well enough to appear at his preliminary hearing on Monday. And once a judge has determined that there are grounds for a trial, I'll be able to wash my hands of this mess until called to testify.

I've been told that Brad's lawyer is already working on a plea deal—reduced sentencing, and the agreement that the state's prosecutor is barred from using the term serial killer. It's not the best news I've ever received, but since he'll be revealing how many babies he helped "rehome," and everything he knew about Justice's operation, it's not something I'm opposed to.

Rumor is, he's also offered to join Glen Coffrey in testifying against Officer Kevin Miller. The statie's facing conspiracy charges—on my behalf. Seems the mustached cop developed such a vendetta against me that he tried to recruit them both to file false complaints, in an attempt to unseat me from my position as the Coyote Cove Chief of Police.

It's unclear whether he hoped to fill the position himself— God knows the townspeople probably would have been all for it —but what is clear is that he intended to bring me down. I guess maybe I should feel flattered that he knew he couldn't do it on his own.

One of the few good things to come from what's happened is Eddie Diaz. He's taken to stopping by the station, sometimes for long talks, sometimes for companionable silence, and sometimes it's to watch the extreme stunts on the new series Micah Jenkins stars in, landing the gig after successfully snowboarding off the roof of Em's Diner and onto the back of the moose statue out front. That episode also included headcam footage from the many attempts it took to get the feat right, including the time his arm got ripped open on one of the moose's antlers, resulting in the need for stitches.

Occasionally, though, Eddie comes for tutoring. He plans

to get his GED. He wants to go to the police academy once he does, but I've urged him to give college a try, first. With instincts as sharp as his, he could go far in law enforcement, and a university degree will help. But if he decides that path isn't for him, well, I've promised that there will always be a spot waiting for him with the Coyote Cove Police Department as long as I'm chief. It's just too bad he's not ready to start tonight.

I remember drawing parallels once between Justice Panettiere and Eddie. I also remember saying that, no matter what your situation is in life, you have a choice. And Eddie proves my point.

There's no denying that his family and home situation has left him at a disadvantage. That he often has the worst assumed about him—I'm guilty of that myself. But he's a good kid. He fights hard to make the right choices. When he noticed Brad watching me, acting like, as he said, a creeper, he decided to keep an eye out on us both.

Eddie said he owed me because I'd stuck up for him with the school principal when he'd been caught with the Swiss Army knife. That when I said I believed him, he thought, for the first time, that maybe there could be more in store for him than just becoming a criminal like everyone anticipated. It just goes to show how tiny actions can have a huge impact. Sometimes when you least expect it.

Like last week, when I received a letter from Cheryl Patton. It turns out that she had stayed in Coyote Cove and climbed Rattlesnake Mountain while on her honeymoon twenty-one years ago. She and her husband had hiked the Glacier Falls trail and picnicked alongside the waterfall. And it had been a perfect, blissful day.

Cheryl hadn't returned to try and recapture that happiness, though. She was there for a darker reason. One that she hoped would make her now ex-husband feel guilty for leaving her after over twenty years of marriage, to have a baby with a yoga instructor half her age.

But as she stood there, staring at the dead before her, she thought about how it could have been a different hiker finding her body. How she had planned to be the one to never wake up or smile or take a sip of coffee ever again. And though she thought her decision had been made, she wasn't quite sure how she felt about it anymore.

Trapped in Coyote Cove, she was filled with anger. First at me, and the town, then at her husband and his soon-to-be new wife. But as she stewed in that tiny motel room at Margot's, her thoughts kept drifting to the people she'd discovered on the mountain. And she realized that she wasn't ready to join them.

In her letter, she told me that she had originally intended to finish the plan to take her life as soon as she managed to escape the Cove. But over the course of her forced stay, that plan had changed. She decided that the best revenge was not to leave her life, but to make the most of living it. I'm glad she found peace. And judging from the photograph she included of herself at the summit of a different mountain, a huge grin spread across her face, she's found happiness, as well.

I get to my feet with a groan and pour myself a cup of coffee, even though I'd prefer a beer. It might be the weekend, but I'm still the only law enforcement officer for over thirty miles in any direction. I watch Steve and the dogs through the window while I drain my mug, then pour myself another before settling back into my seat at the table with a smile on my face.

Because there's a lot to be grateful for. A baby's been safely reunited with her parents. A killer is behind bars. My confidence has returned, because my gut had constantly given me what I thought was an unwarranted funny feeling about Brad. And the picture Steve's mother texted me earlier of Laurel sleeping on top of a throne of pillows has me feeling all the good feels.

Her newfound love of dogs has brought us closer together than I had ever even dared to hope. Even the sharp trill of my cellphone and the likelihood that I'm going to have to head back out into the cold can't dull my happy vibes.

"Chief Riley."

"Um, hi."

I wait a beat. When the speaker isn't more forthcoming about what they need from me, I prod. "Hello?"

"Yeah, sorry. I was just wondering. You had posted a job opening for a lieutenant last month?"

"That's correct."

"Is the position still open?"

I shimmy my shoulders excitedly. It's too early to perform a happy dance, but I have to let it out somehow. "It is."

"Great. That's really... great."

"Are you interested in the position?"

"I am."

"And have you applied before?" I reach for a notepad and pen, pulling them closer across the table with crossed fingers.

"No. Is that okay?"

I punch a fist in the air, try to contain my enthusiasm as I say, "That's just fine. Why don't you tell me a little about yourself?"

"Well, I've been out of the academy for six years. At my current position in Kittery for the last four."

"And you're still currently employed there?"

"I am."

It'll be easy enough to confirm. "Any disciplinary actions?"

"No, ma'am."

"Complaints."

"None."

"Issues with coworkers?"

"Not at all."

"Job burnout?"

"Wouldn't be calling you if that was the case."

Disappointment slips under the edges of my relief. Something about this isn't making sense. "Do you mind if I ask why you want to jump ship, then?"

There's a long pause on the other end of the line. Just when I'm starting to wonder if he's hung up, he exhales a loud breath. "Can I be honest?"

"I wish you would."

"This is kind of embarrassing, but, my fiancée dumped me."

And now my hopes of having a lieutenant are circling the drain. "So you thought a change of scenery would help mend your broken heart?"

"Well... yes and no."

"Listen. I'm sure you'd make a great lieutenant. But it sounds like you have other options. Coyote Cove probably isn't the place for—"

"But it is!"

"Do you have any idea how remote it is up here?"

"I do."

"And how much snow we get?"

"I can't say I'm crazy about inches in the triple digits, but there are worse things."

"Still. This isn't the kind of transition that should be taken lightly."

"But I'm not. I know I could find a job someplace else. But I want this one. I want to be in Coyote Cove."

"Why?" It's out before I can think about it. And said with a little more judgment than I intended.

"Moose."

"Moose?"

"Yeah. I've always wanted to see one. And I read that moose outnumber people three to one in Coyote Cove."

"So you're making a career transition, and a lateral one at best, because you want to see moose?"

"Yeah. Pretty much. I mean, I like the odds. Small town like that? Sounds like the type of place I want to be right now. A place where someone can get their act together. Get their head on straight."

There are alarm bells going off in my brain right now. I've already had one lieutenant go off the rails, I don't think I could handle another. Not to mention that small, remote towns really aren't the best place to get your head straight. They're the best place to lose your head, especially up here. Long nights and short days filled with the same people. The same scrutiny. The same tasks. It's enough to drive anyone mad.

I think about the note that had been pinned to the dummy left hanging outside my office last month.

Lieutenant Lunatic
Deathtrap PD

Sometimes there's a fine line between grief and anger. I know that far too well myself. And as the memory surfaces of watching Lieutenant Murphy's two preteen sons outside my office, stringing up another dummy dressed in one of their father's old uniforms, I also know I'm not the only one hurting out there.

So I already know I'm going to say yes. Because the whole moose outnumbering people, place to get your act together thing? It's the exact same thought I had when I applied for this position. True, my first year here, I thought I might completely lose the last of my sanity. Instead, it ended up working out for me. Why not for him?

"You're hired."

"What?"

"You'll have to pass the background check, but barring any surprises, you've got the job. When can you start?"

"Are you serious?"

I think about nights off. Weekends. Of having a second drink, or even a third. "Completely."

"I'll give my notice now. This very minute. I'll need to find a rental, but I'll live in a motel if I have to."

I think about Brad's empty apartment. "I might have a lead on a place."

"Great! Excellent! You know what? I think I'll drive up tomorrow. Better yet, tonight. I'll leave now."

"Hold on. There's one more thing, first."

I hear him swallow loudly. He sounds dejected when he says, "What's that?"

"Your name?"

"Oh! Kal. Kal Kishore."

"Great. No need to drop everything to rush up here tonight, or even this weekend, but when you do hit town, give me a call and I'll show you around, Kal."

"Thanks, Chief Riley. You aren't going to regret this. Promise."

I kind of already do, but it sounds like this is something we both need, so I stay positive as we end the call. And I can't keep the grin off my face as Steve enters the room, preceded by two terriers skidding on damp paws.

"What'd I miss?" he asks.

"I just hired a lieutenant."

"Seriously? That's great! Congratulations."

"Don't congratulate me yet. Guy sounds like he could be a basket case."

"Then he'll fit right in."

I roll my eyes even if it is true. Shoot an exasperated look at my phone as it starts ringing again.

"Ugh. That's probably him calling to tell me he's already changed his mind." I sigh deeply, then answer the call. "Chief Riley."

Steve crosses the fingers on each hand and stares at the ceiling.

"Maggie?"

It feels like the floor falls out from under me. I have to check to make sure that I'm still seated, that I haven't slid out of the chair. Steve drops his act and crouches beside me, concern etched deep across his features as he mouths questions that I can't answer.

There's only one word on my lips. As soon as I find my voice, I say it. "Mom?"

A LETTER FROM SHANNON

Dear Reader,

First, a most sincere thank you for choosing to read *Their Angel's Cry,* the second installment in the Chief Maggie Riley series. I had a great time writing this book, rediscovering the knowledge and skills from my past as Maggie rediscovered hers. I hope you had as much fun with it as I did, and I can't wait for you to discover what I have in store for Maggie and the rest of the residents of Coyote Cove!

If you enjoyed the story, I would be incredibly grateful if you'd leave a review and recommend the book to your friends and family. I love reading what you think, and it also helps other readers find my books for the first time.

If you'd like to keep up to date with my latest releases, you can sign up at the following link. Your email address will never be shared, and you can unsubscribe at any time.

www.bookouture.com/shannon-hollinger

The idea for this book came straight from the headlines. Tragically, a husband, wife, their baby, and their dog, were all found dead together on a hiking trail in California in August of 2021. As an avid hiker, it really got me thinking. You know the risks when you enter the woods. You do your best to be prepared. My husband and I have even trained in wilderness first aid, which has come in handy a few times. But sometimes, disaster strikes anyways.

What could have happened to this poor family?

Although hyperthermia and dehydration were later determined to have been the cause of their deaths, my writer brain had already started thinking of all the *other* possibilities. Carbon dioxide poisoning or other volcanic fumes from a thermal vent. Chemicals used for gemstone mining. Toxic spores released from the soil. Once I started researching, however, I realized I was somewhat limited by the Maine setting, so I chose the craziest of my ideas and ran with it.

I do try to be as accurate as possible, but I may have taken a teensy liberty with this book. I've always wanted to use succinylcholine in a plot, but please note—although the way I've described its effects in the book are accurate, I couldn't find anything in the literature about the oral application of this drug. It does work if used in the nasal cavity, and I figured one mucus membrane is as good as another, so I went ahead and administered the drug through water.

But be forewarned... if you were planning on using it that way... it may or may not work. Sorry to throw a wrench in your murder plans, but honestly, it's probably for the best. A good pathologist will find it on autopsy, and then you might get caught, and I've heard the reading options available in prison are just horrid, so maybe I just did you a favor?!

In all seriousness, it gets lonely in the writing cave (plus, I might have just saved you from a life sentence of bad books), so please feel free to get in touch with me directly and keep me company! You can find me on Facebook, Twitter, Goodreads, Instagram, TikTok, or my website.

Thank you so much for your support—it really is hugely appreciated!

Until next time,

Shannon Hollinger

shannonhollinger.com

facebook.com/thiswritersays

twitter.com/thiswritersays

instagram.com/thiswritersays

goodreads.com/shannonhollinger

tiktok.com/@shannonhollinger

ACKNOWLEDGMENTS

Writing a book can be a long, solitary process. Sometimes, after all those hours spent staring at the computer screen, occasionally typing a word, you get a little strange and forget how to people, which is why I'm incredibly grateful to my writing companion, who never fails to listen patiently and without judgment to all the odd things I say while plotting murder. And who always reminds me to take snack breaks. Lots and lots of snack breaks.

So thank you to my sweet Sullivan, who's sitting beside me now as I write this, and to my darling "first born" Tempest, who insisted she needed a pup of her own. The two of you made my world a much brighter place and you'll both always have a special place in my heart.

Thank you to my husband, Ben, who married me for the dogs and stuck around for the snacks. The best part of my day is the time I get to spend with you.

Thank you to my parents, who raised me among a crazy menagerie that kept this only child from ever being lonely. My mom and best friend, Stacy, who never censored what I was reading as long as I *was* reading, who taught me to write, and who never worried (too much) when I decided I wanted to be an author and talked about all the ways there were to kill a person. And my dad, who always believed in me. I wish you were here to see all the ways I've managed to kill people... on paper.

Thank you to my grandmother, Marvis, reader extraordinaire, who introduced me to Agatha Christie at an early age and, as I got older, to a bevy of wonderfully dark and twisted authors.

Thank you to Erika from the Wayland Writers Group for the use of her name. It was short-lived but we had a lot of fun!

Many sincere thank yous to my publishing team at Bookouture. I'm so very grateful to have found such an amazing tribe, one that feels more like a family than a publishing company.

Special thanks to my editor, Susannah Hamilton, for her excellent guidance and input and for all the many, MANY times she had to remind me to focus less on the dogs and more on the baby in this one!

Thank you to everyone else on the team whose hands, talent, and skill have touched this book and helped make it into what it is today! Also, to my fellow Bookouture authors, who are unbelievably friendly and supportive across both genres and oceans.

Finally, and most importantly, endless thanks to all the readers, reviewers, BookTokers, Bookstagrammers, book tweeters, bloggers, and librarians out there who spend so much of their valuable time sharing book love!

Please don't underestimate how important you are! Knowing that there are people who enjoyed reading the book you've spent so much time, sweat, isolation, and occasionally tears on is a tremendous feeling, and your kind words mean the absolute world to me! The best part of this journey has been "meeting" you. I love reading all of your posts! Thank you so much for brightening my days!

Printed in Great Britain
by Amazon